MR. SINGER'S SEAMSTRESS

MR. SINGER'S SEAMSTRESS

A WASHINGTON TERRITORY STORY

KARLA STOVER

WHEELER PUBLISHING
A part of Gale, a Cengage Company

LIBRARY OF CONGRESS CIP DATA ON FILE.
CATALOGUING IN PUBLICATION FOR THIS BOOK
IS AVAILABLE FROM THE LIBRARY OF CONGRESS.

ISBN-13: 978-1-4328-8991-3 (softcover alk. paper)

Printed in the USA
1 2 3 4 5   26 25 24 23 22

To my husband,
who gives me time to write
The wonderful settlers
whom I consider friends
And the *Tacoma Daily Ledger,*
gone but not forgotten

CHAPTER 1

Clouds of dust from the hooves of nervous Indian ponies filled the rutted dirt road in front of Mike Murphy's wagon. A crowd of angry Puyallup Indians milled about, shouting, and Mike pulled hard on the reins to calm his team. "Easy there, Sadie. Easy, Big Lou."

"Are those Puyallups?" Nell Tanquist, Mike's passenger, held tightly to the sides of the dray as his horses jerked and danced. "The Puyallups never fight."

"Excuse me, ma'am," Mike said, "but they fought alongside the Nisquallys in the 1855 Injun War, though that was well before your time."

Nell's brown eyes snapped in excitement, as they always did when something unusual was happening, and she only half-heard him. "I wonder what they're all het up about."

"I expect they're here about the kidnappings."

"What kidnappings?"

"Last week Lieutenant Wilkinson snatched some Injun girls and took 'em down to Oregon, to the Forest Grove School."

His words barely rose above the racket of loud voices and barking dogs that darted in and out of the throng of natives, both male and female. Near the sidewalks, white men poured out of businesses lining New Tacoma's main street. They stood with their backs to their premises, talking among themselves, and keeping wary eyes on the crowd, while inside their female shoppers huddled nervously. Nell knew most of the Indians would have come by water, beaching their canoes near the Northern Pacific Hotel and walking up the Wharf Road to town, and she was surprised to see that some of them had ridden bareback from the reservation on their half-broken cayuses. The dirt smell the horses kicked up hung in the warm spring air, mixing with the stench of burning stumps where men were clearing land two streets up from Pacific Avenue, and with the fishy odor of the Indians' clothing. As she watched, one of the Puyallups raised his arms to calm the crowd.

"Who's that?" She turned her head and

bent close to catch his words.

"I reckon it's the Puyallups' Chief Citrell."

Like most of the men, the chief wore a breechclout over buckskin pants, and a dirty cotton shirt. Despite the heat, he had added a Hudson's Bay Company coat, which enhanced his dignity. A red kerchief held back the long hair that hung down past his shoulder blades, and every time he shouted, furrows and pleats came and went in his brown skin.

"*S'Puyalupubshtil-i-kum sol-leks. Tum-tum til. Klone* suns Bostons *chah-ka kap-su-al-al. Tahhumtenasiskum* Oregon."

Mike cupped his hand behind an ear, as intent as Nell was on hearing every word.

"You were right," she whispered. "It's about the children."

"You speak Chinook?"

"Enough to know six girls were snatched, and the Puyallups want them back."

Some of the tribal chief's words were lost as several women began keening wails. Tears ran down their faces, leaving salty streaks. *Why, they're sad.* The realization surprised Nell. *They're sad just like Ma would be if someone tried to take us away.*

"I don't figure Wilkinson shoulda done that." Mike scowled. "The galloping con-

9

sumption is taking kids away right and left at that there boarding school."

While they listened, a schoolboy snuck through the crowd and threw a rock at one of the ponies. It whinnied, reared, and narrowly missed tossing its rider.

Without thinking, Nell jumped off the dray. "You stop that right now, Delmar Manches, or I'll tell your pa."

"Ah, Pa won't give a dern."

"He will if you hurt someone, and he has to get an attorney again, like when you stoned the Chinese."

Delmar started to answer, but he was shoved aside when three of New Tacoma's leaders — General John Sprague, Theodore Hosmer, and Dr. Henry Bostwick — pushed their way through the milling mob.

"*Kla how ya,* Chief Citrell." The general greeted the chief in the Chinook language. He put his hand out, and, after a long moment, the chief took it.

"Miss Nell." Mike jumped off his wagon and hitched the reins to a rail in front of Levin's Saloon. "Come back here. It ain't safe."

Nell didn't hear him over the din, but she probably wouldn't have returned to the wagon, if she had. She was familiar with Indian men from the years she'd lived on

Bush Prairie near Olympia, but she had rarely seen Indian women up close. As always, she was interested in clothes, and she paid close heed to the native women. Those she saw in the crowd wore moccasins laced around their ankles, long deer-hide blouses tied in the middle, and faded skirts of Turkish-red cloth. Nell knew several white women who refused to wear that particular shade of red because they didn't want the association with the local Indians, for whom it was a favorite color.

Taking a position near one of the Puyallups who stood slightly back from the others, she saw that the woman had a papoose wrapped in elk skin. She had fastened the baby to a paddleboard that hung on cedar strips down her back. Nell smiled at the infant and shook her long braid where the child's big brown eyes could see it. The child stared a moment and then wiggled and smiled, showing the beginnings of a tooth. Though Nell had taken care of enough younger brothers and sisters in her sixteen years to make her immune to cute babies, this one appealed to her. She put out a hand, and it clasped her finger. As if sensing the movement, the mother spun around and glared.

"To'ke-tie," Nell said.

The woman looked Nell over as closely as Nell had looked at her. After a pause she said, "*Na wit'ka* — pretty." Her eyes rested on Nell's hair. "*T'kope.*"

"Yes, white." Nell was used to people staring at her moon-colored, pale-blonde hair. Then a movement on the far side of the crowd caught her eye, and she saw her closest friend, Hildy Bacom, waving. New Tacoma had just recovered from a smallpox epidemic, and Nell's ma had sent her and her two sisters to stay with relatives until it was over. She hadn't seen Hildy for several weeks. The Indian woman turned away, and Nell hurried to join Hildy.

"Is it about the kidnapping?" Hildy linked an arm through one of Nell's, and they started south on Pacific Avenue, away from the throng.

"Yes. General Sprague was getting ready to talk to Chief Citrell when I saw you."

"The general is a fine-looking man, isn't he?"

"I've always thought so. I saw him once, back when he was surveying for the railroad, and he hasn't changed much. It's good the Puyallups respect him."

"Do you know who the woman you were talking to is?"

"No. Do you?"

"Yes. Samuel pointed her out once. She's Burnt Face Charlie Paul's daughter, Ramona."

Everyone in New Tacoma knew about an accident at the Hanson and Ackerson Mill that had burned Charlie's face and how, ever since, he and his family carried a deep-seated hatred of all white men. However, Nell was more interested in what Hildy's beau, Samuel, might know about the kidnappings. Samuel was one-quarter Indian. Though not Puyallup, he had friends on their reservation.

"Has Samuel said much?"

"Yes, he's been talking to the Puyallups. Apparently, Captain Wilkinson sent George Boynton and Peter Stanup to the reservation to try and talk the parents into sending their children to the Forest Grove School." Hildy stopped speaking long enough for both girls to smile and nod at Mr. Nolan, who had been sweeping his wooden sidewalk while keeping an eye on the Puyallups but paused to let them pass. Once out of his hearing, she continued. "The parents didn't want their children to be so far away, so the captain appealed to General Milroy in Olympia, and he tried to persuade the parents, too, but it didn't work."

Approaching the Washington Lodging

House, they saw a cluster of men who regularly lounged out front, waiting for working orders from the Tacoma Land Company. Nell hated walking by the lodging house because some of the men stared at her in a way that made her uncomfortable. She picked up her pace while passing it and had to wait for Hildy to catch up.

Noise from the railway car on John Geiger's wooden track had interrupted Hildy. She and Nell stopped to watch him wheel a small handcar loaded with dirt down 7th Street and empty it over the side of the embankment above Commencement Bay. "What's that for?" Nell asked, looking at a hole Mr. Geiger had dug in the hill.

"Papa says Mr. Geiger is excavating for a beer cellar. Papa's not a bit happy about it. After all the trouble at Longpray's saloon last year, he says New Tacoma has an obligation to maintain a God-fearing town."

"Why?"

"I'm not sure." The girls looked at each other and giggled.

Next to the hole, Smith Hall was strangely empty, but across the street from the future beer cellar, a group of women stood in front of the Mann Block looking at the selection of china and jewelry in a window. Forgetting about the kidnappings for a moment,

Nell and Hildy joined them.

"What lovely things," one of the women said. "And to think they're all being auctioned off."

"When?"

"Next month."

"I wonder by whom?"

"The only thing I've heard is that it's by a well-known auction house." All of them grabbed at their hats as a gust of spring air came and went.

"Wouldn't that be lovely to wear to Mrs. McCarver's at-home?" The young woman who spoke pointed to a cameo set in gold filigree.

"Cousin Caddy sent me Mama's hair brooch. I expect I'll wear it with my black bombazine." The speaker looked pensive.

"Is she related to Mrs. Caddy uptown who's been so ill?"

"Distantly, I think." The lady reached a hand toward the cameo, then laughed and let her arm drop. "You don't think it's inappropriate to wear, do you? It's been nine months since Mama passed."

"I think it will be all right."

"General and Mrs. Otis Sprague were invited," said yet another woman as she adjusted her hatpin. "But Mrs. Sprague has been poorly, don't you know, so they probably won't be there."

The women turned away and went into Mrs. Spooner's millinery shop, and Nell and Hildy continued walking.

As they went on their way, Nell observed the changes on Pacific Avenue. Having just returned from a month's stay at her sister's house on Bush Prairie, she was pleased at the number of new businesses going up and at others under construction. *If we keep growing like this, New Tacoma will be a real city just like Portland,* she thought. To Hildy she said, "If every merchant fixed the road in front of his place, imagine how nice the street would look." They dodged a mud hole well known for staying wet long after other marshy spots were dry.

"Mr. Cogswell promised to put gravel in front of the livery stable when it's finished." Hildy looked at Nell and grinned. "I wonder if Fern will think Virginia has better gravel." Fern, whose family had come west some four years earlier, and who had gone to school with Nell and Hildy, rarely failed to make the observation that everything in Virginia was better than anything New Tacoma had to offer.

Behind them, they heard the hoofbeats of approaching horses. The Puyallups who had ridden from the reservation were coming down the road fast, and rocks and clods of dirt flew up. Nell and Hildy stepped aside and watched them pass. "The Indians still look angry," Nell said.

"They probably are." As the girls skirted a pile of wood and some cans, Hildy looked at Nell. "Are you all right?"

Nell smoothed her black dress and sighed. "The house surely does seem quiet with Amos and Isaiah both gone. Poor tykes."

"Mama wouldn't let any of us out of the house while the sickness was on, or I'd have come. You know that."

"I know, but taking care of the twins took all Ma's time. That's why she sent all of us to stay with Indiana and Lumley. Indiana wasn't happy, but she did have us to help with the chores, so that was good."

"Wasn't your mama afraid of getting sick?"

"Ma had smallpox already. After the twins were taken, Pa made a coffin big enough for the two of them, and she did the needful. They took the babies to the Oakwood Hill Cemetery before the rest of us even came home."

"I think that's awfully brave."

"I don't mind telling you, I was scared she'd die, too. She made Pa find a new house for us to live in, and everything seems all pixilated." Nell's brown eyes filled with tears, and she brushed them away.

They continued without speaking, watching the street's comings and goings. In addition to the Indians and the new buildings, Pacific Avenue was being torn up so men could make a sewer system. The road was all but blocked by piles of dirt and wood. Fortunately, their destination was east on 10th Street. At the second building from the corner, Nell stopped. It was the first time she'd seen Hildy's bakery.

Nell hadn't known a time when Hildy wasn't baking. Hildy made all her family's bread and made and sold bread to a number of bachelors who worked for the railroad or on the waterfront. When honey was available, she made and sold jars of honey butter. Now, Nell looked at her friend's new shop and clasped her hands. "Oh, Hildy, you have your bakery at last."

Tall, narrow windows flanked the door, over which hung a sign that read *New Tacoma Bakery*. Hildy unlocked the door, and they went inside. The bakery was small, even by New Tacoma standards. A Barley Sheaf cooking stove took nearly the entire back wall. Pans and utensils hung from hooks on the left wall, and a workspace was on the right. Over the workspace, flour and other baking supplies were stored on shelves to keep them safe from mice. A counter separated the front from the work area. Nell took everything in and beamed. "It's wonderful, and it smells good, too."

"Well, pretty soon I hope it smells more like bread and less like wood, but didn't Chong and Reuben do a fine job? They built all the shelves. Reuben is finally getting handy."

Nell laughed. Hildy was the oldest in her family, and, though her whole family loved and valued Chong, the Chinese lad who had lived with them since they first settled in New Tacoma, Hildy had long thought her brother, Reuben, and her younger sister, Dovie, were completely feckless.

Hildy pulled over two empty boxes and set them in the pools of sunlight filling the front of the little shop. Nell sat on one and faced her friend. "Now, tell me everything I've missed, but start with the Indians. I've never seen them all riled up like that."

"Let me see." Hildy folded her hands on her lap. "After the men failed to convince the Puyallups to send their children off, some of the Indian police went to the reservation. People hid their offspring in the woods, but the police found them. They took six girls to the railroad station and sent them to the Forest Grove School. Samuel said an Indian woman named Mrs. Swan stood up in the middle of the reservation church during services and demanded an explanation, but no one responded. Samuel and his father are joining some of the men to go down to Oregon and bring the girls back."

"Snollygoster. What a fine to-do." Nell knew Samuel struggled between what his French mother wanted and the loyalty he felt towards his father's Indian heritage. "What does your pa have to say about that?"

"He doesn't know. I didn't tell him. Papa knows Samuel's going to work for the Forestry Department. Mr. Hough, the director, wrote and said so, but the department is new, and it's taking time to get organized, so right now he's working for Mr. Blancut, the tanner. The sooner he gets gone, the better, I say."

Nell understood that Hildy meant Samuel. Nell didn't think much of Mr. Blancut, who, according to her pa, was so rowdy on Saturday nights, he could wake snakes. She agreed and changed the subject. "Now, tell me how you managed all this."

"Do you recollect Mr. Dougherty, who had his three-foot-wide cobbler's shop here? Well, he pulled out and left the space vacant. Of course, three feet was too small for a bakery. Remember how he sat in the doorway and repaired shoes? I couldn't cook in the doorway. So, I asked Mr. Cogswell, who owns the building, if he would move the wall over and rent me ten feet of space. He was agreeable because Papa vouched for me." Hildy looked around with satisfaction. "After Reuben and Chong built the shelves, the Baldwins also pulled up stakes, and Mrs. Baldwin sold me the stove. Gold was discovered in Liberty, and Mr. Baldwin aims to pan Swauk Creek. I've been saving my money for four years, but it still wasn't enough. You'll never guess who loaned me the rest."

"Your pa?"

"No. Mrs. Blackwell." Hildy laughed at Nell's surprise. "Mrs. Blackwell thinks women should learn to take care of themselves in case someday they have to. She told me Mr. Blackwell was sent home from the war to die but that she just ignored the doctors and married him. They came West instead, and, when they settled here, she bought a piece of property above their hotel in her own name. Imagine that."

"Goodness. Isn't that something?" Nell was a little in awe of Mrs. Blackwell, who helped run a hotel for the Northern Pacific Railroad. "I don't know any women who own their own land."

The sound of a train whistle carried up from the waterfront, and a wagon rattled by outside, scaring two seagulls foraging in the road. Hildy waited until the noise stopped. "As soon as I can, I'm going to buy some nice chairs, and then people can sit and rest."

"And buy bread."

"Of course."

They laughed, and Nell said, "I'm glad I got to see you before tomorrow. I'm going to Steilacoom, and I might be gone for a couple of days."

"Gracious me, why?"

"I'm going to try and sell some of my needlework."

"Oh, Nell, how wonderful. You make such beautiful things."

"If I sell to ladies directly, I won't have to pay Mrs. Halstead to offer them for sale at the hotel."

"Is your mama letting you go all by yourself?"

"No, Josie's coming with me. Most people forget she's older than I am."

"How long will you be gone?"

"I don't know for sure. We have a ride over, but I don't know how we'll get back. Ship or shank's mare, I expect. Goodness, I hope I sell enough to pay for the trip." Nell rubbed at a bit of pitch on her hand. "Did you hear that the steamer *Mexico* docked yesterday?"

"The freighter?"

"Yes. Pa hired on to help unload it and mentioned seeing a Singer sewing machine. A man named Bulger is the company's agent, and he's going to have a shop down on 12th and Pacific and sell and lease them. Oh, Hildy, it's just what I want to start a dressmaking business, but they're terribly expensive." She sighed and hopped off the box. "I'd better git. Ma'll be wondering where I am."

"I hate for you to go. I missed you so much while you were gone. And we never seem to have adventures like we used to. Remember the bear that spoiled our picnic?"

"And ate all the berries we picked?" Nell stood in the doorway, watching Robert Scott steer his milk wagon around three sheep someone had tied to a hitching rail. "Sometimes I think growing up isn't as nice as we thought it would be."

She said goodbye, climbed the 10th Street hill to D Street, and headed north. The city fathers were building a jail, and the German Methodists were clearing a lot for their new church. Both had debris piled on the road. Fir boughs and last fall's dead leaves mixed with water from the Burns spring, creating quagmires. Truth be told, Nell thought, D Street was barely a road.

Just before home, Josie joined her, coming up from the waterfront. "Oh, Nell, you'll never guess." Josie's round cheeks glowed with sun and excitement. "Mrs. McCarver is going to pay me to play the piano at her party."

Nell took her sister's arm and matched their steps. "How did she learn about your playing?"

"She heard me one day when I was supposed to be dusting." Josie assumed her most innocent expression. "I happened to be dusting right after I heard about the party."

Nell laughed. "Well, we'll have to fix your Sunday dress."

"Oh, can we? Will there be time after we get back from Steilacoom?"

"As if I would let you entertain in a raggedy dress."

"It's not really that raggedy." Josie beamed for a minute, and then, as they reached home, her face fell. "It doesn't exactly feel like home now, does it, without Amos and Isaiah? Can we go out to the graveyard someday and take flowers?"

"Of course we can. I was planning on that already." Nell reached the door first and turned to look at Josie. "I know how you feel, dear, but aren't we lucky Ma didn't catch the sickness? And anyplace Ma is feels like home."

CHAPTER 2

The following morning, Nell and Josie left their house shortly before dawn. Josie carried a small parcel with lunch and fresh clothing. Nell had a box containing her needlework. Despite the starlit sky, they had to pick their way carefully. Deep ruts made D Street seem like little more than a wagon trail. Nell saw Mr. Galliac, New Tacoma's night watchman, walking on 8th Street and felt reassured. Recently, the town had lost several businesses to fires, and a fire at one place generally spread to adjacent buildings, and sometimes meant a robbery elsewhere. Though New Tacoma's streets were never really empty, most people felt reassured by Mr. Galliac's presence.

Halfway down the hill, with Josie close behind, Nell passed the wooden frame of a new livery stable being built. Just beyond it was Pacific Avenue, where they were to meet their ride. Despite the early hour, she saw a man who was leading a horse stop in front of Muntz's Blacksmith Shop. The door stood open, and she caught sight of a boy working the bellows to build up heat in the forge. Several men with fishing poles hurried past Levin's Saloon, and two Chinese men carrying buckets of garbage gave them a wide berth. Some garbage spilled onto the road, and the smell brought a rat out from under the wooden sidewalk near Jacob Halstead's bathhouse. Josie picked up a rock and threw it. The rodent screeched and scurried away.

"How are we getting to Steilacoom?" Josie asked, switching her parcel from one hand to the other.

As usual, Nell didn't know whether to laugh or sigh in exasperation. *She only thought about asking me now? What if I said, "I don't know? Do you?"* She knew Josie would just look puzzled if she did say it, though.

In the distance and coming closer, they heard horses puffing and saw a wagon on the wharf road. "I think this is our ride," Nell said.

"Who is it?"

"Mr. Hegele, who bought the Byrd Mill in Steilacoom."

When the wagon crested the hill, Nell

waved her hand. "Mr. Hegele?"

"I am if you're Miss Nell Tanquist." The middle-aged man reined his horses to a stop.

"Yes, sir, and this is my sister, Josie." Nell took Josie's arm. "Josie, hop up on the seat. Let's not keep Mr. Hegele waiting."

They sat one on either side of him. He snapped the team into motion, and they fell into an easy gait. With the sun just beginning to show, the air was cold. Nell pulled her shawl tighter and watched pink slivers of clouds spike around Mt. Tacoma. A rooster crowed to welcome dawn, and several of his brethren joined him. Every time the wagon hit a rut, the materials in its bed banged together. Talking was difficult, and they jogged along for some time without speaking. Nell was so grateful for the ride, she smiled at Mr. Hegele and eventually said, over the noise, "I understand you bought Andrew Byrd's mill."

"Yes, Miss Tanquist, but I'm only going to run the flour mill, not the sawmill. I figure there's enough of them around already."

"There certainly are, and more starting up all the time. Maybe one day we'll run out of trees."

Mr. Hegele laughed. "Not likely, miss. As soon as we get a ways out of town, you'll see how many there are."

"Why did Mr. Byrd sell the mill?" Josie asked.

"Why, bless me. He didn't. He was murdered not long after Chief Leschi was hung. Tom Chambers took over the mill, and I bought it from him."

Nell gritted her teeth and looked at Josie. Her sister didn't react well to any mention of violence. To ward off trouble she said, "When we lived on Bush Prairie, Pa used to take our wheat to Mike Simmons's mill on the Deschutes River. I don't recollect hearing about any big rivers near Steilacoom, do you, Josie?"

Josie seemed not to hear the question. "Was Mr. Chambers killed, too?" She clenched and unclenched her fists.

"Not him, miss, but he did have a bit of a donnybrook with the Hudson's Bay Company over the land and creek. Mind you, it's a good-sized creek, Miss Tanquist, not a river. Anyway, seems old Tom took over some land the company was leasing to Joseph Heath. After Heath died, the company sent some men to try and get Tom off, and he met them with a shotgun."

Mr. Hegele laughed, Josie made a noise of distress, and Nell said firmly, "What creek, Mr. Hegele?"

"Some call it Byrd Creek, but most call it

Chambers Creek. Between the dam and the mill, I've got a twelve-foot drop to power the wheel." He gestured over his shoulder. "This here is what I need to get the flume repaired."

He turned the team, and the horses started climbing in a southwesterly direction. They crossed a bridge over Gallagher Creek, and tall timber stands began to crowd the rough road. Hilly mounds of moss and deer ferns pressed against their trunks. Pink flowering rhododendrons and mauve wild currant bushes broke the green monotony. Josie looked up at the gently swaying firs. "Listen, Nell, the trees are talking."

"Are they?"

"I don't think they're happy. I think they're frightened."

Nell heard the low, moaning sound of wind high up in the branches. "Why do you think that?"

"Because they know their lives as trees are going to end." Josie squeezed the parcel she held, and Mr. Hegele look puzzled.

On the edge of the road a mother quail and her offspring pecked at the dirt. The sounds of the wagon sent them hurrying through a patch of kinnikinic and into the underbrush. "Oh, look, Josie," Nell said, "aren't the babies cute? The horse's hooves will turn up some fat grubs for them to eat."

"Beggin' your pardon, miss, but quail eat grain."

"Well, for a robin, then."

Mr. Hegele heard the desperation in her tone. "Yes, miss. The robins will be picking at the clumps as soon as we pass."

Over the next half-hour no one spoke. A doe crossed the road and disappeared into a copse of alder trees. Nell smelled smoke from unseen cabins, and the woods began to thin out. First, they saw a lake, and then an orchard of trees showing off pink and white blooms came into view. A man carrying a rifle walked down the road toward them. "You seen any tracks?" he asked.

Mr. Hegele pushed his hat back and scratched his head. "What kind of tracks?"

"The missus and I heard a cougar last night."

"Sorry, mister, we ain't seen nothing."

"Oh, but that's not true." Josie leaned around Mr. Hegele. "We saw quail and a doe."

Nell smiled at the stranger's bewildered expression. "Are all these fruit trees yours, sir?"

"Yes, miss. That orchard is going on eight years old. We come in '73, homesteaded, and planted 'em. You come back in a couple months, and we'll have apples and pears the likes of what you never saw before."

"Thank you so much, Mr. . . ."

"Alling, miss. Frank Alling." He looked at Mr. Hegele. "You got a gun?"

"Under the seat."

"I'd have it on the seat if I was you. Where you headed?"

"Steilacoom. I bought the mill. Hegele's the name."

"These your daughters?"

"Nope. They needed a ride, and I obliged."

"I'm a businesswoman, Mr. Alling." Nell smiled at him. "I hope to sell my needlework there."

"A businesswoman? Is that a fact? My missus would purely love to meet a female businesswoman." He switched his rifle from one hand to the other. "Say, if you have time, why don't you all stop for a visit. Not many women come out as far as Wapato Lake. The missus says sometimes the only way she knows there's other people around is from seeing their chimney smoke."

Before Nell could reply, Mr. Hegele said, "Well now, ain't that nice. I expect I'll be back and forth on this road regular-like, and I'll take you up on the offer, but right now we better be on our way." He made a move, but Nell put her hand on his arm.

"If your wife is nervous about the cougar, Mr. Alling, maybe you could take her mind off it with a pretty piece of needlework." She opened the box on her lap and held it where he could see the piles of white crocheted collars and cuffs.

Mr. Alling propped the rifle against the wagon and poked a leathery finger in the box. "She always did like nice things. New Tacoma's rough after living in San Francisco."

Nell lifted out a white collar with a small button fastener and spread it on her black skirt. "Mrs. Alling might like this because it's detachable. The pattern was in *Godey's Magazine.*"

"By golly, she just might at that. She's a fair one for gewgaws." He fished some coins out of his pocket and offered several to Nell.

"Thank you. I hope everyone in Steilacoom is as generous as you." She closed the box. "And thank you, Mr. Hegele, for waiting."

"If you come back this way, stop and set a spell." Mr. Alling folded his purchase and tucked it in a pocket. "We'd be proud to have you."

Mr. Hegele snapped his reins, and soon Mr. Alling and his orchard were out of sight.

33

After an hour or so, they turned west on a well-traveled road. "This is the Byrd Mill Road," Mr. Hegele said. "It goes straight into Steilacoom, clear to the salt water."

"How much farther?" Josie asked.

"About two hours."

The sun was nearly overhead, and Nell pulled her hat forward to protect her face. The foliage was changing. The fir trees had thinned out, replaced by Gary oaks and the first flush of spring flowers. Prairie land carpeted with blooming camas stretched far into the distance, their violet-blue color competing with the blue sky. Killdeer flew in and out of the grass, catching bugs, while overhead a pair of eagles caught a tailwind and drifted lazily. Then the landscape changed again, and they drove over a bridge so narrow a false move would have tipped one side of the wagon off the edge. The bridge crossed the narrowest part of a large bog full of skunk cabbages and teeming with insects. A quarter of a mile beyond, Mr. Hegele stopped near a small creek.

"I reckon the horses could use a rest," he said.

"So can I." Nell and Josie put their parcels under the seat and jumped down.

"Ouch, I've got pins and needles." Josie waited until Mr. Hegele turned away and rubbed her backside. "Where are we, Mr. Hegele?"

"Comin' onto old Fort Steilacoom and the insane asylum. This is land Joseph Heath cleared back in the 1840s."

"Insane asylum?"

"Didn't you never hear of the Fort Steilacoom Asylum? It's been here for about ten years. Last I heard, fifteen men and eight women live there. Their families say they can't live on their own, and they can't do for them."

Josie began clenching and unclenching her fists again, and Nell tugged at her arm. "Just look at all the strawberries. Let's pick some." She all but dragged her sister to the patch.

Mr. Hegele loosened the horses' tack and led them to the creek to drink. Then he started a fire, filled a pail with water, and threw in come coffee beans. "Likely to be strong," he said. "I reckon we'll have to do without the eggshells to settle it."

When the water boiled and the beans had sent their perfume into the air, the three sat in the wagon's shade to drink coffee and eat bread and drippings along with the fresh berries. The sun was directly overhead, and it was so quiet an unseen man's voice from somewhere carried across the plain. Cabbage Whites, their butterfly wings barely moving, lit on camas flowers. Nell closed her eyes and immediately noticed how different the prairie smelled from what she was used to in town, where the odors of salt water, low tides, and burning wood were always present. *Prairie air,* she thought, *is soft.*

When they finished the meal, Nell took the pail upstream from where the horses had muddied the water and washed it out. She splashed water on her face and neck and flicked some on a hovering dragonfly. *I'd like to stay here all summer; sleep under a lean-to and just be alone for a while.* But the thought filled her with shame. Even with the older ones married and the twins dead, Pa was still Pa, and Ma and Josie and Albina needed her at home.

"Nell. Where are you?" Josie had appeared while Nell daydreamed. "Mr. Hegele is harnessing the horses."

Nell stood and started back, swinging the pail to dry it. Together they hurried to the wagon. "What side of the road is the asylum on?" Nell asked Mr. Hegele.

"The right."

"Josie'd best sit on the left, then."

Josie seemed not to care, and the two girls were ready when the horses were.

By now, they were close enough to Steila-coom to pass others on the road. An occasional homestead came into view. Dogs barked, and, once, two children jumped onto a fence railing and waved. The horses picked their way across another creek with a small, man-made lake on the left. Mr. Hegele gestured toward the right. "Yonder's the mill, but we'll be going into town. Some of this here wood is for Nathaniel Orr, who has a wagon shop."

Nell and Josie looked in the direction Mr. Hegele indicated. Wooden crates and barrels in various states of repair were scattered about a weathered, two-story building. It perched on a leveed embankment, at the bottom of which was a water-soaked wooden bulkhead, with a lively creek lapping against it.

"I'm sure you'll make a wonderful success of it." Nell smiled, and Mr. Hegele looked pleased.

Less than a mile on, the asylum's fenced acreage appeared. Near the road, two women in ragged dresses walked in circles around a plant. When they heard the wagon, they ran to the fence and waved. "I want to go home," one said. She turned it into a chant. Her companion giggled and started rocking back and forth.

"Oh." Josie put her hands to her mouth. "How awful. What could they have done to be put there?"

"Now, never you mind that, Miss Josie." Mr. Hegele snapped the reins, and the horses broke into a jog. "Here, they gets three squares a day and beds to rest in, and sometimes that's all it takes. The doctor will fix them up, and they'll be home before they know it."

"Look." Nell pointed to gulls resting in a cleared patch. "We must be close to the salt water."

"Around the bend and down the hill." Mr. Hegele let the horses slow down. "Steilacoom's been here for almost thirty years. It's a real pretty place. Just you wait and see."

"Pretty or not, we can't thank you enough for the ride, can we, Josie? And you never mentioned the cost."

Josie didn't answer, but Mr. Hegele shook his head. "Never you mind about that; it's nothing. You ladies helped pass the day in a mighty pleasurable way. Look. There's the town down by those madrona trees."

Steilacoom was at their feet, and, in the distance, McNeil and Anderson Islands filled the horizon. Sailing ships and tugboats crowded one large dock while a stern-wheeler floated in front of another. Ducks rode the gentle waves, and gulls screeched and fought while men unloaded their catch of fish. Being so old, Steilacoom looked well settled and affluent to Nell's eyes. Buildings lined neat, north-south roads, and she saw a small church with an adjacent vegetable garden where three nuns and several children were working. Mr. Hegele stopped in front of a single-story shop with a tall false front. From among a cluster of men, one came forward and tied the horses to a hitching rail. Nell straightened her hat and jumped down. Josie stared at a building on McNeil Island with a troubled look.

"That's the prison, isn't it? I hear people talk about it in town, sometimes."

"It's a long way from here, though, way across the water." Nell shook out her skirts and picked up her box.

"But that doesn't matter to those who are there."

"Who do you mean? The residents?"

"Why, the ghosts of all the unhappy people. They don't like the prison. So many sad spirits walk the roads. I can feel them. What do they want?" Josie looked at Nell.

"Don't be silly." Nell tried to be patient, but it was hard, and she sometimes found her sister's fanciful statements exasperating.

"There's no such thing as ghosts. Climb down, please."

Josie pulled her bonnet up so the sides hid her face and joined Nell. "I don't like this place. Once we leave, I'm never coming back again."

Nell looked at her sister with frustration. It was bad enough Josie saw letters backwards and could barely write, but she also had a peculiar superstitious streak. At the same time, though, Nell's annoyance was tinged with pity for the very real pain Josie's irrational fancies caused her. "You don't ever have to come back, but please, let's get on with today," she said gently.

A flock of noisy crows appeared, and Nell's gaze followed their flight. "Look, they're going in and out of the church steeple," she said, hoping to distract her sister. "They must live here with the nuns."

Nell's words carried to the churchyard, and one of the nuns looked up. "They do indeed live here." She dusted off her hands and approached a short picket fence surrounding the white clapboard church and the garden. "I'm Mother Joseph of the Sisters of Charity of Providence, and this is our church." The children who had been helping her pull weeds crowded around.

Nell was unsure whether to curtsy or offer

her hand. To avoid having to do either, she hugged her small box. "I'm Nell Tanquist, and this is my sister, Josie."

"Are you new to Steilacoom? If so, welcome to the Church of the Immaculate Conception." Mother Joseph hesitated for a moment and then laughed. "I know everyone here, so of course you're new, and I welcome you both to Steilacoom even if you're not Catholic."

"Is this really *your* church?" Josie asked.

"Oh, no, my dear. It's God's church, of course. I'm merely visiting. Many years ago, I helped when the church building was moved from Fort Steilacoom, that's all, and now it needs a few repairs." She held out her hands, and Nell saw a blackened thumbnail and several cuts.

"Mother Joseph can do everything," said a girl in a faded pink dress. "She's teaching us to sew."

The nun smiled. "My father taught me all the things he knew: carpentry, farming, blacksmithing, how to work a forge, and even to repair watches. It certainly all comes in handy."

Before Nell could respond, Josie, who had little interest in sewing, said, "I don't understand. What's that — a Sister of Providence?"

41

The elderly nun seemed pleased at her interest. "It means our headquarters are in Montreal, Quebec. Our work is to build missions and bring the word of God to those who don't yet know Him. You aren't Catholic, are you?"

"We're Lutheran," Nell answered. "There's a new Lutheran church in New Tacoma, but we haven't joined yet."

Mother Joseph tipped her head to the side as if considering the words. "Just remember," she said, "the devil loves people who wait."

Nell tensed. "We're not heathens. Ma has told us all about being Lutheran."

She was just about to decide she didn't like Mother Joseph when the nun said, "You're very young to be traveling to Steilacoom by yourselves."

"We're here to see if I can sell some of my needlework." Once again, Nell opened her box.

The nun leaned down. *"Superbe."* She gave Nell a wide smile. "I do needlework myself." At Nell's surprised look she added, "For the church."

Before Nell had time to ask what Mother Joseph made for the church, another nun came up the street toward them. Like Mother Joseph, her head was covered by a piece of white cloth with black fabric wrapped around it. Both the nuns wore long black, robe-like dresses. Nell thought they must have been warm wearing so many clothes.

"Mr. Pincus's boat is here." The second nun stopped and dabbed her perspiring face.

"Ah, just the thing." Mother Joseph beamed. "Thank you, Sister Praxedes." She looked at Nell. "Some fifteen or twenty years ago, Mr. Pincus arrived in Steilacoom with a boat full of miners' supplies he hadn't been able to sell up on the Fraser River. He sold out here in three days, and, ever since, when new supplies arrive, he lets people buy right off the wharf. That way he doesn't have as much to haul to his store. People are so excited when his boat arrives, they often purchase things on a whim. You go on down there, and I'm sure you'll sell your needlework."

Nell wasn't sure if buying her items on a whim was an insult or not. Outspoken nuns were all well and good, and she still smarted from the woman's comment about the devil, but she was also glad to take the advice. "Thank you, ma'am."

"You must call me Mother Joseph."

"Yes, ma'am. Thank you, ma'am." Nell

took Josie. "Come on."

They doubled back on Nisqually Street to the Byrd Mill Road and turned down Frederick Street past a grade school. Josie looked back and waved at the two nuns, then asked Nell, "What does Church of the Immaculate Conception mean?"

"I don't know."

"It's lovely, though, isn't it, that conception could be immaculate?"

Nell made a noncommittal noise. Though neither she nor Josie knew much about the mechanics of conceiving, after watching animals couple, Nell knew a bit about the grunting and coming together that often led to a noisy, messy birth. She considered neither process immaculate.

Their quick footsteps took them to the corner of Frederick and Starling Streets, and a large weather-worn building whose dirt yard was cluttered with wooden pallets and broken casks lying on their sides. Nell knew from the smell that the building was a brewery. On its front side, open double doors were blocked by a wagon with a man standing precariously on its seat, facing backward as he directed men who were unloading the wagon bed. Nell and Josie hurried past the men's curious looks and crossed Rainier Street. From there, they had a view of Commercial Street, which ran along the waterfront.

Commercial was dotted with both homes and businesses. At a quick glance, Nell saw a bakery, butcher shop, and beer hall. Her attention, however, was on one of the docks, where both men and women talked among themselves while watching workers unload crates from a steamer.

Unlike New Tacoma, the ships in Steilacoom Bay were anchored out in the water in front of bobbing docks, accessed by ramps and long wooden walkways. While some men unloaded cargo onto the dock, others transferred the crates onto small carts, which they wheeled to a quay where a crowd milled about, and where a line of wagons waited to be loaded.

"There, Josie." Nell nudged her sister. "That's where we need to go. Come on, now. Hurry." Dodging piles of dung dotted with flies, they hurried down the hill.

The noise was deafening. Longshoremen shouted; heavy wooden boxes thumped on the wharf; children shrieked and chased each other. Seagulls swirled in circles and occasionally broke away to dive toward the heads of the half-dozen fishermen who continued emptying a hull full of thrashing silver bodies into large baskets. *Poor things*

45

gasping for air, Nell thought, and *why in the world did Mother Joseph think I could sell my things here?* She looked at the chaos and then at Josie. "I don't know what to do."

Josie glanced around and found a broken barrel near a pile of driftwood. She pulled it away and scanned the debris-strewn beach. It offered up a battered box and several short planks. By wedging the barrel between two logs, putting the box over the top, and laying the boards on it, she created a table of sorts.

"Oh, Josie. That's brilliant." Nell covered the planks with her black shawl and laid some collars and doilies on it. Satisfied with the display, she smiled at her sister. "Now, I guess we just wait."

They didn't have to wait long. First one woman and then several others strolled over. They held the pieces against their dresses and poked and prodded, all the while talking.

"Isn't this lovely?"

"I think I prefer something plainer."

"Do you have any other colors?"

"I'm sure I could do just as well if I had time."

And so on. Nell was glad the gloves they wore kept her things clean and unsnagged. Slowly at first, and then faster, coins filled her pocket as the ladies made purchases. The sun was high, and the crowd was thinning when two women, their arms linked, strolled up. They wore identical dark-green dresses with large collars, and hats that covered their brown hair. Josie made a small noise, and they smiled. "Have you never seen twins before?" one of them asked.

"No, ma'am." Josie's eyes went back and forth between them. "That is, not grown up and looking the same. Ma had twin babies, but they were different."

"Where are they?"

"In the graveyard."

"Goodness me," said the twin who'd spoken to them first, while the other quickly changed the subject.

"Did you make all these things?"

"I did," Nell said.

"Irish lace, is it?"

For some reason, the words *Irish lace* sounded patronizing, and Nell bridled. "It's something that's popular back East. A recent resident in New Tacoma taught me. She calls it crocheting."

Josie looked startled when Nell said, "recent resident." Hildy Bacom and her family had lived in New Tacoma for nearly five years, and it was Mrs. Bacom who'd taught Nell to crochet. Fortunately, neither twin noticed her reaction. One of them held up a starched butterfly. Nell had put a pin on the back thinking, once tried on, it would be easier to sell. "Look, Rose. Wouldn't this dress up your navy blue?"

"Yours, too."

"Yes, but mine is in better shape." Rose nudged her sister and grinned.

"The butterflies are my favorite," Josie said. "Nell made me a yellow one."

"Do you have any others?" Rose handed Nell some coins.

"No, ma'am. They're all gone."

"Just as well. It'll help people tell us apart." She laughed, and her sister smiled. Nell wondered if the difference between them was that one of them was quieter than the other.

While the quiet twin considered a white doily with purple trim, the wharf was becoming less crowded. Nell took off her bonnet and fanned her face. The temperature had risen, and the water's glare made her squint. The fishermen she'd seen earlier were gone, leaving gulls and crows to fight over any offal. Nell spotted two wharf rats snooping among the beach's refuse and heard birds in a nearby fir tree chatter to each other. She was watching two boys skip rocks when Josie interrupted her thoughts.

"We're almost sold out. Can we go home now?"

The quieter of the twins looked at her. "Don't you like Steilacoom?"

"There's unhappiness here."

The two women looked startled. "My word," Rose said.

"Perhaps she means Albert Balch."

"Oh, of course. Albert Balch."

"We've never been here before, so we don't know who that is. Josie just has fancies, sometimes." When her sister began to pull at her fingers, Nell covered Josie's hands with her own.

"Albert Balch was Lafayette Balch's brother. Lafayette founded Steilacoom." Rose stopped to pin the butterfly to her dress.

"He built the first store here," her sister said.

"Had the wood shipped clear from Maine."

"Goodness gracious, why?" Nell's glance took in some of the many trees surrounding the town.

"He built it in 1851, and there weren't any sawmills."

Josie looked wide eyed at Rose. "Tell me about Albert."

"Why, he was quite mad, you know. Tell

her, Marcella, you knew him better than I."

"Poor Albert." Marcella shook her head. "Well, our father, John Rigney, came out here with the military. He eventually built a farm on the prairie, and that's where he saw Albert. Albert was a storekeeper. Generally, he behaved himself, Albert, that is, and was as sane as you and me. But every time the moon was full, he had a spell and showed the most alarming behavior, claimed his enemies were chasing him and trying to kill him. His family put him in the insane hospital, but the doctors there said he was sane enough to be at home, and they turned him loose. He got worse, though. On nights the moon was full, Albert roamed the woods carrying an ax. Father would hear him near the barn talking to people who weren't there. One day Albert didn't come home. Searchers went out and found him dead, wearing nothing but his nightshirt." Marcella sighed, and the twins shook their heads. Josie clutched at Nell.

"Please, Nell, please. I don't want to stay here anymore. Please, let's go home."

"Josie. Stop it. We'll find a nice hotel and leave first thing tomorrow. I promise. But we don't have any way to get home now. It's so late in the day, no one will be going there."

"Dear me." Rose looked at her sister. "I'm ever so sorry." She began backing away.

Marcella patted Josie's arm. "Where is it you want to return to?"

"New Tacoma."

"Well, it will be fine, dear. The Harmon House Hotel is just down the road." She, too, backed away, and the sisters melted into the dwindling cluster of people.

They certainly didn't want to feel obligated, Nell thought. She began putting away her unsold handiwork. "Oh, Josie. What am I going to do with you?" She rubbed her forehead in distress. Josie sat next to her and put her head on Nell's shoulder.

"I'm sorry, Nell. Please don't be mad. Let's go back to the church. Maybe they'll let us stay overnight. I wouldn't be afraid there."

Before Nell could respond, a male voice said, "I cunna help hearing. I may be able to help ye."

Both girls jumped, and Nell hurriedly put her hat back on. The man standing in front of them looked to be in his early twenties. His black hair gleamed in the late afternoon sun, and he had black eyes with thick eyelashes. He held a cap like those Nell had seen Greek sailors wear, but his tanned face said he didn't often wear it. Fish scales dot-

51

ted his heavy pants and wrinkled shirt.

"Thank you, sir. It's kind of you to offer, but we'll be fine at the hotel."

"Oh, Nell, if he can take us home today, let him."

"We don't even know him." Nell struggled for composure. "Truly, sir, we are most appreciative of the offer, but we can't impose on the kindness of a stranger."

"My name is John Calhoun. I'm from Aberdeenshire in Scotland." His voice was quiet and had a touch of a Scots burr. "The ladies you were just talking to are the Rigney twins," he said, "and they can vouch for me. I just came up from San Francisco with a shipment for Mr. Pincus."

"You see, Nell, he's a friend of those ladies." Josie turned to John Calhoun. "Are you going to New Tacoma? Do you have a wagon?"

"Not a wagon, exactly. You see, it isn't known yet, but Mr. Pincus wants to relocate to New Tacoma, and he hired me to go there and take a look about." John Calhoun glanced briefly at the wharf. "You see the man with the white mustache? That's him. I'll ask him to speak with you."

Before Nell could respond, John Calhoun put his cap back on and walked to where the Rigney twins and Mr. Pincus stood. She watched as they talked, occasionally looking in her direction. After a few minutes, while she and Josie waited, all four returned. The mustached man removed his hat and spoke first. "I'm afraid John didn't tell me your names."

"I didn't give him our names." Nell wasn't sure whether to feel pressured or not. "I'm Nell Tanquist and this is my sister, Josie, and we are planning on staying here overnight and riding back on the *Dashing Wave* tomorrow. I had a little money when we arrived and made enough to pay with some left over. The *Dashing Wave* will be headed for New Tacoma in the morning but generally stops at Steilacoom on the way."

"That's right, but I understand from John that your sister is anxious to return home tonight. He asked us to verify his reliability, and I can vouch for him." Mr. Pincus looked at the twins, and they nodded. "It's approximately twenty miles by water from Steilacoom to New Tacoma," he continued. "The tide is good, and it won't be dark for several hours. Now, dear ladies," he nodded at them and John Calhoun, "I have to get back to the unloading."

Mr. Pincus put his hat back on and walked away with a twin on each arm, and Nell looked silently at Josie. "It's very kind of

you, Mr. Calhoun. Under ordinary circumstances, I hate to be beholden, but, since
my sister insists, we'll accept your offer with
our thanks." She picked up her shawl.
"Which vessel's yours?"

John Calhoun smiled. A dimple in his
cheek gave him a boyish look. "This way."
He started down the wharf to where a
wooden boat had just enough freeboard to
float. "She's not mine; she belongs to Mr.
Pincus, and he has given me use of her."

Nell looked at it in dismay. "Where are
the sails?"

"She doesn't have sails."

"But how will we get home?"

"I'll row."

CHAPTER 3

Nell looked at John Calhoun, at the boat he'd indicated, and back at him. "Row?"

While she stared at him in dismay, John smiled at Josie and offered his arm. "I promise you; you'll be safe with me."

Josie scrambled aboard and sat on a small thwart in the stern. "Don't make a fuss, Nell. Get in and we'll be home before you know it. Won't we, Mr. Calhoun?"

"Aye, that we will."

Nell tucked her box under one arm and clambered awkwardly in, thinking, *I wish Hildy had come with me.* However, when she sat on a seat in the bow, her usual excitement at something unexpected happening returned. *Young ladies aren't supposed to be so impetuous, but it's been a long time since I had an adventure,* she thought. Meanwhile, Calhoun stepped around her and sat in the middle. He pushed off from the beach with an oar, slid it back in the oarlock, and started rowing. A few strong strokes took them to the south-flowing current.

When they'd left Steilacoom behind and passed an expanse of tree-lined shore, Nell looked at him. "How long will it take us to reach Old Tacoma?"

She watched as the tree-crowded beach receded and a stretch of driftwood-strewn shoreline come into view. Two Indian long-boats passed them, headed in the other direction. Farther out in the water, sailing vessels on their way north made use of a three-knot breeze and the Narrows' swift-moving middle channel. The air smelled fresh, and Nell settled her hat more firmly on her head. She and Josie both smiled as a seal broke the water's surface and looked around.

"A few hours."

"Will we pass any towns along here?" Josie asked.

"No, ma'am, only Father and Mrs. Weston's house." Listening to Calhoun's soft Scottish burr, Nell suddenly wished he'd smile at her the way he did at Josie. She quickly put the thought away and was going to ask who Father Weston was when they got caught in a small whirlpool and spun in a circle.

"Lots of wee eddies in the Straits." Calhoun focused on controlling the boat. After that, she closed her eyes against the sun's glare on the water and tried to relax. When the rowing stopped, she opened her eyes and saw they'd come to rest in front of the mouth of a creek. Calhoun was writing in a small book.

"Are you looking for land?" she asked.

Calhoun looked up, tucked the book in his pocket, and picked up the oars. "Aye."

He continued rowing, pulling in long, even strokes that sent the boat skimming. Grebes and Harlequin ducks rode the tide, and cormorants lined snags. An eagle shot down from its hidden perch and grabbed a fish. Though her brother, Ike, had taught her to row, Nell had little time nowadays to use the skill; she was often near the water but rarely actually on it. She enjoyed the new perspective, and the briny and mildly fishy odors.

Ships passed, some leaving gentle wakes. Nell recognized the *Dashing Wave* and the *Gipsy,* both headed south. When John Calhoun wasn't watching the shore, he seemed to enjoy seeing the tugs and masted schooners go by.

"Is that Father Weston's place?" Nell opened her eyes and saw Josie point to a weathered building with a long, covered porch and smoke rising from a chimney.

"Aye."

The house faced the Narrows but stood well up from the waterline. The Westons had cleared enough land to allow for a large barn and good-sized lean-to. Behind the buildings, fruit trees blossomed. "That looks like an orchard."

"Aye, it is."

Josie frowned at the site. "It's awfully lonely way out here, isn't it?"

Nell smiled. "But Josie, you always say you don't like neighbors being too close."

"I know, but closer than that."

She laughed, and Nell felt irrational irritation when John Calhoun said, "I feel much the same." *I'm just tired,* Nell thought. *We should be having a nice dinner in Steilacoom instead of sitting in this boat on a wooden seat that is mighty hard.*

Off in the distance they caught a glimpse of Fox Island and saw more and more ships entering the strait. Nell was surprised at how many she'd seen in New Tacoma, and how much prettier they were on the water rather than tied up at the wharf. All but one had their names visible in large letters. The unnamed ship was a small, weather-beaten steamer. Smoke poured from her stack, and the captain steered her among the other vessels with seeming reckless abandon. Some captains sounded their horns when she came too close, and Nell saw several men waving their arms. John Calhoun, who had been keeping an eye on the steamer's speed and direction, adjusted his strokes to direct the rowboat toward shore.

"What are you doing?" Nell held to the sides after he changed their course and drove the boat up onto the rocky beach.

"Are we near home?" Josie asked.

The beach was a small spit, with an arm ending in a point and salt water washing around it into a channel. "I think this is Day Island. If it is, we have a long way to go," Nell said, looking around with interest. "Mrs. Blackwell comes here to find the shells she trades to East Coast collectors. Look." She leaned over the side and peered down into the water's clear depths. "There's clam, mussel, and quahog shells."

John Calhoun ignored Nell and Josie and watched as men in the derelict steamer began to lower small rowboats over the side. Swiftly, he crawled around Nell, jumped off the boat into knee-deep water, and grabbed a rope. "Get out," he hissed.

"What?"

"Quiet. Voices carry on the water. Get out. Come on. Hurry."

Nell looked at Josie's startled expression and let Calhoun take her arm to help her out. "What are you going to do with us?"

"Nothing, but I can't speak for yon men."

Nell grasped his meaning and shuddered. Josie looked over her shoulder and gave a little squeak. Men were climbing down rope ladders into the bobbing boats. As soon as one was full, a rower headed it toward land. She scrambled out and stood by Nell.

"Come on." Calhoun bent low and hurried up the debris-strewn shore. A small deer trail climbed the embankment from the beach and disappeared in the serviceberries, ferns, and trees. He strode up it and turned to help Nell and Josie. The trail was covered with fir needles, which sent up a pungent odor under their feet. It was so narrow, low-hung boughs caught at their clothing, and low-growing Oregon grape scratched through the cloth. Insects, attracted by their sweat, hummed and hovered. John followed the path until he found a massive downed cedar whose roots had apparently been wrenched from the soil by a windstorm.

"There." He pointed to the resulting hole.

"There, what?"

"I don't think yon men will find you there."

Without a word, Josie climbed in and wrapped her skirts around her, but Nell remained standing. "What about you?"

"Ssh." He scowled. "I'm going back to try and hide the boat."

"What if they see you?"

"They won't."

"But what if they do?"

"If I don't come back but the boat's there, row to Father Weston's house. If it isn't there, you'll have to walk."

He disappeared into the brush, and Josie glanced up. "Are there bugs here?"

"What do you think?" Nell looked at her sister and then at the barely discernible trail. *At least I can find the way to the beach.*

"Why are you still standing there?"

"I'm going to see what he's up to."

"But you can't leave me here." Josie's voice rose, and Nell squatted down to hush her.

"I need to make sure we're safe. We don't even know this man, and now he's left us here in the woods. I'll only be gone for a few minutes and I promise to come right back. Here." She tugged on Josie's shawl. "Cover your head so the mosquitoes won't find you."

Nell pulled her own shawl up to hide her blonde hair and started retracing their footsteps, tamping down fear from the implied danger. It seemed like a long time since she'd been a child and able to run free and no one bothered her. Life as a young woman, she discovered, had too many restrictions.

She heard voices before she caught a glimpse of the water. A round, squat rhododendron in full bloom provided cover, and she hunkered down behind it to look. The first rowboat had beached, and a tall man with a scar extending from his eye to his jaw stood in knee-deep water. "Come on. Get out." He grabbed the arm of one of the passengers. The other boats also beached, and the rowers followed suit, until, eventually, four rowboats lined the shore. The scarred man laughed when some of the passengers slipped on knots of kelp and eelgrass and fell. *Chinese.* Nell wondered why they had chosen to come this way when the railroad hired so many and brought them north by train.

When all the passengers stood on the rocky shore, Scarface pointed north. "That way, boys. This is the end of the line. I suggest you start walking before it gets dark. The tide's coming in."

One of the Chinese men spoke. "Wha?"

"I said, this is the end of the line. Tacoma's

that away."

Something moved in the bushes near where Nell hid, and Scarface looked in her direction. Nell held her breath and waited in terror until a crow flew out and lit near a rotting clam. After a moment of scanning the bushes, Scarface jerked his arm toward the unnamed boat they'd come from, then pushed one of the rowboats off the beach and got in. His crew did the same with the other rowboats. When all the boats were several yards from shore, the Chinese men began milling about, waving their arms and arguing. Finally, they started walking. When their voices had faded into nothing, Nell let out a long-held breath.

"What are you doing here?" John Calhoun appeared suddenly at her side. She hadn't heard him move from wherever he had been hiding. "I thought I told you to stay put."

"You did." Nell stood and worked the pins and needles out of her legs. When she didn't say more, he turned away. They returned to the deer trail, following it back to where Josie waited.

Josie was still down in the hole. The shawl prevented her hearing their approach. "Josie." Nell touched her sister's arm lightly and felt her jump.

"You were gone a long time."

"But I came back. I told you I would, didn't I? It's safe now; the men are gone, and Mr. Calhoun is anxious to start for New Tacoma before it gets too dark." She helped Josie up. "You were very brave."

Josie beamed. "Yes, I was, wasn't I?" Nell rolled her eyes and saw John Calhoun suppress a smile.

He had hidden their boat at a place where the boughs of a madrona tree hanging out of the embankment, almost parallel with the beach, touched the shore. Nell and Josie helped push the boat to the edge of the water and climbed back in. Calhoun gave it a final shove and followed. He resumed his seat in the middle and began rowing. The tide in the Narrows Strait reversed direction twice a day, and now he had to pull hard against it. Josie's head drooped, and she nodded off. Nell put her little box on her lap, propped her elbow on it, and rested her head in her hand. She watched the land pass but neither saw nor heard anything of the Chinese men. *Poor things,* she thought. *I hope they'll know to go in the same direction as the ships.*

The sun had almost set when they rounded the point people called the Military Reservation That Never Was. Out of the strait's strong current, John breathed a sigh of relief and hugged the shore. His face glistened, and Nell saw his fatigue.

"Would you have decided to row to New Tacoma if it weren't for us?" she asked.

"No, ma'am. I'd have slept rough someplace where the fishing was good." He grinned, and Nell smiled back.

"Then it's awfully good of you to do this, especially for Josie's sake."

"Aye, well . . ." He let the sentence trail off, but Nell guessed he was trying to find something polite to say.

"Josie is very — um — imaginative. She sees things that aren't there, hears them, too."

He considered her words, and Nell rushed to defend her sister. "But she plays the piano beautifully, when she has access to one, and she sings, too. It's just that sometimes she needs help with practicalities."

Calhoun lifted an oar over a floating log. "Aye, I can see that, but we can all use an occasional hand."

They were silent until noise from the Hanson and Ackerson Mill reached them. The sounds woke Josie, and Nell asked to be let off there.

"We can walk over the hill."

Josie scowled. "You know I don't like to walk through the woods in the dark."

Nell closed her eyes for a moment and then laughed. Josie never ceased to amaze her. She saw John Calhoun glance at her sister before he turned toward the mill's ladder. "Josie," she said, "we've been up and on the road for twenty hours, and I, for one, am tired of sitting. Mr. Calhoun went out of his way to row us back to New Tacoma just to please you, but we shouldn't put him out any longer. If he takes us on to the Blackwells' hotel, we have to walk half a mile to town on the Wharf Road and then up several hills to get home. From Old Tacoma, we can walk through the woods on a mostly level trail and be home much faster. And, you can hunt for wildflowers."

Josie brightened a little. "Maybe I could take some to Ma."

"That would make her no end happy."

The girls smiled at each other, and John Calhoun shook his head. He pulled up to the edge of the mill's dock at a place where brackish water lapped halfway up a rough plank ladder. Handing Nell the rope, he climbed to the wharf. She tossed the rope to him, and he tied it to a piling. Josie followed him onto the dock, and then Nell handed up her box and the parcel of clothing they hadn't used and stepped onto the ladder. At the top, she had to take his hand in order to climb onto the dock. He held it longer than necessary, staring intently at her face, and his eyes glowed in the drawing-on dark. Nell was suddenly aware that his shoulders were very broad and the hand holding hers had blisters.

"You'll need to put some cream on those." She touched his palm gently.

"Aye, but I've work to do yet this night." His expression changed, and she let go of his hand when he turned to smile at Josie. "T'was a pleasure to meet you, Miss Josie."

Well, of all things. Nell pulled some coins out of her pocket. "How much do we owe you, Mr. Calhoun?"

"Nothing, Miss Tanquist. You ladies came as a favor to me."

"That's awfully kind, but I'd like to pay you for your trouble." He started to protest again, but she suddenly smiled. "I know. My friend Hildy has a new bakery in town. You go there and ask for a loaf of her bread, and tell her I will pay her later. She makes awfully good bread."

"I would enjoy that." He smiled. "At home we have a saying, 'A table without bread is not a table, but bread is a table on its own.' "

Nell laughed. "Well, Hildy would certainly agree. You must tell her that." She watched him walk away and disappear among piles of logs. *Holding my hand and smiling at Josie. The very idea.*

By this time Josie was growing anxious again. "Can you find us a lantern, Nell? It's dark, and you know I don't like the woods when it's dark."

Nell sighed. She didn't know whether to laugh or cry. *Oh, Josie why can't you grow up? You're four years older than me, but I always have to be the adult.* Ashamed of her thoughts and tired from the long day, Nell took Josie's arm, and they hurried across the dock, anxious not to attract the millworkers' attention. A pungent fish odor filled the air, and they saw a group of men and boys admiring an eight-foot basking shark suspended from a pole. "Fought him for going on five hours," a fisherman was saying.

"That'll fertilize most of the gardens in Old Tacoma," someone responded, and the men laughed.

On Old Tacoma's main street, a man walking to work offered Nell and Josie a bottle with the bottom broken out and a candle stub burning in the neck. Nell took it gratefully.

The trail to New Tacoma was still wet and muddy from spring's erratic weather, and the makeshift lantern saved them from several mishaps. Night had closed in. They stepped over downed saplings and around marshy patches of skunk cabbages, stumbling from fatigue. New Tacoma was a welcome sight, and, when they reached their own street, a light shone in the kitchen window. The door opened, and they met their brother, Ike, and his wife Frieda Faye just leaving.

"I thought you weren't coming home until tomorrow." Ike kept his arm around his wife, who was due to give birth soon.

"Josie didn't like Steilacoom."

In the dim light, Nell and Ike exchanged knowing looks.

"I didn't. It was horrid. We saw an asylum, and there's a jail on an island. Folks say the ghost of a man named Albert Balch roams around at night . . ."

Before Josie could say more, Nell gave her a little push. "Go inside. I'll be there in a minute."

"It's too bad you came home early," Ike said. "Grandma Staley is here."

"Oh, no. Why?"

"Ma's hoping she can contact the twins."

"A séance?"

"Yeah. Grandma Staley showed up as soon as Pa left for work."

"Ma can't afford to pay her."

"She'll get the money somewhere." Ike looked at the box in which Nell carried her handiwork.

"She can't. She won't ask for my money, will she? Ma knows how hard I worked all winter making things to sell."

"You can always say no."

But Nell knew she couldn't and knew Grandma Staley could smell money and would charge accordingly. She shoved the box behind the rain barrel. "I'm going for a walk. Give me a minute, then tell Ma, will you, Josie?" Without waiting for an answer, she turned and hurried away, no destination in mind. Behind her she heard Ike saying goodbye to their mother and heard her mother ask Josie if she had any money.

CHAPTER 4

When Nell returned from her walk, the kitchen's oil lamps had been turned low, and her mother sat in front of the fire, staring into the dying flames. Nell saw her mother's rough, red hands — idle for once — and the streaks of white hair gradually pushing out the brown and felt a pang of sadness. Amity Tanquist had less to do now that the twins were gone, and yet she looked more tired than she had when they took so much of her time. Nell hung up her shawl and hat, then went and sat on the floor, resting her head on her mother's knee. "Where's Josie?"

"Gone to bed." Amity smoothed Nell's hair with a work-worn hand, the way she had when Nell was sick as a child. "She gave me a garbled account of a ghost wandering Steilacoom carrying a knife, a nun named Joseph, and a boat ride you took with a strange man."

Nell watched the fire's embers turn red and then black. She thought briefly of John Calhoun's dark eyes and his hand holding hers and half laughed. "It's all more or less true, but I'm too tired to tell you now."

"Were you very successful?"

"Yes, I sold nearly everything I made."

A piece of pitch in a Douglas fir log snapped, sending sparks up the chimney. Nell closed her eyes and felt her tension lessening. "Ike said Grandma Staley was here."

"I asked her to come."

"Why?"

"To do a seeing over the twins."

Nell leaned back and looked up. "Oh, Ma. What could she possibly see? The twins were so young when they died."

"I know that." Amity continued stroking Nell's hair while she searched for words. "Grandma Staley comforts me. After a seeing, I feel like I can rest easy for a while."

"But it never lasts."

"I know."

"Aren't we enough, Ma?"

"Of course you are, each in your own way. But I've lost four babies now, and there's such a hole in my heart where the twins were. Grandma Staley helps fill the hole with her words."

Nell felt sudden tears and brushed them away. "I can't keep paying her, Ma. I make such a little profit, and I'm saving to buy a sewing machine. You know that."

"And what will you do with a sewing machine?"

"Start my own dressmaking business." Nell sat up and covered her mother's hands with her own. "New Tacoma has three millinery shops but no dressmakers. I could be that — have a business of my own, just like Hildy and her bakery. And there is a shop on Pacific Avenue that's going to sell Singer sewing machines. Remember, Pa told us about unloading them. It's just what I want."

"But, daughter, you'll be married long before you have saved up enough."

Nell shook her head. "No, I won't. I don't care so very much about being married and having a husband and children. I never have. I want to make my own way, travel maybe. I hear people talking about San Francisco and Portland and Victoria. I want to see those places."

"Before we came West, your pa and I lived in a big city. Quite often they're not as nice as you think they'd be."

"The biggest town I've seen is Olympia, and it's not much. Just because *you* don't like real cities doesn't mean I won't."

Amity sighed and looked at the fire. Only the embers remained to be banked for morning. "Will you see Grandma Staley tomorrow?"

"Yes, Ma, but I'm going to tell her this is the last time."

"Go to bed, Nell."

"Aren't you going to bed?"

"Your pa will be off work soon. I'll wait for him."

"Good night, Ma." Nell scrambled to her feet and kissed her mother's cheek. "Josie has to do all the dishes for a week; don't let her wiggle out of it."

Amity laughed. "Dare I ask how that came to be?"

"It will be part of what I tell you tomorrow."

Nell woke late the next morning. She rarely slept after dawn and almost never had the bed she shared with Josie to herself. However, the previous night her mother had brought her a hot toddy, and the alcohol warmed and relaxed her into a deep sleep. She stretched and wiggled while listening to Josie singing in the kitchen. Then the door opened, and Albina, her youngest sister, peered in. "Ma says to see are you awake yet."

Nell sat up and held out her arms. "I am now."

"Are you rich, Nell?" Albina asked eagerly. She jumped onto the bed, and Nell tickled her. "Josie says you are. Will you buy me something?"

Nell tossed the covers over her sister's head and jumped out of bed. "I'm not rich, Beanie, but I will buy you something if Ma says you were good while we were gone. Were you?"

"I was entirely good except I bit Billie Yoder on the arm."

"What?" Nell stepped into her corset and wiggled it up under her nightgown. "Why?"

"He poured his slate water down my neck."

"What did your teacher say?"

"Mrs. Stair didn't see, except she saw me bite him, and she kept me after school. I had to write, 'I will not bite' fifty times."

"Do you think little girls who bite people deserve presents?" Nell pulled her nightgown over her head and tightened the corset's ties. Then she stepped into her dress. When the dress was buttoned, she picked up the button hook and began fastening her shoes.

75

"They do if they have to sit in a wet dress," Albina was saying. "It was just awfully cold, and Mrs. Stair didn't care." She sighed heavily. "I think she was glad I was wet because she wants me to get sick and die."

"Oh, surely not." Nell hid a smile.

"I think so." Albina sighed again. "It's because I can't do fractions."

"I didn't know you were learning fractions."

"We just started, and they're terribly, terribly hard." Albina looked at her sister and said,"I struggle, Nell, I really do."

Nell picked her sister up and swung her over her shoulder. "Have you done your homework for Monday?"

"No."

"Well, after dinner I'll help you." She carried the little girl into the kitchen and plunked her into a chair. "You are getting much too big for me to carry. I think you gave me the epizootic."

Albina giggled. "People don't get epizootic, only animals."

While Nell sliced a loaf of bread and put two pieces on a toasting fork, Amity came in with her apron full of eggs. She emptied them carefully into a wash basin. While they soaked, she pulled a skillet onto the stove, added some fat, and cracked two eggs into it. "Look, Albina, a double yolk. Make a wish."

The eggs and toast were ready at the same time, and Nell sat down with her food and a cup of coffee. "Where's Josie?"

"She took some things over to Frieda Faye."

"You'd think no one ever had a baby before."

"It's her first." Amity started cleaning feathers and dung off the remaining eggs. "When you have your first, you'll understand." She handed the eggs, one at a time, to Albina, who dried them and packed them in a basket of straw.

Nell sighed and finished eating in silence. She washed her dishes and picked up her hat and shawl. "I'm off now, Ma."

"Where are you going?" Albina asked. "Can I come, too?"

"No, Beanie. I'm going to Old Tacoma, and it's too far for you to walk." She hugged her sister. "Be good."

Albina beamed. "Oh, I will. I'll be ever so good."

Nell's gaze met her mother's, and they exchanged smiles.

Outside, Nell was glad of the shawl. Clouds obscured the sun, and a slight breeze pushed leaves and tree limbs around. Remembering the previous day's tides, Nell decided to hike the land trail to Old Tacoma and, if the water wasn't too high, take the beach trail back. She climbed the hill behind her home and veered around Old Woman's Gulch. Nell was a little afraid of the community there. The gulch was where New Tacoma's destitute widows built shacks and tried to scratch out livings. The women didn't always get along, and stories of their fights, some involving fists and occasionally knives, regularly made the rounds. As she skirted the gulch, Nell saw laundry draped over bushes and heard a rooster throw back his head and greet the day. A few voices reached her, but the shanty area was mostly quiet. Half an hour later, long before the trail began to drop down the hill to Old Tacoma, she heard noise from the Hanson and Ackerson Mill. What with construction of a new coal bunker, a fish cannery, and all the new houses going up, the mill had more business than it could handle, and more mills were being built.

It was the middle of the day, and Nell saw few people until she started down Starr Street and passed St. Peter's Episcopal Church. Grandma Staley lived on North 30th Street, next door to her former husband, Job Carr. She was the only divorced person Nell knew. Everyone in both Old and New Tacoma had heard the story of Job arriving in December 1864 and settling where two creeks met to create a small lagoon. Two of his sons and one daughter followed him, and then his former wife showed up so she could live close to her children. Nell had never met them but had heard that the daughter, Marietta, was the belle of Old Tacoma.

Taking a deep breath, Nell approached the cottage just as the door opened and a man came out, followed by the psychic. The man had green and yellow bruises on his face, and strips of cloth held one arm fast to his chest. Catching sight of Nell, he nodded and hurried past, leaving the rank smells of fish, smoke, and sweat in his wake. Nell shuddered and hurried to where Grandma Staley stood on a wooden doorstep. This was the first time Nell had met the medium, and the slight, dark-haired woman standing in the doorway wearing a flowered apron over her neat cotton dress looked much like any other woman well into middle age. "Come inside, child," she said. "The teapot is on. It's always a treat to do a seeing for a lovely young lady such as yourself."

Nell followed her into a small, expensively furnished room. She'd heard Grandma Staley made a lot of money being a medium, and the mahogany furnishings, large mirror, and collection of dishes on a sideboard provided proof.

"Sit down. I'll just fetch the tea. Do you mind if I leave the door open for a few minutes?"

"I would prefer it." Nell picked up a small bouquet of sweet peas from the table and inhaled their spicy scent. "Who was that man? He looked as if he'd been in a terrible fight."

"He had." Grandma Staley set two cups on a table and turned to pick up the teapot. "It's been in the papers, so I'm not violating a confidence. The man was Prussian Pete. Would you like milk or honey with your tea?"

"Honey, please." Nell didn't really like tea, but she added some honey and stirred it in. "I read about his fight in the *Ledger.* He wasn't expected to live, was he?"

"No, he wasn't. Wonderful stamina, some of these Germans." The older woman added honey to her own tea and sat down. "Saw it myself in the war."

"The war?"

"The War between the States. I was a

hospital matron."

Nell didn't know how to respond. She sipped her tea and said, "That was very brave of you."

"I absolutely agree, child. I saw terrible things." Grandma Staley put her cup down. "Now, if you will give me your hand, what *seeing* do you want?"

"I'm not here for that. I came to pay for Ma — that is, my mother, Amity Tanquist." Nell put her hand in her pocket. "How much does she owe you?"

The medium named an amount, and Nell counted out the coins. When she put them on the table, she said, "This is the last time I will pay you. From now on, you best ask for your money before you do a seeing."

Grandma Staley put a finger on one of the coins and moved it in circles over the white cloth. "Is that kind?"

"Kind or not, we can't afford them. I can't afford them."

"Even though they bring her much-needed comfort and closeness with the deceased children?"

"Yes, even though." Nell stood up. "They were just babies, and, besides, Ma has Indiana and her family down on Bush Prairie, and Ike's wife, Frieda Faye, is going to have a baby any day, and there's me and

Josie and Albina."

"You sound very heartless."

"I don't mean to be, but . . ." Nell didn't know how to finish the sentence.

"But you don't believe in what I do."

"It's not for me to say. I just know that I worked all winter for what little I made selling handiwork in Steilacoom. I'm saving for a Singer sewing machine. If I can buy one, I can start a dressmaking business. Then I'll be able to . . ." Again, she stopped.

". . . be your own boss," Grandma Staley finished. "Have your own money and do with it what you like."

"Just like you."

"You're right." The medium stood and moved toward the door. "Very well, I'll do as you wish. Cash up front, as they say, and devil take the hindmost. You do what you have to do, too."

"Thank you." Nell stepped out the door and took a deep breath of the sawdust-smelling air.

"Goodbye for now," Grandma Staley said.

"There won't be another time."

The woman smiled and stepped back. "We'll see," she said and closed the door.

Nell tried not to hurry as she walked toward town. Old Tacoma bustled, but not as much as New Tacoma. Most yards were unfenced, and cows wandered wherever they spotted something to eat. Flies swarmed on piles of muck. Some people had tied bits of rags to sticks and pushed them in the ground near their gardens, but the chickens walked around them and pecked at the soil. Seagulls flew in circles above the shoreline, trying to chase away an eagle circling overhead. Turning off Starr Street, she saw Mrs. Steele's hotel and the McCarver house where Josie worked. On the bay to her left, a tugboat pulled a log boom across the water toward the mill. In front of her, men crawled over the frame of James Williams's salmon cannery. The little community, Nell decided, was the same as New Tacoma but somehow different, too.

As the tide was still within six feet of the land, Nell decided she had enough time to walk the beach and reach the Wharf Road that ran from behind the Blackwell Hotel to Pacific Avenue. She started southeast, keeping close to the less rocky, high-tide line. On the hill to her right, businesses and private homes gave way to men's lodging houses. Some half a dozen or so were backed up unevenly against the embankment. Nell remembered an expression her pa had picked up in the war, and she thought it applied to the boardinghouses:

most looked as if they'd been rode hard and put away wet.

The sight of men going in and out, the sounds of shouting and doors slamming, made her uncomfortable. She picked up her steps and was passing the last building — the only one with a second story and a porch running its length — when two men strolled out. The taller of the two was John Calhoun. As she watched, he pulled a sheaf of papers from an inside jacket pocket and handed them to his companion. The other man put them away and removed a small flask that he'd concealed in his coat. He took a drink and passed the bottle to Calhoun, who put the flask to his mouth and tipped his head back just far enough to let the liquid flow slowly down his throat. He handed the flask back. They exchanged a few words, and Calhoun turned, then gave a start and hurried down the stairs. Nell ducked her head and quickened her steps along the beach. Behind her, shells and rocks crunched under heavy footsteps, and a moment later Calhoun took her arm.

"You shouldn't be here," he said.

"If you let go of my arm, I soon won't be." Nell pulled away.

"The lodging houses are dangerous places."

"I had business uptown. I wasn't at a lodging house."

"Whether you were or no', you were seen."

"I can't see how the beach trail is any more dangerous than the trail over the hill."

"I'll walk with you."

"It's not necessary."

He stared her down. "I think it is."

Nell continued walking, and John Calhoun fell in beside her. Neither said a word until the coal bunkers' scaffold came into sight. "I'll leave you here."

"Three workers have fallen off the stringers. Are you sure I'll be safe?"

Unexpectedly, John grinned. "You will be if no one falls on you."

"I'll be sure to watch for falling bodies. Goodbye, Mr. Calhoun. Thank you for the escort."

"It was entirely my pleasure, Miss Tanquist, but I wish you'd call me John."

Nell raised and lowered an eyebrow. "Really, Mr. Calhoun, I hardly know you."

"But we have traveled together." He gave her a slow smile. "It would be a favor to me. I have no family here, and few friends."

Nell's memory flashed to John Calhoun's look as he helped her from the ladder and to the warmth of his hand on hers, but then it jumped to the sight of his sharing a drink with the man at the boardinghouse. "All right," she said, though without smiling, "that is, if I see you again." The implication that she wouldn't was clear.

Calhoun's eyes darkened, and his voice turned cold. "Thank you, Miss Nell." He turned abruptly and walked away.

CHAPTER 5

Several days after the trip to Steilacoom, Nell pulled on a pair of cotton gloves and went outside to work in the garden. Despite a cool spring, the vegetable starts were thriving, but so were the weeds. Nell liked working in the garden; but she worried about her hands and how, if her skin became too rough, they might damage her handiwork. The first time she weeded wearing a pair of old gloves, Josie laughed. She didn't laugh later that night when Nell rubbed her hands with bear grease and pulled on a second pair of gloves. "That smells awful."

"I know, but it will keep my skin smooth, so it won't snag the crochet threads."

"I hope the smell doesn't keep me awake." Josie jumped into bed and turned her back, and Nell grinned as she climbed in next to her. Nothing kept Josie awake. And then, not long after, Josie started doing the same thing because, she said, working for Mrs.

McCarver was ruining her hands for the piano.

Nell was thinking about that when she heard Albina's voice coming from a wagon pulling up in front of the house. She put her trowel down and went to see who her sister was with. On the rutted dirt road, Hildy's brother, Reuben, sat on the seat of a familiar-looking wagon. When Nell appeared, he grinned and pulled off his hat.

"Howdy, Nell."

"Good afternoon, Reuben. Did you give Albina a ride?"

"Yes. I was driving by the school and saw her."

"That was kind." Nell looked at the pony pulling the old dray, and at the pails and jugs in its bed. "Isn't this Mr. Scott's milk wagon?"

"He hired me." Reuben's grin widened.

"What about school?"

"For now, I'm doing his afternoon deliveries. Anyway, school's almost out."

"Well, I thought I recognized Martyr-to-the-Cause." Nell rubbed the horse's nose. "Does he still sulk when you hitch him up?"

"I don't know. Mr. Scott has him ready when I get there."

"Why isn't one of the Scott boys making deliveries?"

"Bob burned his — er — self on the stove and can't drive the wagon."

"Sitting too close?"

"Not exactly. But he was standing close to it when he forgot he had some gunpowder in his pocket, and it caught on fire and burned his britches good." Reuben bit his lips to keep from laughing. "Anyway, Mr. Scott is building a windmill, and all the boys are helping with that. Besides . . ."

"Besides what?"

"Well, you know Mr. Scott's land extends almost to the reservation . . ." Reuben looked toward Albina.

Realizing Reuben didn't want Albina to hear what he wanted to say, Nell nodded at her sister. "Beanie, don't you have something to do?"

"Not until you can help me again with my fractions."

"Well, run inside and see if there's anything you can do to help Ma."

Albina scowled. "You just want to talk about something I'm not supposed to know."

Nell raised an eyebrow and looked at her sister. "That's right, so go on in."

"Okay, but I'll learn whatever it is tomorrow at school, you know. You might as well let me stay and listen."

"What you hear there is out of my control, but home isn't. Now, scoot."

Albina stuck her tongue out and jumped out of the wagon when Nell made a move to swat her. "Same time, same place tomorrow, Albina, and I'll give you a ride, again," Reuben said. When she was out of earshot, he continued. "There's more trouble among the Puyallups, and Mr. Scott wants to keep close to home."

"What kind of trouble?"

"Remember when the little girls were kidnapped and taken to Oregon?"

"Yes."

"Well, the Puyallups want Dr. McCoy replaced."

"But doesn't his wife teach on the reservation?"

"Yes, but the Presbytery of Puget Sound had to go to the reservation and meet with Dr. McCoy and General Milroy."

"Oh dear, that doesn't sound good."

"It isn't. The Puyallups claim Dr. McCoy's cruel, that he stole things from them; one thing was a Henry rifle. He was supposed to get it in exchange for burying the Indian called Old Gambler. Do you remember him?" Nell shook her head. "Well, I guess Dr. McCoy made a poor job of the burial, and everyone was mad. They all met

90

at the church and filled it to overflowing. Reverend Reed from Port Townsend asked for a show of hands from all those who wanted the doctor removed, and they all went up."

"Will he be?"

"No one seems to know, but if the Presbytery doesn't do something, there's likely to be big trouble."

"Well, I can't say I blame the Puyallups."

"Me, either." Martyr-to-the-Cause pawed the ground and bobbed his head, and Reuben took a firmer grip on the reins. "I better go."

"Thanks for the news."

"It doesn't rain but what it pours."

Nell laughed. "You're too young to be so distrustful about things."

"Huh?"

"Never mind."

Reuben went on down the road to finish the afternoon deliveries, and Nell returned to the garden, much perturbed. If there was any possibility of an Indian war, Hildy's beau, Samuel, would know before even the newspaper did. If he was in town, he'd make sure Hildy and her family were in no danger. Nell decided to visit Hildy after supper. A few of Chief Leschi's braves were still alive, and another Indian war was a troubling thought.

However, as it turned out, she didn't make it to Hildy's house.

Nell stood in front of her pa's shaving glass, pinning on her hat, when someone knocked at the door. "Oh dear, now what?" She turned away from the mirror just as the door opened and her oldest sister came in, followed by her sons, eight-year-old Elwood and seven-year-old Frank.

"Indiana." Amity put her mending down and got up to hug her daughter and grandsons. "What are you doing here?"

"Pa's gone to jail," Elwood said. "Grandma, I'm hungry."

"Of course, you are, dear." If Amity was startled, she didn't let it show. "Nell, get them some bread and butter, will you?"

Nell removed Frank's arms from where he was hugging her around the knees and took his hand. "Would you like jam or drippings, Frank?"

"Jam." Indiana cleared her throat, and he added, "Please."

"Jam it is, then. Elwood, how about you?"

"Drippings, please, Aunt Nell. Pa says a man needs all the meat he can get, and drippings has got meat."

"Coffee for me, if you don't mind," Indiana said.

While Nell put the pot on and cut two thick slices of bread, Indiana hung her hat on a peg and held her cloak opened to the fire. "In' it funny how good a fire always feels?" she said. "I'm not cold, but we've been on the road from Bush Prairie since early this morning, and I'm mighty sore and tired."

Nell gave the boys their bread, and they sat on the hearth to eat while she unpinned her hat and hung it back up. She sat in a worn wicker rocking chair and took up her needlework, glad Albina was down the street at the McNeeleys' house, playing with her friend Jane. Albina would interrupt Indiana with a thousand questions. "How did you get here?" Nell asked.

"Alexander Howard brought me. He's been at loose ends since his wife died. I guess he's looking for work."

"What did Elwood mean when he said Lumley was arrested?" Amity asked.

"It's true. They took him away last night."

"Who did?"

"Three men. They said they were from the Puget Sound Collection District."

"What's that?"

Before Indiana could answer, the door opened again, and Josie came in. She looked at Indiana and the boys, but, before she could say anything, Amity asked her about work.

"It was fine." The coffee was done, and Josie poured herself a cup, adding a generous amount of cream. When Indiana cleared her throat, she poured a cup for her sister. "Mrs. McCarver set the date for her at-home, and I'm definitely going to play the piano; 'Light, afternoon music,' she says. I asked what's that, and she said it's like, 'Sailing, Sailing' and *'Funiculì, Funiculà,'* and I said Ike came home from Louis Levin's tavern once singing *'Funiculì, Funiculà,'* and it seemed to me that it was more for the night than the afternoon, and she said she had a sick headache starting, and she'd make up a list of songs for me to play." Josie stopped and changed the topic with barely a fresh breath. "Indiana, what are you doing here?"

"She was just about to tell us," Amity said. "But first, have you eaten?"

"Yes, Mrs. McCarver had made a pot of soup for supper and told me to help myself. It was wonderful soup, and I ate three bowls with bread. I was going for a fourth bowl, but she said I had to stop. I said I thought I was supposed to help myself and she said, 'Within reason,' and I said I guessed her reason and mine were different, and, for a wonder, she agreed. She don't hardly ever agree with me. And . . ."

"Josie, sit down. Let's listen to what Indiana has to say." Amity was well acquainted with Josie's occasional habit of talking like a runaway train. "She was about to tell us what's going on."

"I should hope so." Indiana found Josie tiring at the best of times, and plainly this wasn't the best of times. "So, as I was saying, these three men from the Puget Sound Collection District knocked on the door last night and said they were arresting Lumley on suspicion of smuggling. 'Smuggling,' I says, and one of them says, 'Yes, ma'am. Smuggling Celestials into the territory from Canada.' Now I ask you — who would do that when the railroad brings the Chinee in all the time?"

"Maybe it's 'cause President Arthur won't let them come here anymore." Elwood finished his bread and licked his fingers.

"Don't lick your fingers. What are you talking about?"

"Mr. Britnall told us about it in school."

Outside, day had given way to the soft nightfall. Nell stood up. "I'd better go get Albina."

"Well, I call that heartless of you to leave

95

when you can see I'm here in such distress." Indiana looked at Nell, and her lip quivered.

"Light a lamp, first, won't you, dear?" Ma said.

Nell turned away to hide her irritation. Indiana worked hard when she was at home, but, when she came to New Tacoma, she wanted to be catered to. "It's going to be dark soon, and Albina is too young to be out then. You talk to Ma, and I'll hear the rest when I get back." She picked up a cotton waistcoat Ike had left behind when he married, and to which she'd added sleeves.

"You're not going to wear that thing, are you?" Indiana looked at it in horror.

"It's too warm for my shawl, and the McNeeleys don't live far. No one will see me."

"The McNeeleys will."

Nell giggled. "I like it, especially since I added sleeves. It's comfortable and lightweight."

"Gracious me. Adding sleeves. What an odd thing to do." Indiana looked shocked.

Nell kissed her sister's cheek. "Well, I only just added them on, and you'll be back on Bush Prairie before anyone sees it." She left the house with a sigh of relief. The little family home would be crowded with Indiana and the boys staying.

Overhead, the full moon made a bat swooping on some bugs clearly visible. Nell followed her shadow, picking her way carefully and thinking about her nephew's words and the Chinese men she'd seen dumped off on the beach. She also remembered John Calhoun's interest in the scarfaced man and wondered what the Scotsman had given the other fellow on the porch in Old Tacoma. *Could he be involved in smuggling?* The thought made her sad. Though she'd snubbed him during the walk from Old Tacoma, he had tried to be friendly. *Still, when we first met him, I wasn't sure if Mr. Calhoun was a very nice man despite Mr. Pincus vouching for him, and first impressions are important. His being a smuggler would prove I was right. Maybe I'm psychic like Grandma Staley.*

CHAPTER 6

The following morning, Nell found several reasons to go to town: Albina was whiny because she had to go to school and her cousins didn't, Josie had her dress out for Nell to start refurbishing and was unhappy because her sister couldn't begin immediately, and, when her father found out that Indiana had finished all the coffee, he kicked up a row. Nell needing thread and picking up the mail made convenient excuses.

"I'm off, Ma," she said, pinning on a hat.

"For heaven's sake, don't forget the coffee."

Nell laughed, and Indiana looked chagrined.

The post office was on Pacific Avenue, near the new Alpha Opera House, and she went there first. Mailboxes from San Francisco had just been installed, and it was only a matter of minutes before she'd emptied the neatly labeled Tanquist box. There wasn't much, but on top was a letter addressed to her. *Goodness gracious,* she thought, seeing part of a mark indicating it had come from New York. She put it in her reticule to open later; a letter was too precious to rip open in the post office.

From there, she went to the Farmers and Mechanics Cash Store, which, despite its name, carried a variety of sewing notions. Josie's dress was charcoal gray with a foot of petticoat showing at the bottom. She had given Nell enough money for black fabric to make a new petticoat, and to buy black buttons for the bodice, and braid for the collar and cuffs. Then it was on to A. T. Bede and Company for the coffee because the family ran a tab there.

Finally, with the errands done, she hurried down the boardwalk to see Hildy. The aromas of yeast and cinnamon wrapped themselves around her when she opened the door, a welcome relief from a pig wallowing in muck outside. Hildy kept the walkway in front of her shop cleared. She didn't, however, clean the road. "What's the use," she had said. "No sooner does New Tacoma rid its streets of roaming pigs than untethered horses and the occasional cow take over. And cats and rats hide in the broken boxes, buckets, and piles of rope in front of the other businesses, and they add to the smell. I am, however, sad the Lister foundry's fawn is gone. He was like a mascot for downtown."

Hearing someone come in, Hildy closed the oven door and looked up. Nell grinned. Hildy wiped her hands on her apron and poured coffee into the cups she kept for special people.

"How's business?" Nell asked, sitting on one of the boxes that were still in front of the counter.

"Good. I'm starting to get orders for social functions, and, if I wanted to make nothing but pasties, I could sell them all." She handed Nell a cookie and took one herself. "A friend of yours dropped by, looking for a loaf of bread. A very nice-looking fellow. Who is he?"

Nell removed a few coins from her pocket and put them on the counter, then sighed and wiggled her toes. "I think I'm getting a blister. I miss going barefoot in the summer, don't you?"

"Gracious, yes." Hildy sat on the other box. "Don't change the subject. Who is he?"

"His name is John Calhoun. Josie and I met him in Steilacoom, and he brought us back to town. Mr. Pincus hired him to find a place in New Tacoma for a store. Mr. Pincus wants to move here from Steilacoom."

"He was lovely, so polite, and he had a delicious accent." Hildy pushed a strand of hair off her cheek, leaving a streak of flour.

Nell smiled and ducked her head, thinking that Hildy's adjectives were beginning to be food related. Then she looked closely at her friend and frowned. "You look tired."

"Thanks for the compliment."

"You know what I mean."

"I do." Hildy heaved her own sigh. "It's nice to be busy, but Samuel says I need to learn to say no."

Nell laughed and bit into the cookie. "I didn't know a woman could say no." She swallowed and added, "Ma certainly can't if it's something Pa wants. Why don't you hire a helper?"

"Another woman in my kitchen? I think not." Hildy sounded so indignant, Nell laughed again. "But I do have something to help me," she added. "Look over there."

Nell peered over the counter. "I thought it was an old box."

Hildy huffed. "It is a box, a dough box. I put the flour and things in it and turn the handle and knead it all together. See, the legs are high enough so I don't have to stoop over a table. I can make more loaves with it, and the dough rises right inside. I divide it into pans after that."

"Isn't it hard to wash?"

"You never wash it." Hildy looked shocked. "The more bread you make in it, the better it tastes. I just gently wipe the box out."

"I never heard of such a thing." Nell quashed a pang of jealousy. Hildy had so much to show for her work, while her own business seemed years away. But then, she reminded herself, Hildy had been baking and selling bread much longer than she had been crocheting and selling items. "That's amazing. How wonderful." While Hildy beamed, Nell pulled a fat envelope from her pocket. "Look, I stopped to get the mail, and I have a letter. It's from New York; I think it's an answer from when I wrote *Godey's Ladies Book.*"

"Oh, isn't that nice. I never did find the courage to write Tabitha Tickletooth. I'm sure she wouldn't want to be bothered with a frontier baker like me."

Nell had been hearing about Tabitha Tickletooth almost since the day she met Hildy, who rarely made a decision about baking until she read what the well-known cook had written on the subject. "Well, I think you should just beard the lion in his den and do it."

"Is it *beard* the lion? I've never been sure."

"Me either."

"Aren't you going to open the letter?"

"Of course, but I want to savor it for a minute. This is the first actual letter I've ever received." Nell slit the flap carefully, pulled out several pieces of paper, and started reading the one on top.

Dear Miss Tanquist:
I was very excited to see the postmark *Washington Territory* on your envelope. Most of my mail comes from East Coast states. In answer to your question, the pattern for the mitts isn't difficult for an experienced crocheter such as yourself. You are smart to show an interest; they were very popular here during the recent Easter season. The pattern is enclosed. Please let me know how you get on with the instructions. I am very interested in your life on the frontier. Yours most sincerely,

L. Godey

Nell put the letter back in the envelope and opened the other two sheets of paper. The top one had a sketch of a woman's crocheted glove with most of the fingers exposed. Underneath were numbered lines, each containing instructions.

"Gracious." Hildy leaned over to look at the fine writing. "That looks complicated."

Nell pursed her lips for a moment. "I think if I just cover up every line except the one I'm working on, I will be able to figure it out." She folded the pages carefully and put them with the letter. "I'll worry about it later. Tell me, has Samuel heard anything more from his friends about what's happening on the reservation since the children were kidnapped?"

"Not really. There's to be a meeting between the Presbytery, the Puyallups, and Dr. McCoy. The Indians claim the reservation school is a disgrace. None of the children can even read, and, to pile on the agony, Dr. McCoy made a mash of a burial for one of their people. The Puyallups want him removed."

"What does Samuel think?"

"He says since the Puyallups have no respect for the doctor, he won't get any co-operation if he stays." Hildy stood and went to check her dough. "Is Josie nervous about playing the piano for Mrs. McCarver? The at-home's tomorrow, isn't it?"

"Yes, in the afternoon. Josie doesn't worry about things like playing for a roomful of people. It's things we can't see, such as walking dead people in Steilacoom, that fluster her."

Hildy removed several pans of bread from the oven and slid more in. "What are you doing about her dress?"

"Ma refused to let either of us leave off wearing mourning, but she is allowing Josie to have her mourning dress updated. I just bought the notions. I can do it tonight; it won't take me long. By the way, did I tell you Mrs. McCarver hired me to serve? I'm to wear black and a white apron."

"You're serving? How did that happen?"

"Mrs. McCarver asked Josie to ask me if I would, and I said yes. I'll add the earnings to my sewing machine money."

"How much does a sewing machine cost?"

"The Singer I have my eye on costs at least sixty dollars. Sometimes I visit the C. A. Cook store just to look at it."

"Well, I'll loan the money to you as soon as I can."

Hildy's generosity, not to mention her faith in Nell, brought tears to Nell's eyes. Seeing them, Hildy changed the subject. "You are honored. Mrs. McCarver didn't ask me to bake anything." She laughed and scowled at the same time. Everyone knew Mrs. McCarver was one of Old Tacoma's leading figures, and what Hildy perceived as a slight about her cooking was aggravating.

The bakery door opened, and several women entered. Hildy went to help them, and Nell waved and left. Her steps home were slow. She loved her nephews, but having them and their mother in the house for an extended period of time made it seem so crowded. Then she laughed, and a woman coming out of Mrs. Spooner's Millinery Shop looked up and smiled. *Goodness, I'm too young to get cranky over such an unimportant thing,* Nell thought. Nevertheless, she would be glad when her brother-in-law's trial was over. Judge Wicks was hearing the charges against Lumley and the others accused of smuggling in Chinese men the next day. *What will happen if Lumley's found guilty? Pa will have to build a room on the house because, dollars to donuts, Indiana will want to stay with us. She'll swan around and expect Ma to take care of the boys and Josie and me to do all the work. I wish girls my age could live alone.*

Both the trial and the at-home started at one o'clock. Indiana decided to take the boys to the courtroom, "so," she said, "the judge will see that Lumley's a responsible family man who's needed at home." For Nell and Josie, that meant a scramble getting Elwood and Frank cleaned and dressed in their best clothes and little time to see to their own attire. They left the house at twelve-fifteen, and Josie was uncharacteristically quiet.

"Are you nervous, Josie?"

"No."

"Even though it's the only piano in Old Tacoma and not many folks have heard it?"

"No. People have probably heard me practicing."

"Are you looking forward to people hearing how well you play?"

"No."

"Why in the world not?"

"I play for me. It's my secret thing. In music I can go to places no one else can."

"Then why are you doing this?"

"I thought if you can earn money for a sewing machine, maybe I can earn money for a piano of my own."

"Ma would love to hear you play in the evenings."

"It's what the Carrs do — play musical instruments in the evening and sing. I don't think they have a piano, though."

"Do they — sing, I mean?" Nell held a branch of wild currant out of Josie's way. "I can't imagine it of whiskery old Job Carr."

Josie giggled. "Me, either."

They soon reached the hill above Old Tacoma and saw Mrs. McCarver's white, weatherboard house. Chinese lanterns were strung in the trees on either side of the door and on fruit trees in the yard. They bobbed about in a gentle wind. A boy was pounding croquet stakes into the ground, and the air smelled like lilacs. In front of the house, six steps led to the porch. The front door opened into a small foyer with the parlor on one side and dining room on the other. However, Nell and Josie had been told to walk around to the back door.

"The weather really cooperated, didn't it?" Nell said.

"Where Mrs. McCarver is concerned, it wouldn't do otherwise." Nell giggled, but Josie was serious. Mrs. McCarver put the fear of the Lord in her.

The rear door also stood open, and Mrs. McCarver met them on the threshold. "Finally. Folks are coming up the walk." She handed Nell an apron. "You can leave your things here, in the kitchen. Josie, you look very nice. I'm sure you will play beautifully. Now, remember, not too loudly; folks want to be able to talk without shouting, and keep to the music I told you. This is a dignified gathering of Old Tacoma's best people. Also, I have a distinguished guest coming, a German baron, and I want everything to be perfect. This is an opportunity to show the world that we are every bit as mannered as folks back East. Go ahead into the parlor. Nell, come with me, please."

Nell hung her jacket on a hook and put on the apron. As she always did, she took careful note of what the hostess wore, in this case a lavender silk dress with white ruching, and deep purple glove-mitts. *It's a good thing the pattern arrived,* she thought, *people will be wanting glove-mitts like Mrs. McCarver's, and I have to have some to sell.* She followed her employer into the scullery part of the kitchen, where a little girl stood on a box washing dishes, and where a large wooden barrel with a door in it took a place of prominence. Mrs. McCarver opened the barrel door and cold air wafted out.

"I had this made to keep food cold, and I ordered ice to keep the salmon mousse and ice cream from spoiling. A railroad man is bringing another block of ice down from the mountain, so please keep an eye out for him. Also, please try not to let too much warm air in." She shut the door. "The punch will need ice. After people begin arriving, when you carry in the tray of glasses, add a little ice to each, and be careful. I'm using the cut glass. Keep the icepick here on top so you won't forget. I'll tell you when to start laying out the food. If you see any glasses not in use, please bring them to the kitchen and give them to Annie to wash."

Nell managed a "yes, ma'am" that Mrs. McCarver seemed not to hear.

"Now, let's see, is there anything I've forgotten? Yes. Try not to smile too much. It isn't dignified. Proper servers should be as invisible as possible. Your dress was a good choice. Very discreet." Before she could think of anything else, someone rapped on the front door, and Mrs. McCarver hurried to be in place while a relative answered the knock.

Nell was surprised at how many people had been invited. They soon crowded the parlor and spilled into the dining room. The younger people broke into couples and went out to play croquet. Among them were Howard Carr and his sister, Marietta, who seemed to be the focus of the group. Marietta wore a yellow dress, which complemented her dark curly hair, and, for a moment, Nell was overcome with envy. *Oh well,* she thought. *I bet she never went barefoot in the summer or ran down a hill and jumped in a creek when a bear showed up unexpectedly at a picnic.* Forgetting Mrs. McCarver's instructions, she smiled at the memories.

And, besides, I can't be getting so jealous all the time.

Music filled the parlor, and Nell recognized "In the Evening by the Moonlight." The piano was positioned close to a wall, with Josie's profile in view. She looked good and played beautifully, easily transitioning from one song to another.

For the next half hour, Nell walked through the rooms with her tray of punch, trying not to smile. People wiped their perspiring foreheads, emptied one glass, and picked up another. Every time she returned to the kitchen for more, however, Annie had clean glasses ready. The temperature climbed, voices grew louder, and the tray grew heavier. Nell was glad to rest it on the piano for a minute when Josie beckoned her and said in a low voice, "A man asked to walk me home."

"Who was it?"

"I don't know."

"Gracious me, that's bold. I hope you told him no."

"Yes, but he had the most soulful eyes. I purely wanted to melt in them."

"You point him out, and I'll spill punch on him."

"You'd never." Josie's eyes widened.

111

"No, but if he asks again, you send him to me."

Josie giggled and gave the keys a flourish as she changed songs. "That's him, over there, standing near the door."

Nell made note of which gentleman it was, but, by the time she had circled the room, filled her tray with empty glasses, and returned to the parlor, again, with more punch, the man was nowhere to be seen.

Women's voices rose, and men regularly missed the spittoons. Outside, someone shot off a rifle, startling those inside and scaring screeching crows out of the trees. Then a ruckus in the parlor caught her attention. Approaching the room, she saw Mrs. McCarver holding her skirt up and showing an indecent amount of petticoat and ankle as she demonstrated a jig.

"Yee haw, Julie," someone shouted. "You show 'em."

People clapped, and two men began clog dancing, their boots making marks on the wooden floor. Josie's would-be suitor appeared, and Mrs. McCarver tried to draw him into the action. Before she succeeded, he caught Nell's attention and crooked a finger. Nell nodded and made her way carefully through the dancers.

"Excuse me," she said. "I believe you offered to walk my sister and me home, later."

"Your sister?" He had an accent she couldn't place.

"Yes, Josie. She's playing the piano."

"Oh, ah . . ."

"I just wanted to thank you. We live several miles away" — Nell looked at the man's shoes — "and we must walk through the woods to get there. A gentlemen's company will be most welcome. Fortunately, most of the marshy spots have dried up."

"Woods?"

"Yes, but the trail is almost completely clear. You can take your shoes off, if you wish. Lots of people do."

Before he could answer, Mrs. McCarver slapped him on the back. "Walk you home. Ha, ha. Nell, dear, this is my distinguished guest, Baron August von Schilling."

Nell blanched, and the baron managed to move a short distance away from Mrs. Mc-Carver.

"I yust stop this loffely lady to ask for more loffely punch." He clicked his heels and bowed.

"Of course." Nell turned the tray so he could take the last glass. From the corner of her eye, she saw Josie signaling her. Excusing herself, she hurried to join her sister.

"That's not the right man, Nell," Josie said.

"What?"

"I think he's gone now. He came to bring more ice."

"Not the gandy dancer from the railroad I saw leaving?"

"He had the loveliest eyes."

For a moment, Nell was horrified at the mistake. She peeked at the baron, who was still trying to disentangle himself from Mrs. McCarver's grip. Then the humor of it struck her, and she was giggling when a red-faced man pounded his fist on the piano. "How about something lively, sister?"

Josie started playing "The Vampire's Polka," a song newly arrived in town, and was hard pressed to keep up with the sounds of stamping feet as galloping couples circled the room, occasionally dancing out the front door and returning through the back. Nell hurried to the kitchen for yet more punch and saw Annie pouring a bottle of something into the pitcher.

"What's that?" she asked.

"We're running out of punch, but I found this red stuff for folks to drink." Annie emptied the bottle. "This is the last of it, though."

Nell sniffed the unlabeled bottle and

laughed. "How much of this have you poured in?"

The girl pointed toward several empty bottles. Two of them were Lydia Pinkham's Vegetable Compound, and a sniff told Nell the others were homebrew. *Oh dear,* she thought, *that explains everything. I'd better hide the bottles, or poor Annie will get a tongue lashing, for sure.*

The kitchen door swung open, and Mrs. McCarver, whose topknot had slid and was perched over one ear, leaned against the jamb. "Time for the food, gals," she shouted and ducked back out.

Nell handed Annie a tray of cucumber sandwiches and pushed her toward the dining room. She grabbed the empty bottles and tossed them outside behind a bush and then removed the salmon mousse from the ice box. As fast as she and Annie got the food to the dining room, clusters of people, laughing and talking, shoved past them and began filling their plates. When everything was on the table, Nell drank the last glass of punch and fanned her mouth. *Goodness, that's powerful.* She giggled again and wondered how Mrs. McCarver would feel the next day.

The temperature continued to climb, and the numbers of people inside made the house grow warmer. Nell chipped off some ice and took a glass of water to Josie. Then she stepped outside for a breath of air. She remembered the time she'd impulsively jumped into the bay one August day and wished she could do it again. Her black dress was heavy and hot; her hands felt sticky, and wisps of hair tickled her neck and cheeks. A rain barrel was on the other side of a hydrangea bush, and she splashed her face and neck before re-pinning her hair. At the same time, she watched bees going in and out of several well-developed lilac bushes that leaned against a fence. Behind one of the shrubs she saw a man trying to kiss a girl, and heard the girl weakly protest. *Dignified gathering, my foot.*

With a last deep breath, she returned to the dining room, where she began straightening up the table and picking up abandoned dishes. She was carrying an empty plate toward the kitchen when the baron came around a corner and stopped in front of her. At the same moment, Mrs. McCarver took the man's arm. She beamed, and he looked terror stricken.

"Nelly, dear, you're a brick. You see," Mrs. McCarver said to the baron, "the Indians don't feel the need to adapt to our ways, and the white women would rather marry a ne'er-do-well than work in another woman's kitchen."

"Ah, yes, but haffing such a loffely young woman help you iss delightful, iss it not?" The baron clicked his heels, bowed, and tried once again to disengage his arm from Mrs. McCarver's grip.

They turned away, their voices fading into the crowd. Nell pushed her way through the people and back to the kitchen. "Exactly who is the baron, anyway?" she asked Annie, who had finished washing the glasses and was starting on the plates. "Do you know?"

"He came with the railroad to draw pictures." Annie looked exhausted as piles of clean dishes grew. Her hair hung down around her red face, and she tried to blow it back. Nell put the tray down and reached to gather the damp curls. At her touch, Annie flinched.

"I'm just going to braid your hair so it will be cooler for you." She gathered the wispy brown strands and began weaving them in and out. "How old are you, Annie?" Nell spotted a piece of twine and tied the braid's end.

"Eleven."

"Josie hasn't mentioned you. Do you work here often?" She picked up a towel and started drying dishes.

"Yes, ma'am. I'd stay if I could. Pa beats me sometimes, and Mrs. McCarver is awfully nice. She's teaching me to be a lady."

"Is the baron a friend of hers?"

"No, ma'am. He's a friend of Mr. Calhoun, and Mr. Calhoun is Mrs. McCarver's friend. He draws pictures — so does the baron — but Mr. Calhoun's are better."

Calhoun? Nell put clean bowls on the tray and started filling them with ice cream. "What do they draw?"

"I peeked once when everyone was at dinner, and the baron, he draws rocks and trains and Indians, only they don't look like ours, and sailing ships and Chinese men. Mr. Calhoun draws boats and ugly men. One of them had a big scar. If I could draw, I'd draw pretty dresses. If Pa doesn't take my earnings from Mrs. McCarver, I'm going to buy me the prettiest dress you ever saw." She looked at Nell. "You best take that ice cream out, or Mrs. McCarver will come in here looking like Old Scratch. She does that real well."

"I'll bet she does," Nell muttered.

Back in the parlor, welcome cries and light applause greeted the ice cream's appearance. Even the baron seemed to enjoy it.

"The prairies are covered with wild strawberries," Marietta Carr said, "and the Indians pick them to sell."

"It's the one thing they do well," Mrs. McCarver added.

Hearing her, Nell seethed. *If the Indians are so horrible, I wonder that you still live here in Old Tacoma since General McCarver died,* she thought.

The numbers of people had begun to thin as Mrs. McCarver's guests thanked her and took their leave. Nell picked up the scattered ice cream dishes, took them to Annie, and carried the last of the food into the kitchen. Glancing at Mrs. McCarver's grandfather clock, she was happy to see the afternoon was nearly over. She piled the remaining sandwiches on a tray, covered them with a cloth, and put the tray in the ice barrel. The salmon mousse was nearly gone, and Nell gave what was left to a pregnant cat dozing under the back stoop. Near an apple tree, the baron stood talking with a dark-haired man. The man had his back to her, but the set of his shoulders seemed familiar. Their heads were bent together, and, as Nell watched, the baron passed some papers to the other man, who looked through them quickly before putting them in a pocket.

"Nell?"

At the sound of Josie's voice, Nell jumped and turned around. "Are you all right?" she asked. Josie stood at the sink, her hands in the hot dishwater.

"I've never played for so long before, and my fingers are stiff." Josie took her hands out of the water and dried them on her skirt. "Mrs. McCarver says we can each have a dish of ice cream before we go."

"Oh, you are lucky." Annie returned to the sink and plunged her hands back into the water.

"You, too, Annie."

"Really?" She turned from the sink, her raw, red hands dripping water on the wooden floor. "I've never had ice cream."

"Let's finish cleaning up, and then we can sit on the step and eat and have a well-earned rest."

Josie returned to the piano, and Nell circled the rooms, picking up the last of the dirty dishes. She found a broom, swept up spilled food, and put the furniture to rights while Annie washed the silver. When the younger girl was finished and had dried her hands on her worn cotton dress, Josie joined them. They watched Nell fill bowls with generous helpings of the ice cream, and the three went outside to sit on the stoop and eat it before it melted. A fishy smell from the cannery had replaced the scent of lilacs. With the mousse long gone, the cat lay in the lanky grass sleeping, but, other than that, the yard was deserted. They ate slowly, and, when they were done, Nell returned to the kitchen and took some of the sandwiches out of the barrel. She rearranged those left and carried the others to the stoop. They had just finished eating the sandwiches when Mrs. McCarver's voice reached them.

"Annie. Are you done with the dishes?"

Annie jumped up and hurried back inside. "Yes, Mrs. McCarver." She quickly washed the three ice cream dishes. "I'll just empty the pan now." While she carried the dishwater out and poured it carefully around the roots of the flowers, Mrs. McCarver handed Nell and Josie some coins.

"Josie, you played very well. I might hire you again, and Nell, except for bothering the baron, you did fine, too. Thank you both. You may go home now. Annie, before you finish up, fetch me a headache powder. My, it's hot for June, isn't it?" She fanned her red face and tried unsuccessfully to push her bun back to the top of her head.

"Thank you, Mrs. McCarver," Nell said. When the woman returned to the parlor, she turned to Annie. "You come visit us any time you want, Annie, and I can help you make a dress."

They left Annie beaming and started for the trail home. Nell wasn't prepared, when they reached the top of the hill near where men were sawing wood and pounding nails into the skeleton of the new Annie Wright Seminary, to see John Calhoun coming off the old side road that led to Steilacoom. Headed in the opposite direction and tucking something out of sight was the town reprobate, Potato Brooks.

"Why, Mr. Calhoun, imagine running into you," Josie said. "What are you doing here?"

"I had a wee bit of business to attend to." He removed his hat and smiled at Josie.

"With Potato Brooks?" Nell said. "I can't imagine what."

"I'm sure you can't, Miss Tanquist, but you might be surprised." He put his hat back on. "Ladies."

Josie beamed, and Nell narrowed her eyes as he continued past them. *The only business he could possibly have with Potato Brooks is monkey business,* she thought.

CHAPTER 7

When Nell and Josie returned from Mrs. McCarver's at-home, the smell of salt pork and hot coffee drifted through the open door to greet them. Excited voices filled the kitchen, and, seeing his aunts, Elwood ran over shouting, "Pa's out of jail."

"So I can see." Nell smiled at Lumley, who sat in a chair drinking coffee and looking both happy and tired. "That's good news, indeed." She tied on an apron and started peeling potatoes.

"We're going home tomorrow," Elwood said, "but I want to stay here with you."

"Do you, now? What about your friends on Bush Prairie, won't they miss you?"

"It's mostly girls where we live, and they aren't fun for anything."

Nell snickered, but Indiana scowled. "Our neighbors have been taking care of the livestock, and we've imposed on them long enough, and I need to get back to my garden. Anyway, your grandmother and Aunt Josie are coming with us for a few days."

"But Aunt Josie doesn't tell us scary stories like Aunt Nell does." While Elwood fished a cube of raw potato out of the bowl and popped it into his mouth, Nell was wishing Josie could tell them about Steilacoom.

"Elwood, don't eat raw potatoes." Indiana smacked his hand. "How many times have I told you they cause worms?"

"Ah, Ma."

"They're better fried anyway." Nell dropped a spoonful of bacon grease in a cast iron pan, placed the pan on the stove, and began adding the potatoes. "You can grind the coffee beans. We'll need to brew more."

Josie handed dishes to Frank and silverware to Albina, and Amity opened a jar of preserves and sliced bread. Looking delighted at having someone else do all the work, Indiana returned to her chair. When the potatoes were done, everyone sat around the old puncheon table their father, Obed, had made from flattened barrel staves. Obed, who had just returned from work, sat quietly for once, listening to his son-in-law talk. Lumley, full of himself now that the threat was over, leaned back in his chair and hooked his thumbs under his suspenders. "A'course, they was looking for Jimmie Jones," he said. "He's been plaguing Customs for years."

Albina leaned forward, looking excited. "Who's that, Uncle Lumley?"

"Why, he's the best-known smuggler the territory has ever seen."

"What does he smuggle?"

"Ever'thing. He takes a boat to Canada, picks up whatever plunder he can, and sells it down here. Why once" — Lumley stopped talking and started laughing — "he got picked up, managed to lock the customs agent in the ship's hold, and didn't turn him loose until they reached some podunk settlement near Port Angeles."

"That's enough of that, Lumley," Indiana said. "You'll be putting ideas in the boys' heads. Now come on, Frank, let me serve you, else you'll eat nothing but bread and preserves."

After they finished, Amity maneuvered Indiana into helping with the dishes while Albina and the boys went outside. Obed decided he and Lumley should celebrate at Levin's saloon, and Nell started working on the baby jacket she was making for Ike and Frieda Faye. The baby was due any day, and she wanted to have it ready.

"That's real pretty, Nell," Indiana said.

"Thank you."

"Might be you could make me a collar, sometime."

"Anytime, Indiana. Tell me what you want and what color and I'll tell you what to buy. I reckon you'll be able to find everything in Olympia."

Indiana pursed her lips and looked into the fire, and Nell bent over her needlework. She felt unexpectedly ashamed. She knew she could make something for her sister with little expense, but she also knew how close fisted Indiana was. She loved Indiana as a sister but didn't want her as a friend, and the thought saddened her.

"Daughter?" Amity had seen her distress.

"I'm just tired, Ma. Mrs. McCarver knows how to get the most out of her hired help." Nell stood and put her crocheting away. "Josie's kicking won't keep me awake tonight."

The next morning everyone was up early. Obed helped Lumley harness the wagon and stowed the family's bags. Albina filled bottles with water while Nell and Josie packed a lunch. Before they left, Nell took Indiana aside. "I never thanked you for taking us in while the twins were sick, so I

126

thought of something to make you that won't cost you anything."

Indiana's face lit up. "Oh, that is nice. We certainly work hard, but there never seems to be any spare money to buy something for myself."

Nell smiled and felt a curious lifting in her heart. "It will be my pleasure."

At the last minute, Amity decided Albina could miss a few days of school and so took her youngest with her, leaving Nell to cook for her father. As soon as they drove away, Obed left to go fishing, and Nell found the house strangely empty. *It's as if they took all the house's energy with them,* she thought. She washed and dried the dishes, put laundry in a barrel with a wedge of lye soap, and swept the floor. A robin hopped near the open door, and she tossed it a bit of bread crust with drippings. As she worked, Nell soaked up the peace, and, when the chores were done, she decided to visit the twins' graves. *What with Lumley and his problem, we forgot all about Decoration Day. I'll rent a horse and ride out to the cemetery. I can clean the graves off, and Ma will be happy.* She put on a sunbonnet, loaded a flour sack with her gloves and tools, and walked toward Cogswell's livery stable. As she approached, she saw Rigger, Mr. Cogswell's liveryman, unloading bales of hay from a wagon.

"Good morning, Rigger." Nell stood in the doorway to let her eyes adjust to the stable's dim inside.

"Morning, Miss Nell. Here for a buggy? We have a nice little surrey for rent."

"A horse, please. I thought I'd ride out to Oakwood, to the cemetery, and on a horse I won't have to worry so much about the condition of the road."

"It's a fine day for a ride."

"Is Bobby available?"

"Yes, ma'am, but he hasn't been out for a few days and he's a mite skittish. You sure you can handle him?"

Nell laughed. "I'll make sure he knows who the boss is."

She sat on an old bench, enjoying the smell of leather and alfalfa and watching dust motes ride down beams of sunlight. A horse whinnied, and another answered. Rigger put a blanket on Bobby and pulled a saddle off the door of his stall. Bobby kicked the door, and Nell watched, judging the horse's energy. She remembered when she was young, riding horseback on Bush Prairie with nothing but a blanket between her and the back of a mighty bony paint. After Rigger slipped the bit into Bobby's mouth and led the bay to where Nell waited, she tied her bag of tools to the pommel, stood on the bench, and swung onto the saddle, pulling her skirt down as far as possible.

"Be sure to tie him good when you're not riding. Old Bobby's been known to leave a rider high and dry and hightail it back home if he gets the chance," Rigger said.

"I will." Nell gripped the reins and nudged the horse. He danced sideways for a minute before leaving the stable. Soon they were headed up Eighth Street and then turning south on Tacoma Avenue. After the series of unimaginative, alphabet-named streets going up the hill, Nell was glad to see a street with a real name. She'd passed men clearing the road and making lots and nudged Bobby into canter until he seemed calmer. They crossed the wooden bridge over Gallagher Gulch, climbed a short hill, and changed to a southwesterly direction toward Hunt's Prairie. A marsh beginning at the prairie's north end butted up against a hill on the far west side and continued out to the plains. On the east side, farms dotted the land. Nell headed for the tall fir trees, which acted as the graveyard's fence. She dismounted and fastened Bobby's reins to the sturdy bough of an alder tree near a small spring and patch of grass. Before he could drink, she scooped out several hand-fuls of water for herself, enjoying the cold wetness.

Not having been to the graveyard when the twins were buried, Nell had to hunt for their plots among the markers, few though they were. One was for a man named Ben-jamin L. Brown who'd died in 1852, but a weather-worn stone for a Lucia A. Allen seemed to be the oldest. She'd died in 1830. *Who buried them,* Nell wondered. *Who was here way back then except the Indians?* Several military men had been buried fairly close together: Corporals George E. Barnes and Henry Berg, and Private Richard Bond. *Which war,* she wondered, *or maybe not a war at all.*

Stepping carefully, so as not to tread on any markers hidden in the grass, she finally found the twins' rough stone. It was next to that of Mrs. Sophia D. Bacon. Nell remem-bered how, one day, the thirty-six-year-old Mrs. Bacon had suddenly sickened and died. Someone, she noticed, had recently cleaned the grave.

Nell knelt on the ground by the twins' tombstone and ran her fingers along the names *Amos* and *Isaiah* carved into the rough granite. *They were so young,* she thought, *I barely remember them. I wish I had*

130

been a better sister.

Around her, birds swooped down on bugs, and a garter snake slithered between the camas blooms. A small wild rabbit appeared and disappeared almost before Nell registered its presence. The graveyard was covered with mallows, their pink blooms blending with fragile-looking blue camas flowers. *Camas bulbs are a food staple with the local Indians,* she remembered, and wondered what they tasted like. After a moment she returned to the horse for her tools and started digging up the bunchgrass on the twins' small plot. "I think bunchgrass roots go clear to the center of the earth," she muttered, tugging at a tall, stubborn clump. When it was gone, leaving the nearby flowers still upright and unchecked, she searched for stones to outline the cleaned patch. After that, she returned to the bubbling spring, washed her hands, and splashed water on her face and neck. She found a patch of moss under one of the trees and stretched out on her back. Bobby blew through his nose and flicked his tail at some flies. A squirrel chattered and flicked its own tail. Nell rolled over on her stomach, laid her head on her folded arms, and listened to indistinct voices drifting in the air. Eventually, she fell asleep.

She woke with a start when a horse whinnied, and Bobby pulled on his restraint and whinnied back. A man on horseback was just a few feet away, staring down at her.

"You all right, Miss?" asked the rider. He wore a tattered army jacket and dirty serge pants. When he pushed his hat back, Nell noticed he hadn't bothered to shave in several days. He smiled, showing gaps where teeth should have been.

She nodded. "Just resting." The man nudged his horse closer, and she felt uncomfortable under his scrutiny. "I'd best be getting back." Nell scrambled to her feet, picked up her tools, and smoothed her dress. She untied Bobby and used a log to mount under the man's narrow-eyed gaze. "Good afternoon, sir." She kicked the horse into a trot and turned as if starting for one of the distant farms. When it appeared the stranger hadn't followed her, she changed direction, heading back north toward New Tacoma. The sun's position indicated it was early afternoon. If Obed caught fish, he'd sell them to one of the markets, but fish or not, he'd end the day at Levin's tavern, so she was in no hurry.

At the south end of town, she decided to purchase some honey and turned east toward Robert Scott's dairy farm. Hildy swore by the Scott family's honey. The farm, which abutted the Puyallup reservation, was large and sprawling. When Scott wasn't minding his cattle and delivering milk, he grew hay and sold it off a scow up and down Commencement Bay. The addition of honeybees to the farm had begun five years earlier, and, according to Hildy, keeping the bees alive through winter was proving difficult.

As she rode, Nell heard voices coming from the east side of the property, away from where they might aggravate the cattle. That meant the hives were near the reservation. She wondered how the Indians liked having them so close. Yesterday, the *Daily Ledger* had mentioned a reservation potlatch being held near the mouth of the Puyallup River. *Maybe Mr. Scott will give them some honey,* she thought.

She and Bobby were ambling along when a red-tailed hawk swooped down in front of them and grabbed a mouse off the ground. Startled, Bobby half reared and then took off, throwing Nell back before jerking her forward. The movement yanked the reins from her hands, and she leaned over the horse's head to grab at his mane. Her bonnet slid down the back of her head, and its ties pulled against her neck. Clumps of sod flew up from the horse's hooves, and he continually shied from unfamiliar objects. Nell held on until Bobby jumped a drainage ditch. She flew off then, landing hard on her side and rolling. Her head struck a log, and she blacked out.

The room Nell woke in was so dark, only the light coming through an opening at one end indicated it was still day. A small portion of the roof was open to provide ventilation for the twenty or so cook-fires burning, but the ceiling held down the clouds of smoke coiling up. They filled the room, making her eyes water until they adjusted. The building was a big longhouse, approximately forty by one hundred feet, made from a framework of saplings. Benches lined the side walls, and Nell swung her legs over the edge of the one she was lying on. The motion made her grab her throbbing head. When the pain subsided, she looked around. Poles and a few rafters supported the roof, and shakes filled in the spaces between the saplings. She'd seen many buildings go up in New Tacoma and marveled that the longhouse had no other support trusses or collar beams. Haunches of venison hung from the rafters, along with sacks of flour, potatoes, and fruit.

Aiming her gaze back down at the fires, she saw pots and kettles of all shapes and sizes hung over the flames. Whatever was cooking smelled good. Nell couldn't remember having eaten since breakfast and wondered how long ago that was.

While she got her bearings, a man wearing little other than a breechcloth walked over and stared at her.

"Shikhs," said Nell in Chinook so he would know she was friendly.

He answered with a well-known greeting. *"Kla how ya?"*

Nell rubbed her head, feeling a lump, while she struggled to remember the words for *my horse stumbled.* *"Kiu a tan mam ookwim,"* she said after a minute.

He nodded and looked over his shoulder. *"Klootsh man."*

A young woman glanced up from emptying a kettle of meat into the long trough running down the middle of the room. She put her pot down, brushed splatters of food off her deerskin clothing, and approached the two. Nell looked at her as the woman also said, *"Kla how ya."*

Nell pointed to herself. "Nell."

The woman copied the gesture. "Cheeta." She turned and said something to a little girl who had followed her. The girl disappeared for a moment, returning with a tightly woven basket of cold water. Cheeta found a rag, dipped it in the water, and held it to the lump on Nell's head. Nell flinched but otherwise held still.

"English?" Nell looked at Cheeta, who made a dismissive gesture and nodded toward the girl.

"Piney know."

"Horse running away, you on ground," the little girl said.

"And you brought me here?" Nell looked at Piney in amazement.

"Mother help."

Someone threw more wood on the fires, and the smoke billowed. A dog wandered over and curled up near Piney. The little girl scratched its head, disturbing several fleas. Then, as if responding to a signal she hadn't seen or heard, a large number of men came in, and she turned to watch them. They squatted in lines on each side of the trough, which Cheeta and the other women began filling with food from the kettles. While the men ate, Cheeta started frying batter in a large skillet. She served the men first and then brought two pieces of something resembling Johnnycake, spread with molasses, over to Piney and Nell. Both ate with healthy appetites. When Cheeta gave her a questioning look, Nell smiled and nodded. After she was done eating, she stood up, swaying for a moment. "If my horse ran away, I'll have to walk home."

Cheeta said something to Piney, who translated, "Horse gone. Go by canoe. We take."

With Cheeta in the lead, the three left the longhouse and started toward the spot where the river and bay merged. The fresh air hit Nell like a slap in the face. Several times she had to stop and let dizzy spells pass, and once she threw up. *I've got the collywobbles, for sure,* she thought.

At the river's mouth, dozens of canoes were beached against the incoming tide. Looking back from the water's edge, Nell was able to gauge the size of the encampment. Tents and lean-tos of all shapes, sizes, and conditions surrounded the longhouse. Great piles of oyster shells near them swarmed with flies. Seagulls swooped and screeched over the rotting remains. Dogs barked, horses whinnied, and children chased each other. Two older boys wrestled, egged on by their friends, while others played the bone game. Except for the stinking middens of shells, the scene was like dozens of picnics Nell had attended over the years. It came to her that this must be a potlatch, and she asked Piney.

"Yes." The girl nodded. "Made by James Lick."

"Doesn't the church preach against them?"

Piney scowled. "This Indian way."

"Good for you." Nell didn't approve of Reverend Judy and some of the other ministers in New Tacoma telling the Puyallups what to do and how to live their lives.

Meanwhile, Cheeta had been walking by the various boats until she found the one she was looking for. She pushed a small canoe halfway into the water and gestured for Nell and Piney to get in. Nell made her way to a seat in the stern, holding to gunwales on each side to help keep the vessel steady. Taking her place in the middle, Piney was much more adept at keeping the canoe from rolling. Then Cheeta got in so skillfully, the boat barely moved. Sunlight glistened off the fish scales in spaces of the belly where water sloshed around.

Cheeta used a paddle to shove off from shore, caught the river's current, and directed the vessel into the bay. Nell watched the woman with admiration as she kept them on course, pushing through driftwood of various sizes and clumps of shell-encrusted seaweed floating on the water's surface. They passed indifferent ducks and angry-eyed gulls and came close to a somewhat derelict houseboat from which voices were clearly audible. Despite her aching head, Nell enjoyed the ride and the unfamiliar scenery. She wished she could draw and paint like her friend Sarah, whose pockets were never without bits of paper and pieces of charcoal.

In less time than Nell would have thought, Cheeta pulled up to a ladder leading from the water to the top of the wharf. She said something to Piney while positioning the canoe so Nell could grab a rung.

"Ma says to tell you I'm a hard worker," the girl translated.

Nell smiled. "I'm sure you are."

"And father dead."

"I'm sorry." New Tacoma widows often ended up living in shacks and trying to scratch out a living in Old Women's Gulch. She wondered what happened to Indian widows. Apparently, though, Cheeta had no more to say. While on the bay, she had sent the canoe gliding across the water, changing hands when necessary, and looking at the variety of anchored ships. Now, at the wharf ladder, she seemed uncomfortable. *I hope she doesn't get in trouble for bringing me here,* Nell thought.

"Mahsie," she said in Chinook to Cheeta as she held onto the ladder. To Piney, she translated it to, "Thank you." Cheeta nodded, and Piney smiled. Before Nell scrambled out of the canoe, she kissed the little girl on the cheek. "If you and your mother are in town, I would love for you to come and visit me. I have a little sister just about your age. Walk two blocks up Seventh Street from C Street and turn right. It's the plank house." Piney beamed and repeated the words to her mother, who looked at Nell and nodded. Then Nell gathered her skirt and stepped onto the lowest rung. Climbing the rough ladder was harder than she thought, thanks to her queasy stomach and throbbing head. *A change of clothes and a bucket of water to get the smell of smoke out of my hair and I'll be as good as new,* she told herself.

The canoe was far into the bay when she reached the top and turned to wave.

The quarter-mile road from the wharf to town was full of people and wagons. Nell would have liked a ride, but no one was going in her direction. She walked slowly, stopping several times to rest. At the top of a rise, she met a herd of sheep being driven down to one of the corrals near the Blackwell Hotel where they'd await shipment. A farmer and a dog kept them going. Their smell was so strong, Nell leaned over the boardwalk railing and threw up again.

She straightened, wiped her mouth, and continued on. Before long she reached Pacific Avenue, which was crowded with shoppers. Nell saw her old school chum Fern and her mother coming out of Fisher's Department Store. At the sight of Nell, Fern gave a start and dropped a large parcel she'd been carrying, and Nell realized she'd lost her hat. *Oh, dear,* she thought, *Fern will tell her friend Ellen, and Ellen doesn't think I'm much of a lady, anyway.* With a heavy sigh, she ducked her head and continued on her way until she reached Cogswell's livery stable. Rigger stood outside, filling a horse trough. He saw Nell and walked over. "Old Bobby come back a couple hours ago. I had a mind to get up a search party for you."

"You were right about him being full of the Old Nick." Nell swallowed against another surge of nausea. She didn't want word of her accident spread around town. "I'm glad he's back. A hawk came down in front of us near the reservation, and he jumped a ditch, throwing me." She felt the lump on her head and winced. "Next time, maybe I'd better hire a quieter horse."

"You're not looking so pert, Miss Nell.

Want I should fetch your pa? I saw him going into Levin's Saloon."

"No. Pa's no good when someone's sick. Just as well he's out of the house."

Rigger nodded, and Nell continued up the hill.

When she reached home and opened the door, the house was empty, except for a mouse that scrambled under the stove. Home was dim, cool, and blessedly quiet, nothing to be heard except Amity's prize Seth Thomas clock ticking softly. Nell removed her dress and put it in a bucket of water to soak. Then she washed herself off and, after making sure no one was around, went outside and poured several pails of water over her head. Being careful to avoid the lump, she worked the water through her hair. Leaving the resulting puddle for the birds to enjoy, she dried off, went back inside, and crawled into bed. *What a day.*

Obed finally came home, and she roused from sleeping long enough to tell him she was sick. He fussed around for a while and then left, waking her again some hours later when he returned.

"You feeling any better?"

"Yes, Pa. I'm going to heat some soup. Do you want some?"

"No. I et at Levin's."

"Well, that's good. I'm not really up to making a big dinner. Good night, then. I'll be quiet."

Obed went to his room. Nell stoked the fire, then dipped some of the soup Amity had left into a smaller pan and set it to heat. She sat so quietly, the mouse reappeared and looked about for crumbs. After a few minutes, when bubbles broke the soup's surface, she carried the pan to where a shaft of moonlight came through a window and sat to dunk bread and eat. As she did, she thought about what Hildy would make of her day. *Now that we're all grown up and Hildy has her bakery, I don't suppose we'll have excitement like today's anymore.* Suddenly, she remembered two things Hildy had said: "Mrs. Blackwell helped me buy the stove, and Mr. Cogswell moved a wall in his building and rented me ten additional feet of space."

I wonder if I could start with ten feet of space. That's not much to hold a sewing machine and all the other things a dressmaker has to have. Nell dipped a piece of bread into the soup and thought about a shop of her own. *I don't want to borrow money to buy a sewing machine, probably couldn't find anyone to lend me that much, anyway, so I'll just have to sell enough handiwork to pay for it.* She nibbled at the soaked bread. *Renting space, though, that's different. Pa can make chairs for ladies to sit on and shelves to display my work. Until I have money to buy paint, I can whitewash the walls. The space will have to have a window I can sit in front of, so ladies will see me crocheting and want to come in. Hildy taught me how to keep a ledger; I just need to make more things to sell, but I have every day until Ma and the girls get home to work.*

She finished eating and washed her dishes. Obed's snoring drifted into the room. Her head still ached, so she mixed a teaspoon of pulverized charcoal with a third of a teaspoon of baking soda and stirred it into warm water. The beverage tasted nasty, but Amity swore by it for headaches. *At least my stomach feels better.* Back in bed, she fell asleep thinking about a shop called Miss Nell's Fancy Dress Goods.

CHAPTER 8

Five days after her accident, Nell's family returned from Bush Prairie, and she welcomed the hustle and bustle they made. While they were gone, and with no one to do for except Pa, she had crocheted so many things, including some items Mrs. Blackwell had ordered by way of a hand-delivered note, that she ran out of thread. So, one warm day in early June, Nell left home with a spring in her step, headed for the Blackwell Hotel and then to buy more thread.

Walking down the hill to Pacific Avenue, she paused to watch a new confusion. Men erecting poles for the new telephone line had blocked parts of the road with piles of dirt, and the street was torn up in front of the Gross Brothers' store where additional sewer lines were going in. Digging and grading had resulted in mounds of earth and rocks; wagons, pedestrians, and roaming animals all had to circle around them, adding to the chaos. Ordinarily, Nell loved the activity, but today she was in a hurry. Running parallel to Pacific and mostly residential was A Street, which looked like a better route.

To her left on A Street, men were putting the finishing touches on the Northern Pacific Land Office. Nell watched them for a minute and then turned the other way, slowing to admire Otis Sprague's two-story white house. *Someday I'm going to have a house like that,* she thought, *or like Captain George Clancy's house.* The Clancy residence, which was nearby, had flags hanging from the downstairs windows and potted plants on evenly spaced posts. A picket fence separated the yard from the wooden sidewalk. Even Fern liked Captain Clancy's house. "Almost like in Virginia," she'd said.

On the south end of A Street, Nell passed the home on the bluff where Hildy and her family lived. Nell saw three little girls playing in the yard and heard one of them saying, "Button, button. Who's got the button?" She smiled, remembering how she and Indiana used to play that. The street ended a bit farther south, where it dissolved into a little-known trail that meandered downhill to the southernmost end of the wharf. Hildy had found the trail several years previously, but it was rarely used by white people because it ended at New Tacoma's Chinese community, and, other than the Celestials, no one else had reason to go there. Nell liked the path, though, because the Chinese generally had something interesting to see, and from there she could walk north to the Blackwell Hotel and take note of everything new along the way.

Maple branches shaded the narrow track, and the previous winter's dead leaves made it slippery. Nell picked her way carefully, scaring up dragonflies and robins. New foliage smells diluted the ever-present waterfront odors, but it was easy to tell the tide was out. It was also easy, despite the little trail's remoteness, to remember how close the railroad tracks were. Nell heard a train rattle by and, from the sun's position in the sky, figured it was the daily coal train coming down from the foothills of Mt. Tacoma. Little boys always followed the train, picking up fallen lumps of coal to sell to homemakers. As she walked, their shouts filled the air, competing with a tugboat's whistle, a warning that it was towing a ship into the harbor. On any given day, Commencement Bay was crowded with steamers, tugs, and sailing ships. They anchored, waiting to be loaded or unloaded, and Nell loved the sounds of sails snapping in the breeze. She hurried so she could see which ship the tug was pulling, and maybe find out where it came from and what it carried.

A fifteen-minute walk brought her to the bottom of the bluff. Ahead of her, a couple dozen shacks crowded, cheek-by-jowl, down to where the wharf ended at the head of the bay. Racks of drying fish, lines of laundry, and vegetable gardens filled nearly every conceivable space. Hildy had told Nell about the little store run by Shi Ning, whose name meant honest and genial. She spotted it several yards ahead but stopped short when she saw a woman go in. *Why, that's Mrs. Rector.*

Nell stepped off the path and ducked behind a tree. Several weeks back, a small article in the *Tacoma Herald* mentioned that some of New Tacoma's white women were frequenting the Chinese store, and it was rumored they were buying opium. Nell had pooh-poohed the report, knowing that, though some women did buy silk from Shi Ning, when it came to the white population, the folks who went to his store were mostly boys buying fireworks. Either way, though, she was uncomfortable with her neighbor seeing her in the Chinese community.

After a few moments, Mrs. Rector left the store, pocketing a small article wrapped in red paper. Nell remembered the odd odor hanging around Mrs. Rector when she encountered the matron shopping and realized it was the same smell some of New Tacoma's Chinese had. *Snollygoster. Wait 'til I tell Hildy.*

Mrs. Rector hurried down the wharf, and Nell waited until she was out of sight before continuing. Not far from Shi Ning's store was the combination stationery shop, aviary store, and printing office Hildy had loved. Mr. and Mrs. Money, who ran the business, recently sold it, along with their newspaper, the *Pierce County News,* and moved to Oregon. Tears ran down Hildy's cheeks as she told Nell about the sale. "General Sprague told the Moneys he was tired of parrot tracks on his official railroad stationery and was taking his business elsewhere." She'd sniffed loudly and added, "I don't believe the parrot story for a minute, but, if it is true, an old parrot print would surely make railroad letters more interesting."

Now, as Nell passed the store, she saw that all the printing equipment remained, but the birds were gone, and most of the counters looked dusty and sad. She hurried by the shop, some warehouses, and several corrals full of cattle where men leaned on the rails. A wheat train from eastern Washington came down the track, and three wagons of produce lumbered by. Just beyond the corrals was the Blackwell Hotel. Nell dodged a horse tethered outside and entered the smoke-filled dining room. Clustered at the far end, a group of businessmen puffed cigars and argued while a bartender polished glasses at the counter and listened.

"Good morning, Mr. Mann," Nell said.

"Morning, Miss Nell." He set one glass down and picked up another. "How are you?"

"I'm fine. And you?"

"Doing as well as can be expected for the shape that I'm in," he said, and Nell giggled.

"Mrs. Blackwell asked me to stop by." She had to raise her own voice when the men's voices rose, and she recognized one as belonging to Ezra Meeker, a farmer from the Puyallup Valley. Speaking more softly, she said, "Is Mr. Meeker having trouble with his hops?"

"No, Miss Nell, it's the Chinese. There's a law been passed saying no more can come into the territory, and some people want those who are here shipped back to China."

She watched the hotel's Chinese help going in and out of the kitchen and remembered her nephew saying the same thing. "Who would do all the work they do?"

"I don't know. Most men don't want to do laundry, or wash dishes or carry garbage."

"It doesn't seem fair. The Celestials have been here for a long time. This is their home."

"Well now, some see it your way, and some don't. Take Mr. Meeker, for example; he feels the same as you." Mr. Mann shook his head. "I don't reckon anyone bothered to ask the Chinese what they want, though."

"Surely the Blackwells don't want the Chinese sent back to China."

"No, they don't. Mr. Blackwell stands firmly with Mr. Meeker, but the road crew up town has a problem with them and are talking of a strike. That's sure and certain to stir up trouble." The bartender stared at the glass in his hand and changed the subject. "Now, Mrs. Blackwell said when you came for you to go on up; she has someone she wants you to meet."

Troubled by the conversation, Nell nodded and turned toward the stairs.

The hotel's bedrooms lined each side of a long corridor on the second floor, except at the south end. There the Blackwells had their quarters and a small balcony crowded with flowers. Beyond it was a spectacular view of Mt. Tacoma. As Nell reached the landing, she heard female voices leaking through the door jamb. At her knock, a Chinese man let her in. "Is that Nell Tanquist, Liang?" Mrs. Blackwell called. "Please, show her to the parlor."

Nell followed Liang into a parlor filled with the mahogany furniture the Blackwells had bought from Jay Gould after Gould went bankrupt. Nell always thought it was funny that Gould failed to bring the railroad to New Tacoma, like he was supposed to, but that his furniture ended up there. As the servant left to replenish the tea, Mrs. Blackwell rose and gestured toward a lady sitting bolt upright in a wooden chair. "Nell, I have someone I want you to meet. This is Mrs. Dr. Nolan; she's an obstetrician."

Dr. Nolan smiled and nodded. She wore a small round hat with a plain black ribbon, a jacket, and a black skirt. Sturdy-looking boots peeked from under the skirt's hem. "It's a pleasure to meet another businesswoman," she said.

Nell's face lit up with a smile. "I know what a doctor is, but what is an obstetrician?" she asked as she sat on a chair near the balcony and Mrs. Blackwell did the same.

"A person who delivers babies."

"Goodness sakes." Nell looked astonished, and Mrs. Blackwell laughed. "A doctor just for babies?"

"Yes, indeed. Until the invention of forceps, a midwife or female relative was responsible for births. It's only been the last seventy-five or so years that men have been in charge. It's time we women took the responsibility back. Wouldn't you rather have a female doctor tending you?"

Before Nell could consider the question, Mrs. Blackwell intervened. "I don't think this is an appropriate topic of conversation for a young, unmarried woman." She offered a cup of tea to Nell and refilled the other two cups.

"I disagree." Dr. Nolan turned to Nell. "How many children did your mother have?"

"Uh . . ." Nell stopped to count. "Well, there's Indiana; she lives out on the prairie. And Ike, Josie, Albina, and me — and the twins. They died during the smallpox epidemic. And then two others, Mary and Silas, died before any of us were born. That's nine."

"It must take a lot of work to support all of you?"

Mrs. Blackwell frowned slightly. "Dr.

Nolan, really. Nell came to deliver some needlework I ordered, not to talk about her father's ability to feed his family."

Dr. Nolan flushed. "Of course. You're right." She turned to Nell. "You must forgive me, Nell. I was at Abigail Scott Dunaway's ratification meeting for women's suffrage last night, and I'm very excited about future opportunities for women. Did you attend?"

"No, ma'am."

"Well, never mind. Now, I see you're wearing black, too. Are you going to Dr. Wing's funeral?"

"No, ma'am; it's for the twins. When the smallpox come on, Ma sent Josie, Albina, and me to Mr. Bonney's drugstore. After that, we went to stay with Indiana. Ma already had the smallpox, so she tended to the twins."

"Why the drugstore?"

"He made a sulphur room."

"A sulphur room?"

"Yes, ma'am. He filled a room with burning sulphur and cut a hole in the door so we could breathe the fumes, and that would keep us safe. Of course, when the twins sickened, Ma decided that wasn't enough, and that's when she sent us to stay with our sister. Ike's married, so she couldn't send him away, but Mr. Bonney sold him some carbolic crystals to carry in his pocket."

"Saints preserve us, what a thing to do, and in this age of smallpox vaccinations, too."

Before Nell could ask what a vaccination was, voices coming up from the dining room filled the silence, and she changed the subject. "Mr. Mann says some men here want to send the Chinese back to China."

"The government passed the Chinese Exclusion Act," Mrs. Blackwell said, looking as if she hoped the doctor wouldn't have any radical comments to make about it. "It's causing the men here to argue about New Tacoma's Chinese population."

"Mr. Mann said some people don't want the Chinese here, but, if we didn't have them, who would do all the work they do?"

"The Indians?" Dr. Nolan had apparently recovered from whatever surprised her about Mr. Bonney's sulphur room and carbolic crystals.

"They have their own customs and don't see the need to adopt our ways." Mrs. Blackwell sighed. "Anyway, Mr. Meeker is highly respected, and it's to be hoped his opinion will persuade the other men. Now," she smiled at Nell. "You here with the needlework I ordered?"

Nell opened her workbox and handed Mrs. Blackwell a collar and matching cuffs. Almost hesitantly, she displayed a set of fingerless mitts. Mrs. Blackwell slid one onto her hand. "You clever girl, you made them to match the other pieces. They're lovely."

Nell blushed at the praise. "I wrote to Mrs. Godey, of *Godey's Lady's Book,* and she sent me the pattern."

Dr. Nolan tried on the remaining mitt. "Do you have a shop?"

"Not yet. I make things at home and then find someone who wants to buy them. I'm saving for a Singer sewing machine like the one I saw in town because we don't have a dressmaker here in New Tacoma, and I want to help my sister Josie buy a piano, too."

"Doesn't Josie work for Mrs. McCarver?" Mrs. Blackwell retrieved the mitt from the doctor.

"Yes, but we have to buy groceries when Pa's out of work or doesn't have the money, and pianos are very expensive — more than sewing machines." Nell thought of having to pay Grandma Staley and sighed. "I don't suppose Josie will ever have enough money to buy one."

As she spoke, a whistle sounded, and Mrs. Blackwell stood. "That'll be the train from Kalama. I'll just get your money, Nell, and

I'll buy the mitts, too. Then I have to go downstairs and make sure everything is ready in the dining room."

Dr. Nolan also stood. "I enjoyed meeting you, Nell, and I'd like to ask you a question. Why are there two communities so close together, both named Tacoma?"

"It's kind of complicated. A man named Job Carr came to Puget Sound and settled on the bay west of here. He wanted the railroad to stop there so he could make a lot of money, and he called his area Eureka. Then he sold most of his land to General Morton Mathew McCarver. The general was going to call that place Commencement City, only a man from the Northern Pacific thought Tacoma would be a better name. The trouble was, Job Carr's son, Anthony, had already platted the Carr site and filed it using the name Tacoma, so the general added the word 'City' to his filing, making it Tacoma City. When the railroad came, it decided it should have its own town here, where the hotel and wharf are, and they called it New Tacoma. Most people call the other place Old Tacoma."

"Well." The doctor looked a little dazed. "That explains it. Thank you, and Nell, if you'd like to talk sometime, I have an office on Tenth and Pacific."

"Thank you." Nell wondered what they would have to talk about. She left the room shortly afterward with an order from the doctor for a set of navy-blue collar, cuffs, and mitts like Mrs. Blackwell's.

Back down in the dining room, Chinese men in white pants and jackets were setting the tables with heavy white crockery. The smell of roast fowl coming from the kitchen made Nell's mouth water. Intending to hurry home, she stepped outside near to where the train from Kalama, with steam hissing and brakes squealing, was pulling to a stop in front of the hotel. The conductor lowered steps, and people poured out — well-dressed white people first, followed by roughly dressed laborers, and finally by several Chinese men and a young Chinese woman. Few Chinese women lived in New Tacoma, and Nell looked at her closely. She wore dark-blue pants, and a coat of the same faded cloth that hung almost to her knees. Her hair was pulled into a bun at the back of her neck, and a conical straw hat covered her head. While six of her companions stood near the engine, the seventh went into the hotel. He returned after a few minutes, gesturing and pointing. Suddenly, the woman broke away and threw herself on Nell. Nell's arms automatically went around her, and she felt the woman shaking. Excited voices filled the air as one of the men tried to pull her away, while the others began waving their arms and arguing among themselves, all the while staring at the two young women.

Work on the wharf stopped, and white laborers crowded around. A second Chinese man joined the first, grabbing at the woman's arms and tearing Nell's sleeve. Nell kept one arm around the woman and with her other hand swung her workbox at the men. "Stop that," she shouted. When the men ignored her, she swung it again, this time making contact with someone's shoulder. The man rubbed his arm and glared at her while the others stepped back. "How dare you treat a woman like that? And look at what you've done to my dress." Nell pointed to where the sleeve had been ripped from the bodice. "I have half a mind to have you all arrested."

At her words, the Chinese men stepped further back, and the wharf workers milled about, the anger in their voices increasing. Some of them muttered and made threatening gestures. A few waved tools or lengths of wood. Voices in a variety of languages — Swedish, German, and Gallicas well as English — filled the air as more men joined the gathering crowd. The Chinese men huddled together, looking nervous. Caught in the middle, Nell wasn't sure what to do. She was saved from having to make a decision by the appearance of William Blackwell. He burst out of the hotel door and pushed through the angry throng.

"What's going on here?"

Nell and the Chinese woman stood waiting while everyone else tried to answer. Mr. Blackwell raised his hands as if to silence them and called out, "Jianya," over his shoulder. Seconds later, a middle-aged Chinese man hurried out of the hotel. Mr. Blackwell nodded to him. "See if you can find out what's going on, will you?"

Jianya said something to the Chinese men, and all seven started talking. He barked out a few more words and pointed at one of them. A short conversation followed before Jianya turned to Mr. Blackwell. "Man say woman his wife, bought fo' tree hunded dolla."

"What?" Nell stepped forward. "He can't do that."

"Just a moment, Nell." Mr. Blackwell looked at the woman and the men. "Why are they here, Jianya?"

Jianya started talking again, with the men interrupting each other to explain. After a

160

few minutes, he turned to Mr. Blackwell, but, thanks to noise from the muttering crowd, Nell couldn't hear their conversation. Then Mr. Blackwell turned to her. "Apparently, a Seattle man named Han Yan sold this woman, Fang Hua, to this man, Baojia, for eleven hundred dollars. Baojia paid Han Yan three hundred dollars and then married Fang Hua so he wouldn't have to pay the remaining eight hundred. Han Yan sent men to harass Baojia, causing the couple to leave their Olympia home and go to Kalama. Now, Han Yan is charging Baojia with larceny, and they are all headed to Seattle for a trial."

"They can't do that," Nell said. "They can't buy and sell women like — like cattle or something. These men need to go back to this Han Yan and tell him so."

"I agree with you, but it's a difficult situation. If we send the couple back to Kalama, Han Yan's men will just follow and probably kidnap her. At least this way the situation will go before a judge."

"But . . ."

Mr. Blackwell took Fang Hua's arm. "Jianya, tell her to go peacefully with her husband. Tell her I know Judge Lyts and he is a fair man. There is little doubt but that the case will be dismissed."

As Jianya repeated Mr. Blackwell's words, one of the men stepped forward and took Fang Hua's hand. She looked at Nell, tears rolling down her face.

"Oh, this is horrible, just horrible." Nell handed Fang Hua a handkerchief, wrapped her arms around the woman for a moment, and then stepped back. The Chinese men immediately surrounded Fang Hua, and they disappeared.

Mr. Blackwell waved his arms at the horde of men behind Nell. "It's all over, fellas. Go on back to work." As they wandered back to their jobs, talking among themselves, Mr. Blackwell looked at Nell. "You, too, Nell. Go on home. There's nothing you can do."

"But it isn't right."

"The Chinese brought their customs with them. Learning our ways takes time."

"Well, I hope they aren't made to go back to China. If they are, Fang Hua won't stand a chance."

"It's nothing for you to concern yourself about; let the men handle it. Now, it's getting late, and you'd best be home."

Mr. Blackwell returned to the hotel, and Nell scowled at his retreating figure. *Seems to me that, so far, the men haven't handled a lot of things very well,* she thought. *When I have my own business, I'll make them listen to my ideas. Women should have a voice in how things are done. We live in New Tacoma, too.*

She started toward the wharf-to-town road, thinking first about Fang Hua and then about her order from Dr. Nolan, and mentally counting her savings. As she did the math in her head, she remembered her favorite teacher and giggled. *Miss Sparkle would be so proud of me, but more than that, she'd be amazed.*

CHAPTER 9

Spring kicked and fought its way into summer. As soon as Mrs. Bostwick's fruit trees bloomed, the wind blew the blossoms onto the street where horses trampled them into the dirt. Deer ventured into town to eat her roses, and boys went out to the country hunting the damp woods for trillium to sell. Josie, Albina, and Amity spent the better part of their days helping Frieda Faye get ready for the birth of her first child, but Nell found working in the garden a more pleasant pastime. "I wish I spoke Chinese," she said to Hildy one morning as they thinned carrot starts. "I keep wondering what that Chinese girl at the wharf was trying to say to me."

"Was it a girl? I thought you said she was a woman." Hildy patted the soil down around a tender sprout.

"Well, she was married, so I guess she is a woman, but she looked so young. I only ever see Chinese men, and they scurry around so fast it's hard to tell them from boys."

"I said that to Chong once and he got awfully mad at me. He said, to the Chinese we all look alike, and smell alike, too."

Nell laughed and threw a shoot at Hildy, who picked it up and twirled the small leafy stem between her fingers. "I hate pulling up healthy starts. If they're growing, they're alive and deserve a chance to live and mature like the others."

"And be eaten; either way, their end is the same."

Hildy threw the carrot back, and they continued down the row. "How did your dandelions do?"

"Really well. Ma cooked them with pork, and the greens tasted so good; it was nice to have fresh vegetables."

"It was, wasn't it? They're pretty when they bloom, too." After a comfortable silence, Hildy changed the subject. "Did you tell Frieda Faye about the lady doctor you met at Mrs. Blackwell's?"

"I did, and poor Frieda Faye doesn't know what to think." Nell laughed again. "She can't decide if a woman can be as good a doctor as a man. I'm not sure she even knows where the baby came from."

"Nell!"

"I know. Ladies don't talk about such things, but Frieda Faye seems to think she'll wake up one morning and find a baby in bed next to her, all cleaned and wearing its best bib and tucker."

"Is Mrs. Johnson coming?"

"Yes. Ma could probably do the necessary, but Frieda Faye wants a midwife."

They continued thinning out other starts and throwing the greens to a strutting rooster.

"That rooster seems to think a lot of himself, doesn't he?" Hildy said, after a dozen or so squawking seagulls flew by. "Oh, dear," she added, watching them disappear into some trees. "When the gulls take refuge on land, it's stormy at sea. I suppose it's going to rain again."

"That's okay with me. Our rain barrel needs water." Nell watched the rooster chase a hen. "Pa calls him the Ladies' Man. He lives next door at the Rectors', but he likes it here because Ma has so many hens. Ma wants eggs to sell, and the rooster wants a wife — or two." Nell paused and lowered her voice. "The day I went to see Mrs. Blackwell, I saw Mrs. Rector coming out of the Chinese store."

Hildy wiped her forehead with the back of her hand. "What would she be doing there?"

"I don't know, but sometimes when I'm around her, she smells like some of the Chinese men do."

"What do you mean?"

"Kind of sweet but also musky."

"Oh, that. I know what you mean, but, gracious. That's odd about Mrs. Rector. I could ask Chong if he knows."

Nell envied the Bacoms' having a Chinese servant, but she knew what her pa would think of the idea. She pursed her lips and looked in the direction of the Rector house. "No, you better not. There's something funny about the family. It used to be when Ma cooked too much of something, she usually sent me over there with the leftovers. She thought the daughter, Nona, was too thin. I was never invited in, though. Mrs. Rector would meet me at the door. They never were neighborly, but, since Nona died, we hardly ever see them."

"That is peculiar."

"I know. And Albina was never able to make friends with Nona, and you know Albina, she doesn't take no for an answer. Mr. Hanson hired Mr. Rector as a clerk at the Hanson Mill, and the family moved from Olympia late last year. I guess they decided to let Nona wait and start school in fall. Poor thing; she never had a chance to have friends here before she died."

The two had reached the end of the row of carrots and onions when they heard someone calling from the road.

"That's Dr. Mrs. Clarke. I wonder what she's doing here." Nell stood up and walked to where the doctor stood. "Hello, Dr. Clarke. How nice to see you."

"It's nice to see you, too, Nell. I was wondering . . ."

Before she could finish the sentence, they heard a rifle shot. Another followed, and, after a moment, they smelled sulfur. Startled, they both jumped, and Hildy ran to join them. "It came from over there." Hildy pointed south toward the Rectors' home. "Why do you suppose someone is shooting in town?"

"I don't know." Nell chewed on her lip. "Do you think we should go over and make sure everything is all right?"

"Why don't I go," said Dr. Clarke. "I have been trying to meet the ladies in town, and this will give me a good reason to introduce myself. Can I cut through your property, Nell?"

"Of course."

Nell and Hildy watched the doctor until she reached the end of the chicken coop and disappeared among a copse of alder trees and sword ferns. When curiosity got the best of them, they started after her, stopping when they heard piteous groans. "It sounds like someone is hurt," Nell said. She ran toward the Rector house with Hildy close behind her. When the home came in sight, they saw Dr. Clarke kneeling on the porch where a woman lay.

Nell stopped abruptly. "That's Mrs. Rector."

The doctor gave her a quick glance. "She's been shot. Please see if you can find some clean rags. I need to staunch the bleeding."

Nell darted up the steps but stopped just inside the door. "It smells real strong of gunpowder, and there's blood everywhere." She looked down and realized she'd stepped in a stream that was inching across the floor. Nell felt her breakfast — warm and putrid — rising in her throat. Leaning over, she retched until her stomach had nothing left to expel and her throat tingled and burned. In the gloom, she saw a horsehair sofa blocking all but the head of someone on the floor. "I think someone's been shot in here, too."

"Find me the rags first. Then I'll see to that person."

Avoiding the prone body and looking around the room, Nell spotted several flour sacks folded in a pile near the dry sink. She grabbed them and returned to the porch. "Poor Mrs. Rector." Still shaky, she watched the doctor apply pressure to the side of the woman's face and head. "Is she hurt bad?"

"I can't tell until I have a chance to examine her more closely. Head wounds bleed heavily. Can one of you find a wagon to carry her to my surgery?"

"I'll go." Hildy turned and ran.

Nell hunkered down beside the doctor. "If you tell me what to do, I'll do it while you see to the other person."

"Hold this towel here and this one here." Dr. Clarke demonstrated, and Nell's hands shook as she tried to follow the instructions. Then Mrs. Rector moaned and started twisting. "Don't let her move," the doctor said. "I'll be right back."

"It's all right, Mrs. Rector." Nell tried to speak calmly as the lady opened her eyes and groaned. "Dr. Clarke is just inside. She'll be right back. I know it must hurt terribly, but try not to move."

"Mr. Rector," the woman whispered.

"What?"

"My husband. He tried to kill me." She groaned again, and tears rolled down her face.

Dr. Clarke returned to the porch and took

over from Nell. "It's Mr. Rector in there. I had some dealings with him a while back."

Nell took a deep breath, remembering the rusty smell of blood, the dusty surfaces and dead plants, everything in the house speaking of neglect. She squeezed her eyes shut for a moment, feeling lightheaded. "His face was almost gone."

Dr. Clarke grabbed her wrist. "Don't faint, Nell." In a quick movement, she took a feather from her medical bag, lit it, and held it under Nell's nose.

Nell gagged at the acrid smell, managing to hold the towels in place while she leaned back. "Do you think he shot himself, too?"

"Yes. I think Mr. Rector shot his wife, and used his toe to pull the shotgun's trigger to shoot himself. That's why one shoe is off."

"But why? Why would he do that?"

"Perhaps it was the opium."

"What opium?"

"It's in Mrs. Rector's clothes. Can't you smell it?"

"I didn't know for sure what the smell was."

The doctor lifted the bloody cloth and checked Mrs. Rector's wound. "I hate to ask, but would you get me some soap and water? I'll clean this as best I can here and sterilize the wounds at the office."

"Maybe there's some whisky inside that you can pour on it."

"Carbolic acid is better."

Nell steeled herself and went back inside the house, averting her eyes from Mr. Rector's corpse. She found a clean pot and dipped hot water from the kitchen stove's reservoir. A piece of lye soap lay on a counter, and she carried it and the water out to the porch. Dr. Clarke cut away strands of her patient's hair and asked Nell to find a spider web to help staunch the bleeding.

"We don't have them in spring, just in September and October," Nell said.

"Of course. I should have remembered that."

While they worked, a well-worn Studebaker wagon pulled into the yard. Nell recognized the driver. "Thank heavens you've come, Mr. Bain," she said as he got down and hurried over to them. "Mrs. Rector has been shot, and Dr. Clarke needs to get her to her office."

"Mr. Bain," Dr. Clarke said, "would you mind finding me some blankets?"

Hildy jumped off the wagon seat. "I'll do it."

"No!" Nell grabbed her friend by the arm. The doctor and Mr. Bain exchanged a look. Mr. Bain cleared his throat. "I'll take care of it," he said and ducked inside the house.

He emerged some minutes later with several folded blankets in his arms. "That Mr. Rector in there?"

"I believe so." Dr. Clarke closed her bag.

"Looks like he shot hisself with his toe. Heard about it. Never seen it done, though."

"Well, that's for the sheriff to determine." The doctor stood. "Now, if you girls can spread out the blankets in the wagon bed and you, Mr. Bain, can help me, we'll lay Mrs. Rector there."

Nell and Hildy took the blankets to the wagon and spread them out. Mr. Bain picked up the injured woman and carried her to the makeshift bed. "I'll bet her husband was in the Civil War," he said, while Dr. Clarke tried to make her patient comfortable.

"Why do you say that?"

"Lots of men came home from the war sufferin' from nostalgia. Were shamed somethin' awful if folks got wise, and them blankets is shoddy . . ."

Dr. Clarke interrupted the flow of words. "We're ready. I'll ride back here. Nell, would you come with me? I could use a helper when we get her to my office."

"What can I do?" Hildy asked.

"Shut the door, and then find the sheriff. If anyone asks you about the shots, just say someone was shooting at a weasel going after their chickens. That way people won't come nosing around."

Mr. Bain snapped the reins, and they started down the road, the wagon's creaking and groaning covering the horse's plodding footfalls. *I never realized how much like a corduroy road New Tacoma's streets are,* Nell thought, as the wheels went up and down in rain-made ruts, and she and Dr. Clarke tried to keep Mrs. Rector from being jarred.

On Pacific Avenue, Dr. Clarke had Mr. Bain turn right and after three blocks told him to stop at a single-story, white-painted building with a modest sign reading Dr. Clarke, Physician/Obstetrics. She jumped out of the wagon and hurried to unlock the door.

Their sudden appearance attracted passers-by. "Who is it?" a teenaged boy asked. Nell recognized him as Delmar Manches, the fellow who had tried to interfere when General Sprague talked to the Indians after the kidnappings. Several years earlier, he'd been in trouble for harassing the Chinese. She ignored his question, so he walked closer and took a look. "It's just some woman."

"God-ee Almighty," said one of the on-lookers. "She looks, for sure and certain, to be on the way to the Promised Land."

Dr. Clarke elbowed him. "Here, be useful and help Mr. Bain get her inside."

The two men lifted Mrs. Rector out of the wagon and carried her through the door to a narrow bed along the far wall. Nell reluctantly followed. The office was a single room; a table with several kerosene lamps on it stood next to the bed. A folding screen that the doctor could use for privacy was propped nearby. In the right front corner near the door, a wood-burning stove puffed out heat and warmed benches built into the walls for use by patients, and water in the stove's reservoir steamed slightly. Bottles and beakers, piles of clean rags, and various-sized basins filled shelves on the room's left wall. Nell smelled herbs and kerosene.

The men left, and Dr. Clarke filled a basin with hot water and gestured for Nell. They each washed their hands, and the doctor emptied the basin in a hole in the floor under a small table that held a mortar and pestle. Then she poured something with a vinegar-like odor over their hands.

"What was that?" Nell asked as she carried rags and a basin of clean water over to the bed where Mrs. Rector lay moaning. Together they loosened the bloodied cloths that had dried in the wound.

"It's the carbolic acid I mentioned. It sterilizes the hands."

"What does that mean?"

"It gets them so clean no dirt can get into the wound."

They worked carefully, but once, when the injured woman groaned and twisted, Nell asked Dr. Clarke if she could give Mrs. Rector some whisky.

"I'll give her something presently," the doctor said. "The bullet appears to have gone in one side of her head and out the other but close to the surface. Mostly it's just a superficial wound. Right now, it's more important to make sure both wounds are clean. If you can lift her head, I'll finish cutting her hair away."

Mrs. Rector said something that Nell had to bend close to hear. "Not opium."

Nell repeated the words to the doctor, who nodded while she shaved hair from around the exit wound. "Keep her talking, Nell; it'll distract her from what I'm doing."

"Why not opium if it helps with the pain?" Nell asked.

"After a person has taken it several times,

it's hard to stop. I mentioned that I'd had some dealings with Mr. Rector. He got the habit after an injury." The doctor was quiet for a few moments. "I know a bit of his history. He saw his brother killed and was hurt, himself, in the war — at Chancellorsville. After the war, he started taking Dover's Powder." Mrs. Rector arched slightly, trying to twist away. Dr. Clarke stopped working to allow her patient to rest for a minute. Muted sounds filtered into the room: heavy boots on the wooden sidewalk, voices laughing or arguing, wheels crunching, and carts lumbering. Close to the door, someone whistled.

Mrs. Rector broke the room's silence. "I didn't know 'til we come to New Tacoma . . . people said Dover's Powder has opium in it." Her speech was labored, her voice so low Nell could barely hear. "Ever since we come here . . . he made me go to the Chinese store . . . and buy it for him." She paused, as if gathering her strength. "When Nona died . . . he got so depressed . . . he could hardly work." She sighed and whispered, "Poor man, poor man."

Dr. Clarke started working again. "I'm nearly done. Then I'll give you something to help you rest. Who can we call to help you?"

"Father Hylebos . . . can someone fetch him?"

"I don't think you need a priest, Mrs. Rector."

"Not . . . for me. For Mr. Rector . . . may he rest in peace."

Later, while Mrs. Rector slept, Dr. Clarke and Nell sat side by side on one of the benches. "Thank you for all your help, Nell." The doctor rubbed at a spot of blood on her cuff. "I could have taken care of her alone, but having someone to assist me made the task much easier. I wish I could afford to hire a helper. You'd make a good doctor yourself. Have you ever thought about it?"

"No, ma'am. I don't mind nursing, but I don't like it either. I want to have a dress-making shop and wear pretty clothes and go to the Alpha Opera House anytime I want to. I haven't been even once since it opened."

"And a husband and children?"

"No, ma'am. I like children well enough, but I don't want my own." Nell stopped and looked at the doctor. "Aren't you shocked?"

Dr. Clarke laughed. "Not at all. I never really wanted any, either."

"But you got married."

"I did, and, until my husband died, we were happy. But he had tuberculosis when we married, and I took care to prevent a pregnancy."

Nell thought *she* should be shocked at the blunt words, but she wasn't. It was a relief to talk to someone who understood. Hildy had never said anything one way or another about children and was too ladylike to discuss the matter. "You can do that?"

"Yes, and when you're ready to know, I'll tell you."

Nell rubbed her eyes with her palms, and Dr. Clarke said, "If you ever change your mind about becoming a doctor, I'll help you all I can, but, in the meantime, you were wonderful today. Mrs. Rector may well owe you her life. I certainly couldn't have done nearly as well without you."

"Ma always says neighbors have to help each other."

"Your mother sounds like a wise woman."

Nell looked surprised. "I expect she is." She stood and stretched her tired muscles. "I wonder what time it is. Feels like I've been gone all day."

Dr. Clarke looked at the shadow on the noon-mark carved into a sill. Before she could speak, the Hanson and Ackerman

179

whistle blew.

"Only noon? *Hmph.* Well, I'd better go home now. I'll see you when I finish the collar and cuffs set. What color do you want?"

"Pink, please; it's a gift for my sister. And, here, you'd better borrow a hat. People will talk if you're seen without one."

Nell walked home, thinking about the morning and how she'd misjudged Mrs. Rector's interest in opium. *I have to remember never to judge without knowing the whole story,* she thought. In the distance, she saw John Calhoun talking to a group of men and suddenly found it difficult to breathe. He looked up as she passed, removed his hat, and nodded to her. Nell nodded back. She saw him take in her bloodstained dress and start toward her. Not wanting to talk about everything that had transpired, she quickened her step and soon left him behind. *When I get home, the day will be better. After all, it's just the morning that was bad. The afternoon hasn't had a chance to be spoiled yet. But, oh, I will be so glad to see Ma and Josie and Albina.*

CHAPTER 10

When Nell returned home from Dr. Clarke's office, she spent the rest of the day making cookies with her sister. Albina's chatter helped dispel some of the morning's horrors. Obed had returned from work and was dunking a gingersnap in coffee when someone knocked at the door. He pushed himself away from the table and opened it. A young man stood on the step.

"I'm looking for Miss Nell Tanquist," the stranger said. He wore a rumpled suit and white shirt with ink stains on the cuffs, and a well-worn bowler hat that he'd pushed to the back of his head.

Obed took an instant dislike to the man, based on the hat. "Who's askin'?"

"My name's Dolliver. I'm from the *Ledger.* I wanted to ask Miss Tanquist about the shooting this morning."

Obed ignored Mr. Dolliver's outstretched hand. "No," he said and slammed the door.

He returned to the table and picked up another cookie.

Nell pursed her lips, unsure whether or not to laugh. "Thanks, Pa," she said and refilled his coffee.

"Somethin' else will happen soon enuf, and folks will forget about the Rectors," Obed said.

However, to Nell's dismay, the reporter managed to gather enough information to piece together a fairly accurate article that mentioned both her and Dr. Clarke. For the next few days, Nell stayed home, but Obed was right. When a railroad car fell through the tracks and ended up in the Puyallup River, interest in the Rectors faded. Then Amity decided it was time to clean the stove, an all-day, dirty job Nell hated. "I'd rather be answering questions about the Rectors," she said. "How many years before Albina can do this?"

Her mother laughed as she handed Nell an old towel to tie around her hair. "A few, and, when you have your own home and stove, you'll want it to look nice, too. Your husband will expect it."

"A good reason to be a dressmaker and not to get married, if you ask me," Nell said, wondering why her mother refused to consider the fact that she didn't want a husband or children.

She started by carefully removing the lower portion of the stovepipe. Amity had an old bucket ready, and together they cleaned out the soot clinging inside, saving it to make soap later. Then Amity pushed a long-handled brush up the rest of the pipe to where it exited out the roof. Ashes, dirt, and the remains of a dead bird came down. *Well, I guess the stove will draw better,* Nell thought, knowing how hard cleaning the room was going to be. She reassembled the pipes while Amity mixed some of the black residue with wax. They were rubbing the stove with the messy mixture when a boy appeared in the yard. Nell walked to the open door, wiping her hands on a rag. "What can I do for you?"

"I got this here for Nell Tanquist," the boy said. He held up something red that looked like an envelope. From his grin, Nell figured she had soot on her face.

"That's me." Nell reached for the envelope. "Who's it from?"

"I don' know. Some Chinee give it to me, seeing as how I was headed this way."

"Well, thank you for delivering it. If you wait a minute, I'll get you a cookie."

A few seconds later, the boy took off with two plump cookies. Nell turned the red envelope over, admiring its gold tracery. She found a knife and slit the flap, thinking, *first the letter from Godey's Lady's Book and now this one. I'll soon be keeping the post office on its toes.* Inside the envelope, written in black ink on a scrap of silk, were two sentences: *The presence of Miss Nell Tanquist is requested for tea at 2:00, on Thursday. Ask for directions to the Captain James Quincy home, Old Tacoma.*

"For goodness sakes," Nell said.

Amity, reading over Nell's shoulder, had more to say. "What's this all about?" she asked, looking at the unusual writing.

"I don't know, but isn't the envelope lovely, and imagine writing on fabric." Nell returned the silk to the envelope.

Amity frowned. "Do you know the Quincys?"

"No."

"Well, I don't like the idea of your going to a strange home to see someone you don't know. Old Tacoma has too many seamen's boardinghouses. It isn't safe."

"Since it's for tea, it's probably from Mrs. Captain Quincy. Clearly, I'm expected. How can I decline?"

Amity sighed. "I don't suppose we can find the boy who delivered the letter, or that

184

he could find the Celestial who gave it to him."

Feeling oddly defensive, Nell pursed her lips to keep from scowling. *If every white person had a long, black pigtail and wore identical clothes, they'd be hard to tell apart, too.* "Well, how about this? We ask Ike to check around and see if the Quincys are on the up and up?"

" 'Up and up'?"

"It's a new expression."

"Hmmm. Well, I'll agree to have Ike see what he can find out; then I'll decide."

And Nell had to be satisfied with that.

Amity had Albina take a note to Ike, and the next afternoon he reported that although no one he'd asked knew Mrs. Captain Quincy, the captain himself was well known for being on the Oriental trade route.

"Please, Ma," Nell said. "I'll take the overland trail both ways and be very careful. Please say it's okay for me to go."

"Okay?"

"Another new expression."

"Well." Amity sighed. "I'll let you go if you promise me one thing."

"Anything."

"Quit using these new expressions."

As she climbed the front steps of the Captain Quincy home, Nell wondered how she'd missed seeing the tall, narrow house during her previous trips to Old Tacoma. True, it was on a hill and tucked between tall cedars, but its clean, white paint seemed to glow in the sunlight. A small yard contained a number of cherry trees whose petals were scattered about. A wind chime, not common in New Tacoma, hung silent. On either side of the door were large white seated lions, each with a raised paw. *It's as if they're watching the bay for a ship,* Nell thought. At her knock, a stocky, elderly Chinese man opened the door and stepped back, gesturing for her to enter.

The room Nell stepped into was like no other she'd ever seen. Tan rugs with leaf patterns covered the wooden floor. Two corners in the room had three-paneled dividers, five foot high, with centers of embroidered silk. A skilled hand had created scenes of oddly shaped rock formations, tall cranes, and bamboo. Against one wall was a large figure of a man sitting with his legs crossed, his hands on his lap. In front of him, a bowl of sand held burning sticks whose scent was unfamiliar to Nell. Carved ivory figures and enameled dishes covered small octagonal tables. Half a dozen canaries in a large wooden birdcage made the only sounds.

All the chairs in the room were made of wood. The man gestured towards one with a yoke back. "Please to sit down."

Nell sat and found it surprisingly comfortable. She folded her hands in her lap and waited. Within a matter of minutes, she heard a strange shuffling sound and watched as a petite Chinese lady, assisted by two Chinese men, approached. They led her to a chair opposite Nell and bowed their way out of the room.

Nell and her hostess looked curiously at each other. The Chinese woman wore yellow silk pants and a knee-length red jacket embroidered with yellow and green dragons. Her thick black hair had been pulled into a bun on top of her head with long red sticks poking out on either side. It was her shoes, however, that caught Nell's interest. Flat soled and made of silver with black cuffs, they were barely three inches long. The woman saw Nell's interest and smiled. Before either could speak, the elderly man returned carrying a tea tray. He set it on a table and again bowed his way out.

The woman filled two cups and passed one to Nell along with a plate of bright red, slightly mounded cookies. Nell took one and looked at her hostess.

"That is *Ang Ku Kueh;* it means red tortoise cake." Her voice was high, her words slightly accented. When Nell took a bite and smiled her pleasure, the woman added, "I am Mrs. Quincy. My husband is Captain James Quincy. You were not expecting to be having tea with a Chinese woman, I think."

"No, ma'am." Nell set her cup on a small table and put the cookie on the saucer.

Mrs. Quincy nodded. "There are many Chinese women married to American men in China, also to British men. And most of the wives prefer to remain in China, but, because they live so far away, I do not think many people know about them."

"No, ma'am. I don't suppose they do. Are you sure? I ask because most of the sea captains I know have wives here."

Mrs. Quincy smiled. "Yes, I am sure, because some of the men have two families who don't know about each other; one here and a second one there."

"Goodness sakes."

For a moment, they drank their tea in silence, and Nell accepted another cookie. The house was so quiet, she wondered where the men were. Only the canaries' voices broke the silence. Then Mrs. Quincy spoke again. "You do not know many Chinese women, I think."

"No, ma'am. There aren't many in New Tacoma."

"But you tried to help one."

"I did?"

"Fang Hua."

"The lady from the train." Nell leaned forward. "Is she a friend of yours? How is she? Is she all right?"

"She is a peasant." Mrs. Quincy sounded angry, and Nell wondered why. After a moment the woman added, "She is fine and back with her husband in Kalama."

"Oh, I am glad."

"Why?"

"Why?" The question surprised Nell. "Because no woman should be bought and sold that way. No man, either, for that matter."

The servant entered the room with a fresh pot of hot water and took the other away. Again, Nell hadn't heard him coming. She snuck a look at his feet and saw cloth footwear, not as ornate as that of her hostess and definitely of a more normal size. When Mrs. Quincy saw her looking, Nell blushed. "May I ask you a question, please?"

"Of course." Mrs. Quincy smiled slightly. "You are wondering about my feet."

"Uh . . ."

"In China, beginning when they are

189

young, girls of rank have their toes gradually bent under until their feet are very small, as a sign of their status. They are called lotus feet."

"But how do you walk?"

"Our servants do the walking for us."

"Goodness sakes. Didn't it hurt?"

"Of course, but the man my father chose to be my husband would not have agreed to our marriage if my feet were not bound."

"Captain Quincy?"

"No, another." Her expression shut down.

Nell guessed she'd best change the subject. "How did you learn to speak English so well?"

Relief glimmered in Mrs. Quincy's face. "My husband taught me. It is not an easy language."

"Is Chinese an easy language?"

"There is no one language in China. Each region has its own."

"Goodness gracious, how . . ." Nell hesitated, ". . . unusual. It must be very difficult to travel around."

"People in China do not travel much."

"Oh." Quiet fell again. Uncomfortable with it, Nell said, "Uh, while it's lovely to be here, to have been invited to tea, I'm wondering why you asked me."

Mrs. Quincy nodded. "Because you were

kind to a Chinese lady, and in my world that is rare."

"But you said she wasn't a friend because she's a peasant."

"That's true, but life is very hard for the Chinese, and a kindness needs to be acknowledged. Are you aware that Captain Enell fired all his Chinese workers at the brickyard?"

"No, ma'am."

"Or that hotels in Seattle are firing all their Chinese workers?"

"No. Who will do the work?"

"White men, if they will accept the poor wages." Mrs. Quincy put her teacup down and folded her hands. "That is a lovely butterfly you are wearing."

Nell beamed. "I crocheted it."

"You must be very clever."

"My friend Hildy's mother taught me to crochet when we were in school, Hildy and I, that is, and I've been making things to sell ever since."

"You are a businesswoman?"

"Not yet, but I want to be. I'm saving to buy a Singer sewing machine so I can be a dressmaker. We have several milliners here but no dressmakers."

"There is a new bank in town, I think. Can you not borrow the money?"

Nell's smile disappeared. "I tried." And she told Mrs. Quincy about her visit to the bank.

Nell had passed the Bank of New Tacoma many times. It was a substantial-looking wooden building with three windows on a second floor and more windows, protected by awnings, on each side of the door at street level. The day she called in, both the president and vice president had been out, leaving her to talk with the cashier, A. J. Baker. "You are seeking a discount?" he'd asked, after inviting her to sit.

"Pardon me?"

"A discount. That is, a loan. That's what they're called."

"Yes, sir. Enough to buy a sewing machine and rent a small space."

"Do you have any collateral?"

"No, but I am a hard worker and would pay back every cent."

"Can someone — that is, a man — sign for you, guaranteeing the loan repayment? Your father, perhaps, or a brother, or . . . ?"

Nell was pretty sure the bank wouldn't accept Obed's guarantee of repayment, and that Frieda Faye would never let her brother sign. She'd felt a blush rising. "No, but . . ."

"I'm sorry, Miss Tanquist" — and Nell hated the condescending look in his eyes —

"but banks don't make loans to single women, even one so young and lovely as yourself. Not that being lovely is a deterrent, of course."

Nell narrowed her eyes. *Don't you patronize me, you little gump, you,* she thought, forgetting her promise to her mother about slang. Standing, she said, "Thank you for your time," and pulled away when he put his hand under her elbow while walking her to the door.

To Mrs. Quincy, she said, "If Mr. Bostwick or Mr. Blackwell — they own the bank — had been there, things might have been different, but probably not. They just would have been nicer to deal with."

Mrs. Quincy nodded. "In China women have very few opportunities, but by tradition, they are in charge of silkworm farming."

"Goodness, I didn't know silk came from worms."

"Do you know the story?" Before Nell could answer, Mrs. Quincy continued. "According to our legend, one day in the twenty-seventh century, the Empress Lei Zu, wife of the Yellow Emperor Huang Di, was sitting under a tree when a silk cocoon fell into her cup of tea. She, of course, removed it, and some of the cocoon's silk thread wrapped around her finger. She unwound the thread and discovered a tiny pupa. *Is this the source of silk?* she wondered. She persuaded her husband to give her a grove of mulberry trees and began to domesticate the worms that made the cocoons. Because the silk was difficult to unwind, she invented a silk reel to join the fine strands into a thread that was strong enough to be woven. Lei Zu became the Silkworm Raising Goddess, and thereafter the skill of raising silkworms belonged exclusively to women."

Nell tilted her head. "Is that true, do you think?"

"Only the bones of Lei Zu know."

"That's very mysterious, isn't it?"

Mrs. Quincy nodded. "China is full of such stories."

"Maybe someday, if I get to be a dressmaker, I can make silk dresses." Nell smiled at her hostess and leaned forward. "At first, I was nervous to come here. But it's been lovely. Thank you for inviting me."

"Thank you for coming." Mrs. Quincy rang a small bell, and one of the ubiquitous Chinese men came into the room. "Please show Miss Tanquist out."

Walking home, Nell thought about the visit and realized how skillfully she'd been dismissed. *I would like to come back, but she didn't ask me. Maybe Chinese ladies don't do that.* The only Celestial she knew well was Chong. *I'll ask him. And, anyway, I guess if a lady can do all the things Empress Lei Zu did, I can make enough money to buy a sewing machine. And if Albina ever gets old enough to help with the chores, maybe I can get a job, maybe at the new Tacoma Hotel.* Nell jumped over a branch and looked back to see how far she'd leapt. *I know how much I need to buy a sewing machine and rent a place to sew. Until I can afford fabric, maybe I can remake dresses to the latest style. I bet if I write Hildy's Aunt Glady, she can tell me about Mr. Butterick's new paper patterns. Hildy says Aunt Glady likes knowing more things and more* about *things than anyone else. Oh, I love having plans, but I'd love having enough money even more, and a sister who can do chores, too.*

CHAPTER 11

A few days after tea with Mrs. Quincy, Nell walked to town for pink crochet thread. New Tacoma smelled as it usually did, of dust and dung, fresh-cut wood, and salt water, but she found them all welcome after lingering memories of Dr. Clarke's medicine and Mrs. Rector's blood.

On Pacific Avenue, a team of oxen attached to a wagon with doubletree yokes crossed in front of her. Bricks filled the wagon's bed, and the yoke's chains strained against their rings, the grinding noise startling a horse nearby. Two new brick buildings were going up, and the town was puffed with pride. Across the street, a door slammed when a Chinese man left the American Hotel carrying an armload of dirty sheets. He piled them in a small cart and pushed it toward one of the Chinese laundries. Nell's thoughts jumped from the Chinese to opium to the Rectors. *Lordy, I wonder what's going to happen to Mrs. Rector. Pa can make a coffin for Mr. Rector; he's good that way. Someone will tote it out to the cemetery, but who will nurse his wife? I wonder if Ma would let me. Their house is close enough so Ma could keep an eye on things. Poor lady; first her daughter dying and now this.*

A man came out of Bauerle and Braden's Furniture Works and Coffins Store, stood in the doorway for a moment, and then went immediately back in. *When I have my shop, it's going to be right here on Pacific Avenue,* Nell thought, *so I can see everything that's going on.* As if to agree, a bullfrog under the wooden sidewalk croaked loudly. Nell laughed, and two women walking by eyed her frostily in disapproval. *Oh, dear,* Nell remembered, her hand going to her head, *I have on my worst looking hat.*

It wasn't just the hat, though, Nell knew. It was also her family. Both her father and Ike frequented Young Dutchey's Boxing Parlor and changed jobs regularly, looking to improve themselves and their circumstances. Only they never seemed to succeed, and on occasion they drank away their earnings. *Most of New Tacoma sees me as Obed Tanquist's hoyden daughter,* Nell thought, *but they won't always.*

She continued walking. Riley's Soda Shop lay just ahead. She walked faster, feeling in her pocket for enough money to buy a sarsaparilla.

Fred Riley, the shop owner's son, was standing out front when she reached the place. "I'll be glad to treat you," he said, when her search proved unsuccessful.

Nell smiled. "Thank you, Fred. But I don't like to be beholden."

"You'd never owe me, Nell. I promise."

"That's kind, but I left home wearing such an old bonnet. I feel right uncomfortable with it on display."

"I think your head should always be on display; your hair is too pretty to hide under a hat." Fred blushed at his bold words.

The compliment pleased Nell but also made her feel uncomfortable. "That's a very nice thing to hear, but I had best make my purchase and get home. There's no knowing what my little sister will be up to." She smiled at the flushed young man, then crossed the street, scaring up a flock of pigeons pecking hopefully on the sidewalk, and hurried to S. M. Nolan's mercantile.

Half an hour later, as she reached home, Amity met her at the door. "Where have you been? Ike sent word; it's Frieda Faye's time, and the sheriff has been here asking for you."

Albina peered around their mother. "He looked awfully stern."

"Why would Ike look crabby?" Nell winked at Amity.

"Not Ike, the sheriff. Is it because you left the house wearing your gardening hat?"

"Of course not, Beanie, don't be silly. I expect he wants to ask me some more questions about something that — er — I saw."

"What? I saw the sheriff poking around over by the Rectors' house. Did something happen there?"

"Stop it, Albina," Amity said, "and go stir the stew."

"But . . ."

"You heard me."

Albina started toward the kitchen, scowling at her mother and sister over her shoulder. "I can always find out, you know. Even if school is over, someone will know. I think you should tell me now. It'd save me an awful lot of work."

"Albina. Stir. Now."

Leaving Albina in charge of the stew, Nell and her mother went outside and walked toward the chicken coop. "Frieda Faye's time? Lordy," Nell said.

"We'll have to take turns being with her."

Amity didn't mention Josie's helping, and Nell didn't expect her to.

"Her mother will be there, too, won't she?"

Amity shook her head. "She's on a quick trip to Portland with Emma Kinnear and Mrs. Kinnear, to shop for Emma's bridal gown."

"You see." Nell hugged herself against the cooling late-afternoon air. "That's exactly why I have to get my dressmaking business started. Then Emma wouldn't have to go clear to Portland. I just hope that by the time I get enough money saved, there will still be a Singer sewing machine in town for me to buy."

"Time enough to think about all that later. Right now, we have to focus on Frieda Faye."

"Did Ike fetch the midwife?"

"It's too early for that, I think. First babies usually take their time. I don't expect the baby will be here before tomorrow."

"Then she won't need us right away."

"Of course she will, to keep her company and walk her. I'll have a bowl of stew and take some to them. You can relieve me when your pa gets home from work and stay the night, and I'll go back in the morning. I've helped with births before, and Frieda Faye should be getting close by midday. I don't want you there then."

"But you might need me, and I've seen animals born."

"It isn't proper for you to be there." Amity sighed. "I don't talk much about my life before I married your pa, but my family was much like Hildy's." She was quiet for a moment, her expression thoughtful as if looking into the past. Her next words sounded sad. "My parents didn't want me marrying Obed. They thought I could do better, but I was headstrong and in love. The men they thought suitable seemed dull in comparison. When Obed and I wed, they told me to leave the house. Things might have resolved themselves if we'd stayed in New Harmony, but Obed wouldn't have it. I wasn't prepared for life on the frontier, and, with babies coming along, I was just too tired to keep up standards."

"Oh, Ma, don't talk that way." Nell's heart ached at the words, and she hugged her mother. "We have a fine life. You taught us everything that's important. Indiana is a good wife and mother, and Josie is a lady; we'll just have to make sure Albina is one, too. I'm your only harum-scarum."

Amity smiled. "And I couldn't get along without you. However, I am going to give you one piece of advice. I know you plan to be a businesswoman, but think long and hard about whether that's really what you want out of life, and be careful what you wish for. It sometimes proves not to be what you wanted after all." She laughed. "Now, that's two things, isn't it?"

Nell laughed with her, just as a cannonade of thunder echoed off the hills. The unexpected sound made them both jump and brought a frightened Albina out of the house. Then a dense, gray cloud opened and hail pounded down, and the three raced inside.

The storm played itself out while Amity ate a quick bowl of stew. She left to attend to Frieda Faye while Nell washed the dishes and then sat close to a lantern with her needlework. Josie came home from Mrs. McCarver's and went to bed with a sick headache, and Albina started grating a block of sugar into granules and pouring them into a lard bucket.

Eventually, Albina broke the silence. "It's getting cold."

"You're right." Nell got up and added wood to the stove, then fetched her shawl and wrapped it around her shoulders.

Albina finished her chore and pulled the rocker close to the heat. "I wish I could sell something and earn some money." She rocked slowly, watching Nell's crochet hook fly in and out of the thread.

"Well . . ." Nell looked at her stitches, pulled several out, and worked them again. "What do you think you could do?"

"I don't know."

Albina continued rocking, and Nell thought about how other children in town raised money. Reuben, Hildy's brother, killed rats on the wharf with his slingshot. Eddie O'Reilly pounded old nails straight and sold them for less money than stores sold new ones. People raised rabbits and sold them to local markets, or trapped animals for their pelts, but those jobs were for boys. Girls were expected to stay home and tend to the house.

"I saw Mrs. Halstead today." Albina giggled. "She has a new hat. It's enormous and has all kinds of flowers and bows on it. I heard her husband say the only thing not on it was the antlers from a deer he shot last fall, and Mrs. Halstead scowled and said what did he know about style."

Nell laughed. "Hats are getting bigger and fancier all the time." She looked out a window, briefly resting her eyes. A small goldfinch lit on the sill, looking disgusted at how wet his feathers were. When the pane rattled in its frame, he flew into a bush. "Feathers," Nell said suddenly.

"What about feathers?" Albina stood and went for a cookie.

"You can dye feathers and sell them to hatmakers like Mrs. Spooner." When Albina remained silent, Nell added, "When I was in town today . . ."

"With your tacky old hat."

"Let's forget the hat thing, shall we? Anyway, when I was in town, two ladies came down the street. I didn't recognize them, so maybe they came off the train. Anyway, they were wearing spring hats with pink, yellow, and green feathers."

"They sound lovely." Cookie in hand, Albina settled back in the chair, rocking again as she nibbled her treat.

"They were, but if Mrs. Spooner wants to decorate hats with colored feathers, she has to send away to Portland. Why not gather feathers and dye them here? Think, Beanie, who do you know has white chickens?"

Albina's eyes sparkled. She stopped rocking and sat up straight. "Ma has some leghorns."

"So do lots of people, and Mrs. Ouimette has geese, too. Why, Mr. Ouimette might even buy colored feathers to sell along with his dress trimmings."

"Where will I get the dyes?"

"You can make them. I'll help you. I know a few things, like juice from strawberries and raspberries makes things red, and Oregon grape berries make blue . . ."

"And onion skins make yellow."

"That's right, good for you. Why, I bet if we experiment, we'll come up with all kinds of colors."

Albina jumped up. "Gosh, I wish it was light enough for me to go look for feathers right now."

Nell gawped in surprise. "Albina, that's practically swearing. Ma will wash your mouth out with soap if she hears you."

Albina ate the last bite of her cookie. "Well, the boys at school say 'gosh' all the time."

"Nevertheless, a lady doesn't. Now, clean your teeth and face and put on your nightgown. It's your bedtime."

"Will you tell me a story?"

"Why don't you tell me one?"

"I don't know any."

"I bet you do. After you get in bed, think about one you used to hear at school. It will be nice for me to listen."

Albina washed up and changed in front of the stove. She climbed into bed and was asleep almost immediately, as Nell knew she would be. The stove needed more wood, so Nell added some, and it snapped and whistled companionably. Outside, the peepers started their high-pitched croaking. A heavy mist formed, and tree limbs whooshed with passing breezes. Nell rested her head on the back of her chair and closed her eyes. *Just until Pa gets home,* she thought. It wasn't her father who woke her, though, but Ike pounding on the door.

"Nell, wake up."

Nell came to with a start and hurried to lift the bar. "Ike, what are you doing here? Shouldn't you be with Frieda Faye?" She pushed her hair off her face. "What time is it, anyway?"

"Nell, listen. There's been an accident. Pa's been hurt."

Nell froze while the words sank in. Turning back to the room, she said, "Let me get my jacket. Where is he? How bad is it?"

"Wait." Ike closed the door and went to warm himself by the fire. The room soon filled with a wet wool smell. "I stopped at home on the way here, and Ma will be back as soon as you go there. Pa fell off a piece of scaffolding, and I think he broke a leg. Some of the men are bringing him here on a makeshift litter, and I'm to go get Dr. Bostwick. Ma says to make some switchel for the men to drink. It'll help warm them up."

Nell dropped her jacket on a chair. "All right, but before you go, I need a bucket of water. Oh dear, I hope we have enough ginger."

While Ike went for water, Nell found the ginger, vinegar, and a block of brown sugar, and started making the switchel.

"Here." He set the bucket down and shook his head. "I'm leaving. Lordy, what a bag of nails tonight's going to be."

"Not to worry, everything's under control." Nell ground enough brown sugar for the drink and found her father's bottle of whisky. By the time someone pounded on the door, she had the drink ready. Four men carried Obed in, and she gestured toward his bedroom. With much huffing and grunting, they maneuvered him there and put him on the bed. Obed yelled in pain all the while, only remembering to watch his language when he saw his daughter. Once Obed was settled, Nell handed each of the men mugs of the well-spiked drink and took one to her father.

"Here, this, this should help with the pain." She held his head up while he drank. Then he dropped back onto the pillow and closed his eyes.

"Thank you, daughter."

The men put their mugs on the table and left, and Nell woke Josie to tell her what was going on. "Ma will be here soon." She sat on the edge of the bed. "Don't let anyone in unless you know who it is."

"Is Pa bad hurt?"

"I don't know. Ike went for Dr. Bostwick. We'll have to wait until he tells us. Try not to wake Albina. You know how she is. You won't be alone long. I forgot to cover Pa. Can you do that? I suppose his boots should come off, too; just be careful of the broken leg." Seeking comfort, Nell wrapped her arms around Josie. "If the sheriff comes, you might as well tell him where I am."

"The sheriff?" Josie jerked away.

"I think he wants to ask me more questions about the Rector shooting. Gracious me, this will be a busy night." Nell kissed her sister. "Remember, keep the door barred."

Leaving Josie to dress with shaking hands, she put on her jacket and hat. Outside, the mist had vanished, and a full moon helped light the road. A falling star crossed the Milky Way, and she quickly made a wish that everything would be all right. New Tacoma was never quiet at night, but the voices she heard were muted. She was hurrying down the road, dodging puddles, when a small, emaciated dog appeared out of the brush. She stopped to pet it, and the dog licked her hand, and Nell thought they each were probably grateful for the other's presence.

"Come with me and I'll give you something to eat," she told the little animal. Nell started walking again, and, as if it understood, the dog followed. When they reached Ike and Frieda Faye's house, lamp light from every window welcomed them. She knocked, and Amity opened the door. The dog followed Nell in.

Frieda Faye gave it a dirty look. "Where'd that dog come from?"

"He's mine."

"When did you get a dog?"

"Not long ago." Nell crossed her fingers. Her mother said nothing.

"It isn't sanitary to have a dog in the house."

"I was afraid to walk here alone in the dark," Nell lied. She hung her jacket and hat on a hall tree and was glad to see that a generous amount of the stew Amity had brought over was left. She scooped some into a bowl and set it on the floor. Frieda Faye's squawk of protest ended in a groan, and she clutched her stomach. Amity put on her own jacket and hat, saying, "She wants to lie down, but the more Frieda Faye's on her feet, the better. Is your pa home yet?"

"Yes. I gave him some of the switchel — I put whisky in it, and it seemed to help."

"That's good." Amity kissed Nell's cheek and looked at Frieda Faye. "Remember, keep walking."

Nell sighed. *It's going to be a very long night.*

CHAPTER 12

While Nell and Frieda Faye looked at each other, the dog, who proved to be a male, licked the bowl of stew clean, curled up near the stove, and went to sleep.

"Where did he come from?" Frieda Faye started to sit, and Nell took her arm to keep her standing.

"A man who was about to sail gave him to me because his wife didn't want him," Nell said. "The dog, I mean. I'm really glad to have his protection when I have to go out at night."

Frieda Faye had nothing to say to that. She knew as well as Nell that New Tacoma was both a port town and a frontier town, with more than a few unsavory characters and not always safe for females, especially at night.

"What's his name?" she asked finally.

Nell hadn't thought of one. "Uh, Pup."

"Isn't that a little — um — common?"

"Probably." To distract her sister-in-law from further comments about the dog Nell said, "I haven't seen your baby clothes yet."

"You mean my layette?"

"Is that French for baby clothes?"

Her sister-in-law gave her another dirty look, and Nell helped her into the bedroom and let her sit on the bed for a few seconds to rest. The room was small but cozy. A framed print of roses hung above a well-polished, four-drawer dresser that faced the bed. The bureau held a vase of wild currant in full bloom. One side of the bed was close to the wall, the other by a table with a blue-globed lamp on top. A print of birds hung near the door and braided rugs covered the floor.

"Your bedroom is lovely," Nell said.

"Isn't it?" Frieda Faye patted the bed cover with a pleased smile. "This is called a Crazy Quilt."

"What a good way to use many different shapes and sizes of cloth."

Frieda Faye scowled. "I could have pieced squares, but Crazy Quilts are all the rage back East. They aren't usually quilted, never mind the name, but I quilted this one for extra warmth. See." She flipped up a corner. "And the solid border was my idea."

"Well, it's lovely, and did you make the

curtains, too?"

"Yes. Mama thought I could use some of her flour bags for curtains, and then I added a border to match the quilt."

"You certainly did a nice job."

Her sister-in-law grabbed her stomach and groaned again. Nell helped her to her feet. "Where will the baby sleep?"

Frieda Faye pressed her lips together, then drew a deep breath as the pang ebbed. "Ike is making a crib, but, until he's done, I expect I'll have to use a dresser drawer. Look." She shuffled to the bureau and opened the top drawer. "I have this one ready." She groaned again and held onto the bureau for support, just as the front door burst open and Ike came in. "Oh, Ike!" Frieda Faye wrapped her arms around him. "I'm so glad you're here." A wail followed the last word. "I didn't know there'd be so much pain."

"It's the curse of Eve," Ike said. "You must bring forth your child in sorrow."

"Good grief, where did you hear that?" Nell took Frieda Faye's arm again and walked back to the main room.

"From the Reverend Mr. Judy."

"Well, it's a horrible thing to say to your wife."

Frieda Faye had stopped to pant, and Nell

hoped she hadn't heard Ike's words. "I think you'd best go for the midwife."

Ike nodded and left. Pup whimpered in his sleep, and Nell made Frieda Faye drink a little water. "It won't be good if you get too thirsty," she said.

"How do *you* know?" Frieda Faye moaned and doubled over.

"Ma told me. Now let me wipe your face with a cool cloth, and I'm going to time your pains."

"I don't think you have to; they're plenty close, and I feel pressure."

"Nevertheless, the midwife will want to know." Nell led Frieda Faye to a chair. "Don't have the baby yet. I won't know what to do, and I forgot to start the water boiling."

While Frieda Faye tried to rest between contractions, Nell filled all the pans she could find with water and added wood to the stove. Fifteen minutes later, when Ike returned without the midwife, the room was steamy and hot. "She's not there," he said, looking wild eyed.

Nell wrung her hands. "Oh dear. Ma'd be here if she could, so that means Pa still needs her. Where is Mrs. Johnson, anyway?"

"Helping someone else."

"Well, she's got some nerve. You scheduled her."

"Babies can't help it when they come, so you'll have to do the necessary," Frieda Faye said. She started to cry. "I wish Mother was here."

"Oh dear," Nell said again. "Don't cry. Let me think." After a moment, she said, "I know, how about if I help you change into a nightgown and get in bed. Ike, you go get Dr. Clarke, and hurry. Borrow someone's horse and buggy if you can."

With Frieda Faye groaning and panting, the two returned to the bedroom. Nell unbuttoned her sister-in-law's dress, undid the stays, and pulled the dress off of her, then tugged a nightgown on in its place. She turned the bed covers back and motioned Frieda Faye to sit down, then unbuttoned Frieda Faye's boots and pulled them and her stockings off. "Be careful of those," Frieda Faye said between gasps, indicating the stockings. "They were hand-embroidered in Philadelphia."

Well, la-de-dah, Nell thought. She went to the kitchen for a basin of cool water and wiped Frieda Faye's face and arms with a dampened bit of flour sack. This went on for a time, while Frieda Faye screamed, arched her back, and swore at the absent

215

Ike. If Nell hadn't been so scared, she would have laughed at hearing all the bad language her very proper sister-in-law knew. Then the front door burst open, just as Frieda Faye shouted, "It's coming!"

Dr. Clarke hurried into the bedroom, followed by Amity, who pushed Nell out of the room and shut the door in her face.

"Thank God," Nell whispered as she dropped into a chair. However, after a few moments, curiosity got the better of her. She went outside, followed by Pup, and peeked through the bedroom window. Frieda Faye lay flat on her back with her nightgown hiked up and her knees bent. Kneeling on the floor in front of her wide-spread legs was the doctor, while Amity held Frieda Faye's hand and wiped the sweat off her face. Nell didn't notice when it began to drizzle, soaking her hair and dress. She heard Dr. Clarke say something, watched as Frieda Faye took a deep breath, and saw something wet and slimy, attached to a grayish cord, emerge from between her sister-in-law's legs. Amity took it in her hands, which were draped in a towel, and did something with her fingers. After that, she smacked it on its bottom, and Nell heard outraged cries. Dr. Clarke made two ties on the cord and cut it in the middle. That done, she massaged Frieda Faye's stomach. More slime poured from between Frieda Faye's legs, and the doctor caught it in a basin.

"Oh, my God." Nell leaned against the side of the window. Amity had her back turned, but Dr. Clarke glanced up and met Nell's gaze. She gave a brief nod and turned back to put strips of cloth on Frieda Faye's crotch. Then she picked up the basin holding the discharge and left the bedroom.

A few seconds later, she came outside, the basin in one hand and a large spoon in the other. Away from the house, she used the spoon to dig a hole and buried the discharge slime. Then she set the basin down and joined Nell. "Are you all right?"

"I don't think so." Ignoring the wet ground, Nell slid down the wall, sat in the mud, and hugged Pup. "That was awful. All the pacing and pain and screaming for hours, and then to have a baby come out from between your legs, like that. I can't believe it."

Dr. Clarke squatted next to her. "Haven't you ever seen an animal give birth?"

"Yes, but it seemed so much easier for them." Nell looked at the doctor. "How did the baby get there, anyway?"

"Oh dear." Dr. Clarke huffed a small

laugh. Under her breath, she said, more to herself than to Nell, "I wonder how your mother would answer that?" But she knew, just as much as Nell did, that sex and childbirth weren't things decent women talked about. When a woman went to her marriage bed, her husband taught her all she needed to know. To Nell, she replied, "It's best if your mother tells you, but if she won't, come to me. Now . . ." She stood up. "Let's go in so you can see your new nephew."

Nell tried unsuccessfully to clean off the back of her skirt and then, with the dog close by, followed the doctor back inside. In the bedroom, Amity helped a very sleepy Frieda Faye eat some buttery sops. The baby was swaddled and lay at her side, sucking its fist. "Is it a boy or a girl?" Nell asked, then remembered that Dr. Clarke had referred to her nephew.

"A boy," Frieda Faye said, her eyes barely leaving the baby's face.

Nell looked at her mother and tried to smile. "Another grandson, Ma," she said, "but Ike will be thrilled."

Amity laughed and put the bowl of buttery sops down. "I guess I'll have to wait for you to give me a granddaughter."

Nell gave Dr. Clarke a horrified look. "Ah,

or Albina," she said. "How's Pa? Hadn't I better get home to him?"

"Dr. Bostwick gave him something to make him sleep. He said it was a clean break, and Obed should be up and about in five or six weeks, but, yes, go on home, and I'll be there in a bit." She turned back to the baby and Frieda Faye. Nell grabbed her jacket and hat, and she and Pup left.

I didn't ask Dr. Clarke how Mrs. Rector is or ask Ma if I can help with the nursing, she thought as she dodged puddles and wet tree limbs. *Seems like I've been running all over and accomplished nothing. And I'm so tired I just want to go to bed and forget everything.*

One evening, several days after the birth of baby Theodore, Amity asked Nell and Josie to join her and Albina in the kitchen. She poured them each a cup of coffee, closed the bedroom door where their father slept, and sat at the table. "Dr. Bostwick dropped by this morning."

Josie looked alarmed. "Is Pa all right?"

"He came to present his bill." When neither Nell nor Josie responded, she added, "I'm going to post a notice that I will take in ironing. If I get enough customers, the money will cover our expenses until your father is able to return to work."

"Oh, Ma," Josie said. "Is that necessary? Don't we have any money?"

"I used what we had to help pay Dr. Clarke."

"But . . ." Nell knew what she should say, that she'd give her mother the money she'd earned selling her needlework. She bit her lip and looked at Amity.

"Don't worry, dear. I won't ask for your savings, or Josie's either, unless it becomes absolutely necessary. You two work hard and are entitled to keep your earnings. This is just for a few months."

"But ironing is so much work, and why couldn't Ike and Frieda Faye pay the doctor or Frieda Faye's own parents help pay for the baby, anyway?" Nell had been the victim of her sister-in-law's snide remarks about her family's superiority more than once.

"They don't have the money." Amity looked almost amused. "Your grandmother had an expression she liked to use to describe some of the ladies in town: 'She has the biggest purse with the least amount in it.' "

Nell's eyes widened. "Zounds, just wait until Frieda Faye starts swanning around and putting on airs. I guess I'll put her in her place."

"No, you won't, Nell. It's enough that we know, and that she knows we know. Just smile sweetly, and she'll get the message. And what have I told you about slang?"

"It's all right, Ma. It's Shakespeare. Shakespeare didn't swear."

Obed groaned from his bedroom, and Amity stood. "It's all settled. I'll put some placards up around town tomorrow, and we'll go from there. Now, I'd better see to your pa."

"May I go visit Mrs. Rector?" Nell asked.

"Yes, but don't be long. Josie can go with you, and you can check on the chickens at the same time."

Nell and Josie each grabbed a shawl and walked into the yard. "I call this a dirty trick," Nell said.

"We can help Ma iron." Josie swooped down and picked up a surprised hen. "In the coop with you, missy."

"That's not the point." But Nell knew Josie wouldn't understand, and she stomped off fuming toward the Rectors' house.

As soon as Dr. Clarke had contacted Father Hylebos, the priest organized his small congregation. One of his parishioners, a man named Barlow, arranged for a coffin and saw to Mr. Rector's burial while Mrs. Barlow moved in temporarily with Mrs.

Rector to nurse her. Men supplied the new widow with firewood, and their wives brought over food. The situation satisfied everyone but Nell, who had been looking forward to taking charge. She passed a patch of wild violets without seeing their blooms and arrived at the Rectors' yard just as Mrs. Barlow was draping a towel over a large Oregon grape bush. "Hello, Nell," Mrs. Barlow said. "It doesn't rain but it pours, does it?"

"Beg your pardon?"

"Jacob Halstead died this morning. Didn't you hear?"

"No, I've been home all day. Oh, I am sorry. What happened?"

"His heart, the doctor says." Mrs. Barlow sat on a stump and sighed. "He'll be missed for sure and certain. Mrs. Halstead has been trying to notify all the children, especially Jeanette. She's his daughter by his first wife, Brittania. Brittania's buried down in McMinnville, Oregon, don't you know. Jane was only thirteen when she married Jacob, and they came here in 1873." Mrs. Barlow rattled on until she ran out of breath and Nell had a chance to jump into the conversation.

"What will happen to their hotel? It's almost as important as the Blackwells'."

"I don't suppose Jane has had a chance to think about it. Deary, deary, first Mr. Rector and now Mr. Halstead. It's a sorry time for the town." She went on in that vein, but Nell stopped listening. Her brain was giving birth to an idea, and she needed time to let it develop.

CHAPTER 13

Last Tuesday a cougar came into the dooryard of a family living near Kalama, seized a child about five years old, and started into the woods with it. The screams of the little one alarmed the mother, who gave chase. The cougar dropped the baby, which was badly lacerated about the head and face. Medical aid was sent for from Kalama.

"Golly," Nell whispered to herself. "At least here, we never see cougars unless it's at the top of the Eleventh Street hill."

She put the paper down and looked out the Halstead Hotel's front window toward the street where people, horses, and wagons — their wheels squeaking when the loaded drays hit ruts — crowded Pacific Avenue. And her eyes lit with excitement when she saw two draft horses pulling a gypsy wagon come by. Pots and pans roped on its outside bounced and added to the street's general clamor. With its curtained side windows and a stovepipe poking out the top, the wagon looked like a little moveable house. A woman wearing a faded blue blouse and a yellow and red skirt drove the horses, while three small children leaned over the wagon's end frame, looking around. A man dressed in baggy pants tucked into boots had brightened up his leather vest and white collarless shirt with a bright-red ascot. He'd pushed a dusty bowler to the back of his head and brought up the rear, leading a string of ponies. *Uh oh. People will be locking their doors now,* Nell thought. Gypsies were a frequent sight in New Tacoma, and every item that went missing was blamed on them.

"Pardon me," said a female voice beside her, and Nell jumped. "Are the streets safe for a lady?" The voice belonged to Mrs. Angelo Fawcett, the only woman currently staying at the Halstead. Mr. and Mrs. Fawcett had registered at the hotel the previous evening.

"Yes, Mrs. Fawcett, they're perfectly safe." Nell looked at the young woman standing by the registration desk. She held a plump infant, who was snoozing peacefully against her shoulder. "But, if you'll pardon me for saying, it's difficult walking with a baby."

"Really, even for just a block or so? He's not heavy." Mrs. Fawcett frowned. "I have a lovely Wakefield Rattan buggy, but it hasn't been unloaded yet."

"A buggy wouldn't help a lot." Nell paused. "You see, New Tacoma only has one main street, and it's just about five blocks long — from here on Fourth up to Ninth, where Mr. Bonney has his drugstore. Also, a good many of the stores are perched high."

"I don't understand."

"They're not level with the wooden sidewalks. Mr. Bonney's store, for example, has five steps up."

"Why?"

"I don't know. That's just the way it is. And then some of the stores are a few steps below the street, and the sidewalks aren't even, either."

Mrs. Fawcett laughed. "You make it sound quite an adventure just to shop."

"Yes, ma'am, I guess it is."

"Would it be possible for me to leave little Angelo with you for half an hour or so? He's been fed and changed, and he'll sleep for a good hour now. I wouldn't ask it, but I want to see what shops New Tacoma has."

Nell looked around for something to put him in, and to cover her sigh. *Why do I always find myself around a baby,* she thought. But the hotel had no chamber-maids, and half an hour was bearable. "If you'll wait a minute, I'll get the big basket Mrs. Halstead uses for laundry; the baby should be fine in it."

Mrs. Fawcett beamed. "How very kind of . . ." Before she could finish, a herd of goats ran onto the wooden sidewalk. Their hooves clicked and clattered while their bleating drowned out her words. "Goodness me," she said when a barking dog drove them back to the road.

Nell laughed at her startled expression. "I heard Luther Kirkpatrick was going to take goats to the Humptulips to keep down the brush. I expect that's them."

"Humptulips?"

"It's where he lives — west, near the ocean."

Mrs. Fawcett looked bemused. "And I thought we were already out west."

"Well, you're as far west as matters. New Tacoma is going to be bigger than San Francisco someday."

Nell found the laundry basket in the kitchen and put it behind the desk, and Mrs. Fawcett tucked Angelo Junior into it. In his sleep, he gurgled and waved chubby little fists. "If I'm going out, I'd best get go-ing," Mrs. Fawcett said. "Are you sure you won't be too inconvenienced?"

Nell smiled at the young woman. "You just go right along and see the sights. We'll be fine. If he fusses, I'll make him a sugar teat."

After Mrs. Fawcett left, Nell gave her charge a wry look. *I must be the only person in the whole world who doesn't like babies very much.* For a minute the sight of Frieda Faye giving birth flashed before her eyes. *Boy, am I slow. I saw animals being born when we lived on Bush Prairie. Why would it be different for people? But how did the baby get inside Frieda Faye? It can't be how animals do it, can it?*

She put the questions aside and rang a bell on the desk. A man came out of the kitchen, wiping his hands on a towel tucked into his waistband.

"I'm sorry to disturb you, Fred, but would you mind bringing me a cup of coffee? Mrs. Fawcett left her baby for me to tend, and I best not leave him alone."

"Right away, Miss Nell." He left the room and soon returned with a white enamelware mug. Nell accepted it gratefully. She'd been working since five in the morning and it was now after two in the afternoon. Mrs. Halstead would be down soon to relieve her but, in the meantime, she welcomed the hotel's usual quiet hours between dinner and supper. Blowing on the coffee, she thought about what a difference a week had made in her life.

The changes started the morning after Frieda Faye had her baby. While Josie slept, Nell crept out of bed and found her well-thumbed piece of paper from *Strawbridge and Clothier's Quarterly.* In it was an ad for a wickerwork dressmaker's dummy. When she first saw the ad, Nell had written a letter to the company ordering one, and tucked the letter away until she'd saved enough to pay for the purchase. Now, she counted out the required amount, put it in an envelope with the order, and picked up her clothes. Outside, a dog barked, and several others joined in. Nell held her breath until Josie turned over in bed and resumed her gentle snoring.

As quietly as possible, she carried her clothes to the kitchen to dress. Pup jumped up, ready to go, but Nell closed the door on his eager face. She had to hurry, and having the dog with her would slow things down.

Her destination was Fife's Store for the necessary postage. She met few people on the road and was glad not to have to answer questions about what she was doing out so early. "I'll be glad when the new post office has postage and not just mailboxes," she muttered. At Fife's, the door squeaked when she pushed it open, and the smells of pickles, fish, ground coffee, and kerosene came to meet her.

Mr. Fife looked up from a rifle he was polishing. Nell knew Ike had his eyes on it because, as he'd said, "it's a Henry repeating rifle," as if that was enough explanation. "Good morning, Nell. What brings you out so early?"

"I want to mail a letter." Nell handed him the envelope and fished a handful of coins from her pocket.

Mr. Fife turned the envelope over and looked at the address. "Philadelphia, is it?"

Nell bit her lip. Mr. Fife was a bit of a gossip, and she wanted to keep her purchase under wraps — *or under my hat,* she thought, and smiled. "Yes, a crocheter needs supplies, doesn't she? Now, if you'll tell me how much the postage is, I need to get home. Pa broke his leg, you know, and I want to get back before he wakes up."

Mr. Fife put postage on the envelope. "Right you are, then." Nell paid him with a sigh of relief. She wasn't ready for the town to know her business.

"By the way," she said, "do you know of

anyone who is looking to hire?"

Mr. Fife handed back her letter and leaned on the counter. "You wanting to find work?"

"Yes, sir, at least until Pa's leg heals and he's able to work again. I've been wondering if Mrs. Halstead could use some help."

"Jane? Mebbe. I heard she wants to run the place with her son, but he's up in the foothills, and the family is having trouble getting word to him about the death."

"Isn't there a daughter, too?"

"Jeannette, but I heard she's — ah — er . . ."

The storekeeper's embarrassment reminded Nell that Jeannette was in the family way. *Good, she won't be able to help with the hotel.*

"Hmm. Well, I'll pay my respects later, and if you hear of any work coming around, please let me know."

Outside the store, Nell paused to let a group of men pass her. They walked unevenly with their arms around each other, singing at the tops of their voices and hooting at intervals. *How disgusting,* Nell thought, and then one of them caught her eye and waved his hat. "Miss Nell," he shouted. "You're my eye's delight this fine morning."

Nell stiffened. "And you're drunk, Mr. Calhoun, so I imagine you'd find any woman a delight."

"Ah, Miss Nell, you underestimate both yourself and my eyes. As I gaze on you, all my old dreams come back to me." He gave her a deep bow.

Old dreams, my Aunt Fannie. Nell stepped off the sidewalk and, pointedly holding her skirt aside, hurried down the road to post her letter. Once out of Calhoun's sight, her eyes unexpectedly filled with tears. *I don't know why I thought he'd be any different. Drat all men and their need for drink.*

At home, Nell found her mother making up a breakfast tray for Obed. "Where have you been?" Amity asked.

"I went to see Mr. Fife." Nell tied on an apron and took the turning fork from her mother, just as Josie came out of their bedroom.

"I heard you counting your money," she said. "Are you giving it to Ma? I am. Here, Ma." Josie set a string-drawn bag on the table.

Nell turned the pork sizzling in the fry pan. "I went to see Mr. Fife about finding work."

"Work?" Amity looked up from spooning scrambled eggs onto a plate.

232

"I asked him if he thought Mrs. Halstead would hire me, at least for a few weeks. Mr. Fife says she and Charles want to run the hotel, but it's a big job for two people."

"What about your crochet money?" Josie asked, returning to her previous question.

"I spent most of it."

"On what?"

"A dressmaker's dummy." Nell put a piece of pork on a platter and took the pan off the stove. "Where's Albina, by the way?"

"Still in bed."

"Well, if we're both working, she'll have to start being more helpful. Albina, get up!"

"I don't want to," came Albina's voice. She made her tone as plaintive as possible.

Nell went into her little sister's bedroom and pulled back the covers. "Get up and get dressed. There's chores needing done."

"What chores?" Albina tried to grab the blankets back.

"Oh, no you don't." Nell held onto the covers. "Come on, get up. We're going to have a pow-wow."

Albina swung her feet over the edge of the bed. "The floor's cold."

"I know. I'm up hours before you every day."

"You're awfully crabby." Albina caught the dress and underthings Nell threw at her and

233

started changing clothes.

Back in the kitchen, Nell poured herself a cup of coffee and spooned some eggs onto her plate. While she sat eating, Pup nudged her legs, looking for bites. He was such a likeable fellow, the whole family had taken to him.

"When did you buy a dressmaker's dummy?" Josie asked.

"You are a dog with a bone." Nell swallowed a forkful of eggs. "If you must know, this week."

"Before or after Pa's accident?"

Albina came out, dressed and looking sulky. "Wash up, and then you can help yourself to the food, Albina," Nell said. "I have to go to town, so you'll have to do the dishes."

"But . . ."

Nell gave her a look, and Albina muttered, "Bossy boots" before shutting up.

Amity returned to the kitchen with a tray of empty plates. She sat with a quiet sigh and ate her own breakfast, now half cold. "Your father's in quite a lot of pain."

"Did Ike explain how the accident happened?" Nell put some eggs on a piece of bread and popped it into her mouth.

"No, only that the wood they were standing on was wet and still green. Each man had a quota of work to be completed, and Obed was hurrying to finish his. Somehow, he slipped and fell."

"That's the third accident on the coal bunkers since the work there began." Finished eating, Josie carried her dishes to the washbasin. "Why are they in such a hurry?"

"From what Ike told me, Charles Crocker — he owns the Carbon Hill Coal Company — has been putting pressure on Mr. McClellan to get things done," Amity said. "Then, after Mr. McClellan's accident, construction was held up, and the bunkers are behind schedule."

"And now, thanks to Mr. Crocker, Pa has a broken leg, and I have to wash the dishes." Albina managed to pout and look mulish at the same time.

Nell narrowed her eyes and turned slightly to face her sister. "After the twins died, we all spoiled and coddled you until you've become rather selfish. You make me ashamed." She stood and cleared away her dishes, then walked toward the bedroom. "I'm going to change now and go see Mrs. Halstead about a job. I'll be back as soon as I can. Ma, do you need me to pick up anything?"

"No, Nell," Amity said quietly. "As soon as Obed is asleep, I'll go help Frieda Faye.

Josie only works half a day today. Albina won't be alone long."

She looked troubled, and Nell felt chagrined as she walked into the girls' bedroom. *It's true, though, what I said. We have spoiled Albina, and now it's hard to change. And she doesn't understand.* Nell sat on her bed and rubbed her hands together. *I guess I'm a bad person. I spent my money when I knew we would need it, and I wasn't at all nice to Beanie. But I shouldn't have to feel guilty about that. In the long run, she has to learn what we all have had to learn. Oh dear, I hate it when something's for your own good.*

Putting her remorse aside, Nell found her brown dress and checked it for spots. *I suppose Ma will want me to wear black because of the twins' death, but brown looks better with my eyes.* She dressed carefully and, before leaving, turned to her little sister. "After your chores are done, why don't you look for feathers so we can start work on them."

"Okay," Albina said, but Nell left the house followed by reproachful looks from both Albina and Pup.

The Halstead Hotel's front desk was vacant when Nell walked in. Apparently hearing her, a man came out of the kitchen, and Nell asked for Mrs. Halstead.

"She's upstairs, Miss."

"Thank you." Nell spotted the stairs at the back of the room. Already the hotel had a deserted feel, but muted voices led her to the Halsteds' rooms. The door she stood in front of had a black swag draped across the top and a black wreath just above the knob. She squared her shoulders and knocked.

A woman who looked to be in her mid-twenties, her belly rounded with pregnancy, answered the door. "Yes?"

"I've come to see Mrs. Halstead."

"We're not receiving."

Nell stood her ground. "I'm here to see Mrs. Halstead on business."

They stood eye to eye for several seconds before the woman stepped back. "Very well. I'm her daughter, Mrs. Geiger. You can come this way and, please, try to be brief. We're in mourning for my father."

"I know, and I'm sorry. He was a delightful man," Nell said, though she had barely registered his presence in town. She sat in the chair Mrs. Geiger indicated and prepared to wait. The woman who eventually followed Mrs. Geiger into the parlor was middle-aged and spare. Her hair was slicked back in a bun, and her eyes seemed to have sunk into her head. Nell stood and extended her hand. Mrs. Halstead took it briefly and sat on a lumpy horsehair loveseat, with Mrs.

Geiger joining her. For a minute, no one spoke.

"Jeannette says you wish to see me," Mrs. Halstead said.

"Yes, ma'am. My name is Nell Tanquist, and I would like to work for you, temporarily, of course, helping at the front desk."

"Why?"

"So you can adjust to your bereavement and, truth be told, to help my family while Pa recovers from a broken leg. He was working on the coal bunker and fell."

"Have you had any experience?"

"No, ma'am, just in sewing and keeping house, but I'm hard working. I can read and write. If you make a list of duties, I'll see that they're done."

"My son Charles and I are planning to run the hotel."

"I know that. Mr. Fife told me, but until after — uh, Mr. Halstead's services, perhaps you'll be needing help. It will give you time to — um, rest and plan for the future."

Mrs. Geiger laid a hand on her swollen belly. "It would be nice, Ma, not to have to worry about things, just for a little while."

Mrs. Halstead stood and clasped her hands at her waist. "Come tomorrow morning at four thirty. We'll talk then."

"Thank you, ma'am," Nell said to Mrs.

Halstead's departing back.

Outside and out of sight of the hotel's windows, Nell danced a little jig. "Wait until I tell Hildy. I finally have something to brag about."

CHAPTER 14

The Halstead family buried Jacob on an unseasonably bleak day when rain overflowed trenches being dug for sewers and was blown sideways against windows. Nell was on duty during the funeral, and Hildy had stopped by, sitting with her near the front desk while they drank coffee, ate cookies, and watched the activity on Pacific Avenue.

"These are good." Nell spoke with her mouth half full. She broke off a small piece and fed it to Pup, who lay by her feet. "The cookies I had at Mrs. Captain Quincy's house were red."

"Never mind the color; how did they taste?"

"They were good. Maybe you could bake red cookies at Christmas."

"It's an idea. I'll ask Chong about the recipe. This one is from *Miss Parloa's New Cook Book.* Aunt Glady sent it to me — the recipe, not the book."

Nell looked at Hildy in surprise. "What happened to Tabitha Tickletooth's cookbook?"

"She's still my hero, but it's good for business if I can say something is newly popular back East."

"I'll remember that."

They were silent for a moment, looking at what little traffic there was outside, and then Nell gave a little laugh. "Do you ever think of all the things Mrs. Stair taught us?"

Hildy, who was used to Nell's abrupt changes of subject, also laughed. "Every day when I'm figuring ingredients. Why?"

"I was just remembering Milton."

"Milton?"

"The poet. He wrote about clouds having silver linings. I tell you true, Pa's accident has been my silver lining. I get to be in town during the best part of the day and talk to the people who stay here in the hotel. I'm making notes of what the ladies wear, and I have been able to keep a little of my earnings. Ma is teaching Albina to do things around the house, and Frieda Faye's mother is helping with the baby. Right this minute — for just this moment in time — I think I'm as happy as I'll ever be."

"Oh, I don't think that's true." Hildy

turned serious for a moment. "You have such a capacity for happiness, for finding all the silver linings. I think you'll grow old finding the fun in everything. I envy you."

Hildy's words caught Nell off guard. "Why, Hildy, you enjoy life, too."

Hildy sighed and made circles on the windowsill with her finger. "Pa is often sick and unable to work, and Reuben had to quit school and find a job. He's smart and should have been able to go to school more, maybe to the new college here. Cousin Elsie is still with us, and Samuel's job keeps him away for weeks at a time. It's hard, sometimes."

Nell knew Hildy's cousin had come to stay with them several years earlier to recover from the effects of an ill-advised love affair, but her friend's depression caught her by surprise. "But Hildy, you have a beau and your own income; Cousin Elsie won't be with you forever, and, at least when your pa works, he doesn't drink the money away."

"*Hmph.* It seems as if Elsie will never leave." Hildy went quiet for a minute and then burst into laughter. "There you go, finding the silver lining. It's a good lesson for me."

Relieved, Nell asked the latest about Cousin Elsie.

"She's talking about becoming a mission-ary."

"Goodness gracious, why?"

"She met a missionary lady named Gertrude Denny who survived the Whitman Massacre and was smitten with the idea. Mrs. Denny and her husband used to live in China, and now Elsie thinks she needs to go there and preach the Word." Nell giggled, and Hildy continued. "Aunt Glady is horrified. She still has hopes Elsie will return home and make what she calls 'a proper marriage.' She's threatening to come here and drag Elsie home."

"Oh, good grief; what an idea."

"I know, but what with Elsie's giving thanks for each little thing and amen-ing all over the place, a week or so of Aunt Glady might not be so bad." The rain had stopped; Hildy stood and picked up her wrap. "Isn't it time for you to leave?"

"Mrs. Halstead asked me to work late so she and the family can have a pow-wow at her daughter's house after the funeral. I'm hoping that means they're discussing keeping me on."

After Hildy left, Nell looked around with satisfaction. The hotel lacked a lobby; the bottom floor was just one big room with a door to the kitchen in the back, a bar to the left, and stairs to the second floor on the right. The reception desk was close to the front door and faced a small area. On her first day at work, Nell had gone into the kitchen and asked for a bucket and some rags. When the staff looked at her with suspicion, she smiled. "I certainly don't plan on just sitting out front when I can help keep things clean there. You keep on with what you're doing, and I'll be back for a cup of coffee when I'm done." She'd carried the items into the main room and washed the windows, tables, and walls. Every day, she swept the floor and made sure the tables were spotless. She also brought in flowers to put at the registration desk.

At the end of the first week, she asked Fred, the cook, to tell her how the hotel was run. Mistrust written all over his face, he'd given her a quick rundown before discussing the kitchen. As it turned out, Fred had been a chuckwagon cook on trail drives. His expertise was sourdough biscuits with white gravy, sowbelly, baked beans, stew, and coffee.

When he finished speaking, Nell said, "The Blackwell Hotel doesn't serve dessert, so I'd like to." Before he could protest, she added, "But I don't expect you to make pies for the whole hotel. You have enough on your plate." Then she giggled. "That was a pun, and I didn't even intend it." At her words, Fred relaxed. "Anyway, if you think we can raise prices just a little bit, I'd have them delivered from Hildy Bacom's bakery."

Fred was warily willing to give the change a try, and, soon after, Hildy's brother Reuben began dropping off pies before doubling back to deliver milk. Every day, from then on, Nell made sure Fred had a large slice of whatever type of pie was delivered. Slowly, being careful not to step on toes, she made improvements: sending the laundry out more frequently, cutting old sheets into squares and stitching the edges to make napkins, even visiting the bathhouse next door to suggest hours for women and children only. The one area she didn't touch was the bar. And when piano prodigy Madame Julie Rive-King arrived in town to play at the new Alpha Opera House, the hotel was as welcoming as Nell could make it.

Miss Rive-King's company included an Oregon man named William Kinross, who was advertised as "a professor of voice culture and vocal music"; Mrs. Augusta Stetson, a good friend of Mary Baker Eddy; and Miss Annie Griffin. Nell never did find out what either woman's position in the company was. However, not to matter. As she looked at the two new oil lights men had put up at either side of the opera house door, and saw people dressed in their best going in, she thought how exciting her life had become. *How can I ever spend my days at home again?*

Twenty-five-year old Madame Rive-King wasn't beautiful; her arms and hands were too plump, and her features were plain. But the small, curling bangs she wore softened her face, and the Apollo Loop in which she'd arranged her hair added style. Nell noticed that all three women wore black with plenty of lace trim, and that their sleeves were up to their elbows. The oddest thing they did, though, was leave money on the table when they'd finished eating. The first time Nell saw money left behind, she called them back.

"My dear." Mr. Kinross bowed slightly. "This is for you."

"But Mrs. Halstead pays my salary." Nell tried to hand him the money.

Mr. Kinross smiled. "It's a tip, dear." When Nell looked puzzled, he continued, "In finer establishments back East it is customary to leave a little something to say 'thank you' for exemplary service."

"Goodness gracious." At first, Nell didn't know what to think. She added a hasty thank you as the musical troupe walked toward the door. When they were gone, she counted the cash they'd left her. *More savings toward my sewing machine!*

The day dragged on, too quiet with Hildy gone. Late that afternoon, three men came in and headed for the bar. One lingered near the front desk and tried to make advances, but Nell chilled his ardor with a look. When she grew sleepy, she opened the door and stood just inside, letting the cool air wash over her. Night in town and the change in street traffic was, Nell thought, a different kettle of fish. She stared with disgust as the door of Levin's saloon burst open and two brawling men continued their fight on the street, egged on by fellow drinkers. When one of the fighters fell into a horse trough, the other helped him out of it, and they headed up Pacific Avenue singing, their arms around each other's shoulders. The sheriff came by, pushing a drunk in a wheelbarrow to the city's new jail. A woman appeared, and a man approached her. After a moment's conversation, they disappeared into the darkness. Nell thought about Hildy's friends, Miss Rose, Miss Lily, and Miss Violet, and sighed. When she'd tried to talk to her mother about babies, Amity turned red and repeated what she had said before, that when a woman married, her husband would teach her what she needed to know. Nell wondered about that but had yet to approach Dr. Clarke on the subject.

In the hotel, diners came, ate, and left. After tidying the dining room and readying it for breakfast, Nell found some leftovers in the kitchen and fed Pup, then went back to the registration desk, where she sat down and closed her eyes. A cool draft roused her as someone opened the door, and the Halstead family crowded in. Nell looked at the clock and saw that it was near ten. Trying not to yawn, she hopped off her chair.

"I'm going to my room, Charles," Mrs. Halstead said. She looked at Nell. "Thank you for helping out, Nell. Your extra hours will be reflected in your pay packet."

Followed by her daughters, Mrs. Halstead headed for the stairs. Charles hung his greatcoat on the coatrack. "You mustn't mind Mother sounding so abrupt," he said. "It's been a long day, and the weather didn't help. She's tired."

"Of course, Mr. Halstead. I understand completely, and I admire your mother greatly."

Charles Halstead smiled at her words and

took Nell's place at the registration desk while she tied a length of rope around Pup's neck and put on her cloak. Outside, she stood under the awning a moment to let her eyes adjust. Nell had never forgotten advice Hildy's mother had given her years earlier and found the hatpin she kept ready to grab if need be in her cloak. Holding the pin in one hand and the rope in the other, she started down the wooden walk toward Seventh Street. The Alpha Opera House's streetlights made puddles of light in the darkness, but Nell kept to the shadows where possible. After the rain, the humid air smelled clean, and she pushed off the hood of her cloak. Pup kept close to her side as they crossed Pacific Avenue, dodging pools of water, and started up the hill.

At Railroad Alley, Nell's attention was caught by a young woman across the street. The woman walked quickly and kept her head ducked, except when she looked over her shoulder as if fearful she was being followed. Something about her seemed familiar, and, after a second, Nell realized it was her friend Ellen, a girl she'd gone to school with along with Hildy, Fern, Kezzie, and Lucy. "Now, where do you suppose she's headed?" Nell asked Pup. "There's nothing on Railroad Alley except Howe's Book

Bindery, the Baker Hotel, and a storehouse." She decided to follow Ellen and see where her chum was going. Staying on her own side of the road, Nell let Ellen get slightly ahead and then started walking.

Unlike Pacific Avenue, which was a wide thoroughfare running north and south, Railroad Alley was a sparsely developed, narrow road that turned west a few blocks from town and ended abruptly in a flat, logged-off field overgrown with grass and weeds. They'd been trampled down, Nell saw, and several wagons and a few tents made a semi-circle behind a number of campfires. Nell recognized the gypsy wagon she'd seen earlier. Horses loosely tethered off to one side, where there was decent grazing, pulled at their restraints and nudged each other. Sitting on a hunk of wood and barely visible to Nell, a man played a violin for a woman who smacked a tambourine and danced. Nell watched in admiration. *She's as agile as a wet willow switch.* Flames flickered and swayed, and embers hissed and crackled, sending up sparks. Little boys played games of their own making while little girls tried to imitate the dancer. A baby cried and was hushed; voices rose and fell; a man burst into laughter, and others joined in. Sarah could paint this, Nell thought, enjoying the scene playing out before her.

In the meantime, Ellen circled the fires and stopped in front of a woman. They exchanged a few words, and then Ellen dug in her pocket and handed over something. The woman bit it, nodded, and tucked it into the bodice of her dress. Then the two sat down, and Ellen stuck out her right hand. *Why, she's having her fortune told! I wonder why she didn't go to Grandma Staley.* But then Nell remembered how word got around town when anyone did that. *She must have wanted to keep this secret.*

Ellen and the gypsy woman were so close that their heads almost touched as they leaned over Ellen's palm. The fire, stars, and a quarter moon provided the only light, and Nell could barely make out their distant figures. Suddenly Ellen jumped up. "You're lying," she said, her words carrying clearly to where Nell stood. The woman also stood, but her response was too soft and low for Nell to hear. Whatever it was, it didn't soothe Ellen. She held her right hand in her left as if it had been burned and said, "I don't believe you. I don't think you even know what you're talking about. You're a fraud, and I have half a mind to tell the sheriff you took my money."

Beside Nell, Pup growled softly. She laid

a restraining hand on his head. Men appeared from out of the shadows and closed in on Ellen and the gypsy woman. Keeping a tight grip on Pup's rope and on her hat pin, Nell left the shadows and crossed to where Ellen stood. "Ellen, come with me. You don't want to start trouble."

"Yes, I do. This so-called fortune teller doesn't know what she's talking about."

"Be that as it may, you paid her for what she had to say. You can't expect to get your money back just because you didn't like what she told you." Nell took Ellen's arm.

"I can, too, because it was all a lie." Ellen shrugged her off.

Someone spoke to the fortune teller in an unfamiliar language. She spit and then responded. Ellen's eyes widened, and Nell took her arm again and smiled at the gypsy woman. "You may remember me. I waved at you from the window of the Halstead Hotel when you drove into town. I'm going to take my friend home now and leave you to enjoy your evening. The dancing was beautiful."

Nell's grip was firm, and she held onto Ellen until they were well down Railroad Alley. "What was that all about?" she asked when Ellen jerked away.

"She didn't know what she was talking

about," Ellen repeated.

"Well, what *was* she talking about?"

Ellen halted, hesitating. "Never mind." She started walking again. "You'd just make fun of me."

Nell hurried to catch up with her. "No, I won't. I have so many things on my own mind; I don't have time to bother about other people's problems."

"Promise?"

"Cross my heart."

Ellen stopped again and heaved a sigh. "I went to ask her when George was going to propose." She eyed Nell warily.

"Oh." Nell knew Ellen had been pursuing George Meyer as ardently as he in turn pursued Hildy and sometimes herself. "Well, what did she say?"

"That only trickery will make him marry me."

Nell kept the surprise off her face, though Ellen's anger made sense now. "Oh, I doubt that, but if not George, there are plenty of men in New Tacoma who want wives. You'll have your choice of a farmer or logger or fisherman or —"

Ellen interrupted her. "I want George. I want to be his wife, a minister's wife."

Nell, who had also gone to school with George, knew he had spent the winter at divinity school and was fond of telling people what God thought. *He'd be the most officious preacher New Tacoma has ever experienced.*

Men's voices reached them, and the girls resumed walking. "Why did you follow me?" Ellen asked.

They turned off Railroad Alley and saw the Grotto Saloon in the distance. "That saloon was robbed last night. The paper said highway robbers were responsible, and I was worried about you."

Ellen muttered under her breath, but Nell was so tired she didn't pay attention. When they stopped at Eighth Street, Ellen said, "Don't forget your promise."

"I won't, and I wouldn't worry if I were you. You will make a wonderful preacher's wife."

Ellen gave Nell a quick hug, and they parted, each headed to her own home.

Nell's house was dark when she reached it. She opened the door cautiously, hoping no one would be awake.

No such luck. "Nell, is that you?" Obed shouted when the door squeaked.

"Yes."

"Well, before you take off your cloak, I need you to go to Longprey's and get me a bucket of beer."

Nell sighed and hung up her hat and cloak. "It's late, Pa, and I've been working since before dawn."

"It won't take long."

"Where's Ma?"

"Ike dropped by and asked her to help with the baby. He has colic."

"Ike or the baby?"

"What?"

"Never mind. Anyway, I'm tired, and I'm going to bed."

Nell heard the springs creak as Obed wiggled around. "Not without my beer, you aren't."

"How are you going to pay for it? You haven't been able to work."

Obed let loose a string of swear words ending with, "Now you listen to me, daughter. I need the beer for my pain."

In spite of herself, Nell shook her head and laughed. "You have the pain medicine Dr. Bostwick left, and I'm saving every cent not needed to support our family to start a dressmaking business. You know that."

"Stuff and nonsense. Women belong at home."

"Not this one."

"I'll remember this, daughter. I will, and when I'm up and around, I'll tan your hide."

"No, you won't because I'm your favorite.

255

Now take your pain medicine and go to sleep."

Ignoring another string of oaths, Nell went into her own room and shut the door. Whenever she was working nights, Albina slept with Josie, and Nell had Albina's room to herself. It was barely as big as a closet, but being alone was a luxury she hoped to keep. She counted out the household money from her pay packet and hid the rest. *Imagine Ellen as an old maid,* she thought as she changed for bed and braided her hair. *No, I can't. It would be terrible for her.* She snuggled under the blankets and felt Pup jump up next to her. *Not for me, though. I'm going to have my own shop and make beautiful clothes. No colicky babies in my future.* With her hand on the dog, she fell asleep.

CHAPTER 15

Not long after Jacob Halstead's funeral, his widow leased the hotel's bar to a man named George Towle. Nell was hemming new napkins when Mrs. Halstead appeared in the dining room and sat at one of the tables. She wore a plain black dress, and Nell's fingers itched to crochet her a collar. Fred came from the kitchen carrying two cups of coffee. He set them on the table, and she beckoned to Nell. Nell's heart sank. *I've had such a good time working here,* she thought. *I suppose this will be my last day.* She sat across from her employer and folded her hands in her lap.

Mrs. Halstead handed her one of the cups and wrapped her hands around the other. "Charles and I are going to run the hotel ourselves," she said, and, in spite of herself, Nell's eyes filled with tears. She pressed her lips together and waited. "However, we both can't be here all the time, and that's where

I hope you can help us out."

Nell blinked the moisture away, hoping Mrs. Halstead hadn't seen it. There was hope yet. "I will if I can."

"We need someone at the desk in the late afternoon and evening — say, from three until eleven. You have been an exemplary employee; the staff likes you, and the guests like you. Word gets around, you know, and more families are staying here since you have come. I hope that continues." Mrs. Halstead stopped talking and waited.

Nell broke into a broad smile. "Thank you so much, Mrs. Halstead. I am glad to stay and work evenings. I love it here, and, truly, everyone has been so kind." She set her cup down, twisted her fingers, and then said, "There is one thing, however."

Mrs. Halstead waited, and Nell wondered if the woman thought she was going to ask for more money. "A Humpty Dumpty picnic is coming to town, and I want to take my little sister," she said. "I would like an evening off to go."

A rare smile lit Mrs. Halstead's face. "Ah, yes, the pantomime. Have you ever seen one?"

"No, ma'am. I've never seen any show except the ones put on at the school. Did you see the notice in the paper? It's called the Andrews and Stockwell's Ideal Pantomime and Star Specialty Company."

"That's quite a name, isn't it?"

"Yes, ma'am, it is. There's a man known as Frank Moore, the Gymnastics Marvel, and performing dogs, and a Columbine. Do you know what a Columbine is?"

"Why, yes, as a matter of fact I do. I saw a Humpty Dumpty picnic when I was a girl. Two of the characters are the Harlequins, that's a sort of clown, and there's the Columbine, who is a mischief-making girlfriend. She takes pleasure in stirring things up, and, of course, the various performers then react."

"What fun." Nell clapped her hands. "The company is performing on the fairgrounds east of Pacific Avenue at the bottom of the hill on Friday. May I go? I can work a day and night to make up for it."

"That won't be necessary. Charles and I will manage. You may go with your sister and enjoy yourselves."

"Thank you so much." Nell jumped up and hugged Mrs. Halstead, who looked startled at her exuberance. "Excuse the liberty, but I just had to do that. Oh, I'm so excited."

"There, there." Mrs. Halstead patted Nell's arm. "No need to thank me. You have earned a day off. It's little enough I can give you. Now," she pushed back from the table and stood. "Let's just get on with the day, and you can start the evening shift tomorrow."

Mrs. Halstead took her coffee and went to her rooms. Nell, with a happy smile, took hers to the front desk. The interval between meals was generally quiet, giving her time to spread out some of the feathers Albina had recently dyed. Once Albina put her mind to the project, she'd canvassed the neighborhood, and several ladies let her gather their birds' feathers. She'd experimented in dyeing them until most of the plumes were evenly colored. Mrs. Spooner bought the best ones for her millinery work, and Albina sold the others to her friends.

Spreading them out on the desk and using a lice comb, Nell carefully separated the barbs from the quills. When she was done, she tied together the ones Mrs. Spooner would most likely want and put them in a small bag with the others. Then Charles came out of the kitchen to take over, and Nell pinned on her hat. The day's warmth had carried over tonight, and she easily made do with a shawl. She pushed the door opened and knocked it against a man who was coming down the sidewalk.

"Here, now." He struggled to regain his balance. "What do ya think you're doin', crashin' into a man like that?"

Nell dropped her bag of feathers and hurried to help him. "I'm terribly sorry." She took his arm, and the fellow steadied himself. "I didn't look where I was going. Are you all right?"

The man straightened up, emitting a powerful odor of fish and unwashed body. "Well, well, well. You must be the pretty little front-desk gal I've been hearing about."

Nell stiffened and let go of him. He had a hatchet face with deep-set eyes over a crooked nose. A scar ran from his right eye to his chin. She shivered, her eyes narrowing. "I must be on my way."

"What's your hurry?" He stooped to pick up the fallen bag, out of which several feathers had escaped. "What have we here?" He opened it and looked inside.

"They're feathers. My little sister dyes them and sells them to milliners." Nell reached for it, but he wouldn't let go.

"Little sister, you say." He grinned at her, showing tobacco-stained teeth and gaps where teeth should have been. "Is she as much a looker as her *big* sister?" He laughed and grabbed the bundled feathers out.

"What say she sell a few to me?" He tucked the feathers in his shirt and dropped some coins into the bag. "How about you and me go back inside and have a drink?"

Nell rubbed her hands on her dress, conscious of the fact that her hatpin was in her cloak back at home. She'd left Pup there, too, at Albina's request, and regretted it. Not that the man had done anything except insult her. She snatched the bag out of his hand. "Good day, sir."

He laughed as she stepped off the sidewalk. "I think I might just have to take a room in the hotel."

Nell held her head high and pretended not to hear. She'd recognized his voice and face — he was the man she'd seen a few months back, dropping off the boatload of Chinese men near Day Island when she and Josie were coming back from Steilacoom. Despite the heat, she shuddered again and was glad to turn a corner and be off Pacific Avenue. *I'll be safe in the hotel, of course, even if he does take a room, and Pup will protect me. But thunderation, why can't he go to the Villard House or the Saint Charles Hotel?* Nell walked up the hill so fast she barely saw the people she passed. *I need another pin for when I don't have my cloak,*

262

but where can I hide it? She thought about the problem all the way home.

The night of the Humpty Dumpty picnic, Nell changed into a new dress and pulled on half mitts. Amity had finally let her out of mourning for the twins, and her dress was cream and brown sprigged cotton, brown being a color she enjoyed wearing. The top was a jacket with long sleeves, a snug bodice that buttoned in front and that came to points down each side, and which was attached to a ruffled skirt. To match, she'd dressed up an old hat with brown ribbons and yellow feathers.

"You look beautiful, Nell," Albina said. She stood in the doorway, waiting.

"Thank you, Beanie. So do you." Nell hugged her sister. "Are you ready?"

"I've been ready for ages."

Nell laughed. "Well, then, let's go."

In the main room Obed sat at the table looking at an old copy of the *Ledger.* A pair of crutches Ike had made were propped next to him. "We're going, Pa." Nell leaned down to kiss him goodbye, but Obed jerked his head away. "Oh, Pa." Nell half laughed. "Look at how much better you feel now that the drink is out of your body."

Obed put the paper down. "Come 'ere,

Beanie, and give your old Pa a kiss."

"I don't want to mess my dress." Albina pecked him on the cheek.

"With Ike married and gone, this place is nothing but a house of women." Obed sighed and picked up the paper again.

Not quite, Nell thought wryly as she and Albina left. *You have the presence of three men all by yourself.* More than once she'd dodged her father swinging a crutch at her; he was certainly someone who could carry a grudge.

Holding her skirt off the ground, Nell started down the street, nodding to acquaintances they met. Albina copied the gesture. "Are we going to take the streetcar?" Beanie asked.

"No, we're going to walk."

"You just want people to see your dress."

"Of course, and yours, too. Besides, it's not too hot and not too cold. It's . . ."

"Just right." Albina laughed and skipped a few feet ahead.

They joined Pacific Avenue's foot traffic and fifteen minutes later reached the fairground. Nell bought their tickets from a person wearing a pointed hat, a ruff around his neck, and enormously baggy pants. He'd also whitened his face and drawn in giant red lips. While Albina gawked, Nell spotted

264

guards posted to keep non-payers out. Rudimentary, tiered seats to a height of four levels faced west and made a half circle around a large patch of dirt where foliage had all but given up the ghost. The seats were opposite cloth backdrops on wooden frames that circled the other side. Nell looked around, noticing most of the early arrivers had chosen the third and fourth levels. Though she and Albina were early, many of the best places to see were already taken. She felt lucky to find two places near the middle on the second tier.

"I wish we were higher," Albina said as she settled her skirts.

"I think we're safer here."

The setting sun felt pleasantly warm as Nell looked for familiar faces. People kept coming and crammed onto the seats. Dusk fell, and men lit kerosene lights where the entertainers would be performing. Their flickering flames brought the painted backdrops alive. Eventually, when the crowd showed signs of growing restless, an emcee appeared.

"Ladies and gentlemen." He removed his hat and bowed left, right, and middle. "Welcome to the Andrews and Stockwell's Ideal Pantomime and Star Specialty Show." Applause greeted his words. "Pantomime, as you know, is the art of using music, exaggerated movements, and facial expressions to convey meanings. During the show you will see trick skaters and rope skipping feats, amazing calisthenics, and antipodean deeds of dare-doing. We have performing dogs and clowns. We have musicians and comedians, and, most of all, we have the lovely Ida Maussy as the Columbine. Ladies and gentlemen, prepare to feast your eyes, but keep your ears open, too, because, with the Andrews and Stockwell's Ideal Pantomime and Star Specialty Show, anything can and will happen."

More clapping followed as he put his hat back on, turned to one side and then the other, and waved his arms. Musicians stepped around the backdrop at one side of the stage and began to play. From the other side, Humpty Dumpty appeared, followed by Old King Cole, Mary carrying a fake lamb, Georgie Porgy, and other easily recognized figures. Then a Harlequin came out, dancing and cavorting among the others. He wore white, wide-legged pants and a large white jacket, both adorned with black pom-poms. The jacket had a ruffled collar that matched his face mask. Behind him, a head in a pointed hat appeared and looked about, and, finally, the Columbine tiptoed out. Albina gasped. "Nell, I can see her ankles."

Nell was also taken aback. The Columbine wore a red bodice and skirt of multiple layers of red and black, which ended a mere twelve inches below her knees. Red ribbons crisscrossed from her slippers up her black stockings. Several men in the audience whistled.

With exaggerated gestures to show the audience she was up to no good, Columbine used a magic wand and created havoc among the nursery rhyme figures by making them do a number of silly things: sleep and flirt and interact with the performing dogs. Albina laughed and laughed when a clown did somersaults under flying bottles and chairs. When the audience seemed to grow tired of the antics, someone broke into song, and the actors froze in place. Then the Antipodean, wearing red pants and shirt and a short blue robe, stood on his head and began whirling round and round until Nell grew dizzy watching him. Other acts followed before the show concluded with fireworks. Attached to the Antipodean's robes, they shot red, white, and blue sparks into the sky. Nell stared, enchanted, as they lit the darkness.

A slight breeze came up, blowing some

sparks back onto the cloth scenery. Nell squinted, suddenly anxious. Was that smoke? Then someone screamed as the painted cloth caught fire. With the flames rapidly spreading to the backdrops on either side, the audience panicked, pushing and shoving to get off the seats. A woman in the top row tripped, and her skirt snagged on a piece of wood, suspending her upside down. "I can see her bloomers," Albina said with fascinated horror, as men rushed to help. It wasn't funny, really, but Nell had to stop herself from laughing as she grabbed her sister's hand. "Golly Moses, this is a stampede."

Albina looked at her, wide eyed. "Nell, you sweared."

While the performers forgot about the show and hurriedly ripped down the burning cloth, Nell pulled Albina to safety at the edge of the crowd and let the people go by. "That was certainly more than I bargained for."

"I thought it was wonderful," Albina said. "I want to be a Columbine when I grow up. Will you make me a dress?"

"I will, and you can send all your female admirers to me. What color?"

"Pink — no, purple, with bows."

"And feathers?"

Albina giggled. "Of course."

By this time, only the entertainers remained on the fairgrounds. Most of the audience was far ahead of them when Nell and Albina started walking. As they approached Eighth Street, a figure slouched out of the Grotto Saloon. "My goodness me, if it isn't the hotel gal."

Though she couldn't see the speaker's face, Nell recognized the voice and shuddered. She held tightly to Albina's hand and would have kept going, but Albina pulled them both to a stop. "You have one of my feathers in your hat."

"You have very good eyes." The hatchet-faced man moved a little closer, grinning. "You must be the little sister, the one who dyes them feathers."

"Yes, I am. My name is Albina." She turned to her sister. "Nell, you have to introduce me to your friend."

"Nell" — the man emphasized her name — "doesn't know me yet, but I have a room at the hotel now, so I think we'll become good friends."

Nell started walking again, pulling Albina. "Come on. Ma will be waiting up for us."

His laughter followed them.

At Eleventh Street, Nell stopped to catch her breath. "You weren't very nice to that man," Albina said.

"That's because he's a bad man and not someone either of us wants to know."

"How do you know that?"

"I saw him do something terrible once." Nell leaned down and took her sister's other hand. "Listen to me, Beanie. If he tries to talk to you, I want you to run as fast as you can. Go into a store, or find someone you know and ask them to help you get away."

Albina's eyes grew round. "Would he hurt me?"

Nell hesitated. "I don't know, but he might, and better safe than sorry."

At that moment a man called out, "Miss Nell?"

Nell jumped and turned around. "Oh, Mr. Calhoun. You startled me."

"I'm sorry, but I saw you hurrying away from the fellow who stopped you. And it's John, remember? Are you all right?"

"Perfectly fine, thank you."

"No, we're not," Albina said. "A man with one of my feathers in his hat tried to talk to us, and Nell says he's bad."

John raised his eyebrows. "Oh?"

Before Nell could answer, they heard footsteps coming down the street, headed toward the Wharf Road. Soon, seven Chinese men wearing ill-fitting Western suits and carrying scruffy suitcases came into sight. "Where are all those men going?" Albina asked.

"I hope, home to China." John looked thoughtful.

"Why?"

"Remember how we learned that President Arthur signed a law stopping immigration?" Nell said. "Well, the Chinese feel, and rightly so, that they're not welcome anymore."

"Look." Albina pointed at a man following them. "There's the man who talked to us."

John eyed him. "Ah, that's Thurlow Monk."

"You don't think he's going to take them back to China, do you?" Nell felt sick inside.

"I'm willing to bet he told them he would. Whether they get there or not is another thing."

"You mean . . . ?"

He looked down. "I don't like to think so."

"If he takes them to California, they could eat all the oranges they want, instead of just at Christmas," Albina said.

Nell sighed. "I think that's quite enough from you. Little girls shouldn't be so forward. And it's really not an appropriate conversation."

However, John laughed. "I often find oranges when I travel. I'll bring you some, if you like."

"Yes, please." Albina beamed.

They turned away from the rapidly disappearing group of men. "It's late," John said. "I'd like to walk you ladies home, if I may."

"Of course you can," Albina said before Nell could answer, then turned to her. "You didn't introduce us, Nell. Is this another man you don't really know?"

Chapter 16

When Albina and Nell returned from the Humpty Dumpty picnic, Nell found a note from Mrs. Halstead: her daughter had called the midwife, and Mrs. Halstead wanted Nell to come in the following day and work the morning shift. Knowing the hotel kitchen would have coffee, Nell skipped breakfast. She also ignored Pup's pleading eyes. Pup didn't have a collar yet, and, since the town council was now cracking down on any dog that looked like a stray, he had to stay home.

As she hurried down the hill toward Pacific Avenue, the rising sun lit Mt. Tacoma. Nell loved to see the mountain's seasonal changes and had heard Hazard Steven speak about his climb to the summit. His successful ascent had been the talk of the town. *I'm going to climb it, too, someday,* she thought, *in late summer when the snow is gone, and the wildflowers are in bloom.*

At the bottom of the hill, while turning left on Pacific Avenue, Nell saw three things: the many pits, dips, and holes in front of the hotel had been filled with sand and gravel, two blocks of road were leveled off, and Thurlow Monk was climbing into the hotel's new equipage. Just before his death, Jacob Halstead had ordered an omnibus to carry people from the train depot on the wharf to the hotel and back. Nell had heard Charles Halstead tell his mother the vehicle cost more than eight hundred dollars, and that the team of horses required to pull it would have to be stabled — an exorbitant expense.

Nell stopped and stared. *I guess that means he really does have a room in the hotel.* She sighed and started walking again. *At least he's leaving right now. Maybe I can avoid him altogether.*

When she arrived, the dining room was almost full, and she hurried to the kitchen for a pot of coffee. She was filling cups when a newly arrived family, Mr. and Mrs. H. C. Patrick and their son Oliver, entered the dining room and sat near a window. *I wonder what the initials H. C. stand for,* Nell thought as she returned to the kitchen for Oliver's milk. The Patricks, she knew, had bought out Mr. and Mrs. Money's stationery/aviary/printing shop and newspaper business down on the wharf. She re-entered the dining room and had just put down Oliver's milk when five ox-drawn covered wagons passed by in clear view. The boy jumped up to watch and pointed to writing on one wagon's worn canvas cover. "What does that say, Mama?"

Mrs. Patrick looked at the faded writing. "In Bunch Grass We Trust." The wagon's driver, a middle-aged woman in a faded cotton dress and sunbonnet, looked their way and nodded. Oliver waved vigorously.

"But what's it mean?" he asked as they sat back down.

Mr. Patrick put down his fork and wiped his mouth. "It means they are putting all their trust and faith in bunch grass rather than God." He scowled. "I'm not sure but what that's not blasphemous."

His wife looked at her plate and sighed. "Eat your food, Oliver, and don't do that again."

Nell grimaced as she turned away and went to the kitchen to get more coffee. Mr. H. C. seemed a bit too pious for her liking. However, back at their table, she smiled at the boy as she refilled the cups. "Bunch grass is just what it sounds like," she said. "Grass that grows in clumps. Ranchers and farmers depend on it to feed their livestock. But those folks are on the wrong side of the mountains. It grows on the east side. Our prairies don't have bunch grass."

"What will happen to them?" Mrs. Patrick asked.

"On the prairie south of New Tacoma, they'll most likely find decent land that the sheep herds haven't grazed down." A man at an adjacent table held up his coffee cup, and Nell nodded, then looked at the wide-eyed boy. "Don't worry, they'll be all right. The other farmers will help them."

The hour grew late, and the dining room cleared out. Nell emptied the coffee cups in the pot that held Mrs. Halstead's prize aspidistra plant, and Fred was clearing the last of the tables, when Otis Sprague, General Sprague's son, and an unfamiliar man came in. "Coffee, gentlemen?" Nell asked.

"If it's not too late." Mr. Sprague pulled out a chair for his friend, and they both sat down. "So, here's what happened," he said, picking up a conversation that had evidently started outside. "Henry dug a hole on Pacific Avenue to test the soil for the sewer system. Pa's Jersey cow got loose and fell in it. Took three men to get her out."

Nell's ears perked up as she set clean cups

on their table and filled them.

"Who's Henry?" asked the unknown man.

"The roadmaster." Otis Sprague laughed. "Anyway, I went to the city council meeting and casually mentioned what happened, and old Henry stood up, raised his fist, and said, 'Any man who would dig a pitfall in the street for any purpose whatever and failed to make it safe for Jersey cows ought to be prosecuted.'

"When I pointed out the fact that he'd dug the hole, Henry didn't say a word, just stood up, grabbed his hat, and stormed out."

The men laughed, and Nell hid her smile. What with animals and people falling in the ditches, the sewer system had caused more than one problem. She poured her own coffee, sat with it at the registration desk, and was taking a first welcome sip when Thurlow Monk pushed open the door. Nell hoped he'd head for the bar. Instead, he walked to a nearby chair, turned it to face her, and sat splay-legged in it. Close up and in the bright morning light, Nell had no doubt he was the man she'd seen leaving the Chinese men to fend for themselves the day of the Steilacoom trip.

"I see it's not too late for coffee," Monk said.

Nell gave him a steely-eyed look. "It is, actually."

" 'It is, actually,' " he mimicked her. In a fluid motion, Monk surged to his feet, reached across the registration desk, and grabbed Nell's wrist. He narrowed his eyes and kept his voice low so it wouldn't carry. "It seems to me, Little Miss Counter Girl, that you're playing favorites."

Nell wrenched her arm away. "You can probably get coffee at the bar, if you ask nicely."

"Oh, I always ask nicely — unless it's something I really want — then I just take it." When Nell rubbed her wrist and remained silent, he leaned an elbow on the desk. "You like to walk at night with that Chinee lover, do you?" He turned and spat, missing the spittoon. "Maybe some night I'll be here when you get off work, and you and me can take a little stroll."

She glared at him. "Get away from me."

"Now, now. Is that any way to talk to a paying guest?"

Nell knew Monk wouldn't create a scene with Otis Sprague in the room, but her stomach tightened a few seconds later when Sprague and his companion stood to leave. When they opened the door, they came face to face with Aksel Bernhart, Frieda Faye's cousin. Aksel and his twin sister, Annika, and their parents had moved to Tacoma from Wisconsin to build a dairy farm. At the sight of him, Nell's stomach unclenched.

Monk returned to his seat and looked Aksel up and down. Aksel returned the favor on his way over to the desk. "He bothering you, Miss Nell?" Aksel asked.

"Mr. Monk came in looking for coffee," Nell said. "The dining room is closed now, so I suggested he try the bar."

Monk put his hands on his knees, taking his time to stand up. His glance dismissed Aksel, but not Nell. "You remember what I said about that walk."

He moved away, and Nell shuddered. "Odious man." Then she turned to Aksel. "How are your ribs?" Until the previous week, Aksel had worked for the coal company, helping blast out stumps near Old Woman's Gulch. Unfortunately, one explosion sent a piece of wood flying into his ribs, breaking two of them.

"They's all right as long as I don't breathe." He handed Nell an envelope.

"What's this?" She lifted the flap with her finger and removed a sheet of paper. It read: *Mr. and Mrs. Ike Tanquist are having a necktie party in honor of Mrs. Tanquist's cousins, Annika and Aksel Bernhart, Sunday next at*

3:00 at their home. The honor of your presence is requested.

"It's a party." Aksel beamed. "Will you come, Miss Nell?"

Nell folded the sheet of paper and tucked it back in the envelope. She was aware that Aksel was starting to like her more than she wanted. "If I don't have to work." She smiled and slipped the invitation into her sewing bag. "What are you doing with yourself while your ribs heal?"

"Fishing. I can sell all I catch; I maybe won't go back to the coal company."

Nell laughed. "You might change your mind come December and January."

Aksel left soon after that, and Nell's thoughts returned to Thurlow Monk. She picked up the red collar she was crocheting for Pup. *He's coming to work with me from now on.*

Deciding on a dress for the necktie party was easy for Nell; she had but one that was new. The rest, she'd remade. The cloth to stitch up a necktie was harder. She knew the ties would be auctioned off to the young male guests, and the man who bought her tie would be her dinner partner. Nell wanted cloth no one had seen before. After rummaging through her scraps, she decided to see if Hildy's mother, Verdita Bacom, had something she could use. Mrs. Bacom's East Coast sister-in-law regularly sent the Bacoms packages of items for which she no longer had need, and the packages often included articles of clothing. Verdita was a skilled seamstress and made use of most of the garments; nevertheless, her scrap bag was always full.

"I'm so glad to see you. It's been ages," she said when Nell knocked on the Bacoms' kitchen door. Despite hard work and her husband's ill health, Verdita still looked like the young mother she'd been when the Bacoms moved to New Tacoma from Johnstown, Pennsylvania, some five years earlier. Her face was unlined, and her dark-brown hair showed no signs of gray. She welcomed Nell with a hug and gestured toward a chair.

Nell removed her hat and sat in the big old rocker. She'd always loved the Bacoms' kitchen with its squat stove, plants on a sill, and the perennial smell of baking bread. Her shoulders, stiff with tension, began to relax. "Where is everyone?"

"Dovie and some of her friends took a picnic up to the site of the new Central School, Reuben is at Scott's dairy, Ira is at the office, Chong went to Puyallup to visit a friend and . . ."

"Hildy is at the bakery," Nell finished.

Verdita laughed, sighed, and shook her head. "Hildy works too hard. She comes home exhausted."

"I know. I suggested she hire a helper, but she doesn't want someone else working in her kitchen."

Verdita filled two glasses with iced tea, piled a plate with cookies, and resumed her seat near her mending. Nell rocked and sipped her tea. For a few minutes, they talked about various things happening around town: Nell about the new blacksmith shop going up between the Halsteads' hotel and the Williams and Grainger Stables, and how a man named E. T. McKinstay, a representative for the Singer Sewing Machine Company, had been in town, and Verdita about the wheat warehouse being built behind the Blackwell Hotel and the railroad switchyard the Northern Pacific was building in front of the hotel.

Nell shook her head. "Poor Mrs. Blackwell. She will never have a moment's quiet."

"I think that's why she and William bought property on C Street. And there are so many hotels now. Besides, theirs is showing its age."

The old Seth Thomas clock ticked, and sunlight came through the window, falling on a noon mark. One of Dovie's chickens wandered into the kitchen and then back out again. Nell, feeling her eyelids growing heavy, decided she'd better state her business before she nodded off. "Frieda Faye and Ike are having a necktie party to introduce her cousins. I came to see if you have a piece of material I can make a tie out of."

"Are the ties for sale?" Verdita asked as she went for her sewing basket.

"I don't know. The invitation doesn't say. Hasn't Hildy been asked?"

"Yes, but she doesn't know, either."

Nell looked at the fabrics. A piece of brown toile with large begonias and cabbage roses on it caught her eye, and she giggled as she picked it up. When Verdita looked at her, she blushed. "Sorry. I'm sure — um — whatever this came from was lovely."

Verdita snorted. "I highly doubt it." She folded the cloth, and Nell put it in her pocket. As she started to leave, Dovie came in. "How's the school coming on?" Verdita asked.

"It's going to be huge." Dovie untied her bonnet strings and hung the bonnet on a hook. "And it's in the middle of an ugly cleared lot with nothing else around it. But there are separate staircases for boys and girls, so that will be good." She sat in the chair Nell had vacated and finished her mother's tea. "Do you think New Tacoma will ever have ice in summer?"

"Once, there was a plan to build a flume from the mountain to town that chunks of ice could be slid down." Nell smiled at the recollection. "Your sister and I were going to climb to where it began and ride on the blocks back to town. We didn't think about how cold it would be."

She left to the sounds of their laughter and met Hildy coming home. "I thought I'd see you robbing Mama's sewing basket," Hildy said. "Did you find anything good?"

"If by *good* you mean something really horrible, I did, and I'm going to make a tie so peculiar, the boys won't know what to think."

"Have you met the two cousins yet?"

"Yes. Frieda Faye brought the whole family down one day last week right at supper time. We were hard-pressed to stretch the meal."

"She doesn't miss a trick, does she?" Hildy shook her head. "I chose the prettiest fabric I could find because Samuel will hate it. Let me see yours."

When Nell pulled it out of her pocket, they looked at it and at each other and grinned.

"Mama is going to make mine, so it will be beautiful," Hildy said.

"You'll have to keep it where Samuel won't see it."

"I will, though I'd rather have him buy my tie and get to eat with him than anyone else. Gosh, I hope George doesn't bid on it."

"Let's help Ellen out and pretend your tie is hers."

"That's a wonderful idea. It just seems like the designs she's had on him since our school days have been wasted. Well, she's welcome to him, but what about you? He's a bit soft on you, too."

"Huh! Who wants a man who can't make up his mind?"

"Who do you want to buy your tie?"

An image of John Calhoun flashed in Nell's mind, but she hurriedly banished it. "I guess I don't care." She paused and turned her head. Faint music was coming from somewhere. "Listen. Do you hear that?"

Hildy nodded. "Mama told me Mrs. Bailey is giving piano lessons. She said if Mrs. Bailey can't make enough to support herself, she's likely to end up in a shack in Old Woman's Gulch. She's been hard-pressed since her husband died."

"It's awfully difficult for women, isn't it? We can do lots of things just as well as men. Remember Kezzie? She did sums better than all the boys in our class combined."

"My bakery still isn't making enough to live on, but maybe someday."

"I can't wait for my dress form to come. I'm going to talk to Mrs. Spooner about having a small display in her hat shop."

"And then you'll be in business."

"Not quite, but I will be able to maybe start taking some dress orders."

The two turned to watch a wagonload of gravel come slowly down the road. Several Chinese men followed, shoveling it into holes in the street. *I don't suppose I will ever know what happened to the men I saw headed for the dock after the Humpty Dumpty picnic,* Nell thought. *I hope they get home all right.* Turning to Hildy, she said, "I'd better get going. I promised to help Albina with her feathers, and Mrs. Halstead wants me to work afternoons and evenings."

"Aren't you afraid to walk home in the dark?"

Remembering Thurlow Monk's presence at the hotel, Nell gave an involuntary tremble. "That's why I have Pup. He's really good about sleeping under the desk.

And when it's quiet, I can crochet or comb out some of Albina's feathers."

"Is she selling a lot?"

"Actually, yes. I was surprised at what a good salesgirl she is."

Hildy repinned her hat, which was in danger of sliding off her heavy, fine hair. "I'd best be going, too. See you at the party."

Nell grinned. "And don't you dare give Samuel a sneak peek at your tie."

Hildy laughed, and they headed in different directions.

That evening and for the next few nights, things were quiet at the hotel. Once all the feathers were combed out and ready for sale, Nell designed and began work on a bow tie. With careful cutting, she managed to position a flower in the knot in the middle where the exaggerated folds on either side came together. She was admiring its ugliness when knuckles rapped on the desk. "Well, aren't you the industrious little lady."

Nell looked up to see Thurlow Monk.

His smile was more of a sneer. "First, I see you combing feathers, and now I see you making some kind of tie."

"Idle hands are the devil's workshop," Nell said. "Proverbs 16, verse 27."

Monk might have said something else, but

a man at the bar waved him over. Mercifully, he stayed there a while. When it was time for her to leave, Nell watched until Monk's attention was diverted before slipping out the door. Walking home, she avoided the few streetlights. She was daydreaming about a shop with pale-green walls, lots of mirrors, and piles of fabric when she made the turn toward home and saw a girl sitting on the step. Next to her was a ragged blanket with its corner tied in a knot, as if the blanket held unseen items. Pup ran ahead, and the girl stood up. Nell recognized her immediately. "Annie. What are you doing here?"

CHAPTER 17

As Annie stood in front of her, Nell couldn't believe how the girl had changed in such a brief period of time. She'd grown enough so her dress was too short and strained against budding breasts. Dirty strands of hair framed her face, and dark rings lined her eyes, one of which was bruised. She held one arm protectively and cried out in pain when Nell hugged her.

"Oh, Annie." Nell sat on the step and beckoned the girl closer. Pup gave Annie a cursory sniff and ran to piddle on a piece of wood. Nell patted the empty space beside her. "Sit down and tell me all about it."

Annie sat near Nell, but not close enough to be touched. "Pa wanted the money Mrs. McCarver gave me, money for a new dress." As she talked, tears made streaks through the dirt on her face. "I told him Mrs. McCarver said I had to have a new dress because this one is too small and she said I wasn't decent, only he wouldn't listen. He grabbed me by the arm, but I wouldn't give him the money, so he hit me. Then he pulled my arm behind my back until I dropped the coins. When he let me go, I tried to snatch 'em back, but he pushed me into the stove, and I fell. My arm and side hurt somethin' awful."

Pup ambled back to them and hunkered down near Nell, and she rubbed his ears absentmindedly. "What a perfectly dreadful thing."

Annie wiped her eyes and managed to blow her nose on the hem of her skirt. "I don't know what to do, Miss Nell. I don't want to go back home. But if I can't work, Pa'll just beat me some more."

"Of course you won't go back there!"

"But Pa is the only family I got. Where can I go?"

From a nearby snag, an owl hooted. Pup's ears lifted, but Nell didn't hear it. Nell pursed her lips, considering the situation. "Well, first, I'll get you something to eat. I bet you're hungry; I know I am. Then I'll send for Dr. Mrs. Clarke."

Annie looked at her feet. "I don't have any money for a doctor."

"Don't worry about that." Nell ignored a mental image of some of her savings going to pay the physician. "Come on. I'll help you indoors."

She stood and extended a hand, but Annie flinched and stepped back. "I can do it." She staggered a little, catching her balance against the house with her good arm. Pup trotted over, and she patted him.

"Pup doesn't like just anybody," Nell said. "But he likes you."

"That's nice," Annie said, with no real enthusiasm. Taking a deep breath, she followed Nell inside.

Amity, Josie, and Albina were away, visiting friends, and the house smelled of stale cooking odors. Nell looked in a pot on the stove and saw slightly congealed stew. She stoked up the fire to heat the food and had Annie sit at the table. "I don't think you'll be able to work for Mrs. McCarver anymore." Nell sat where she could watch both the stove and Annie. "Your pa'll go there looking for you, but I'm sure she can put him gone. Anyway, we'll send her a note and tell her what happened, and that you can't come back."

Annie listened, her body hunched over and her head drooping. Nell put her fury at Annie's father aside for the moment while pity for his daughter overwhelmed her. She checked the stew and stirred it, sliced and buttered some bread, took three bowls out of the cupboard, and filled them. "Eat slowly," she said to Annie, putting a bowl in front of her.

Annie picked up a piece of bread and dipped it in the stew's juices. She ate in small bites, chewing slowly and swallowing carefully. Gradually, some color returned to her face.

Nell gave a bowl to Pup and sat to dip her own piece of bread. "When did you last eat?"

"Yesterday, at Mrs. McCarver's. She had me clean the icebox and said I could have anything that looked like it was on its last legs. She's good to me that way." Annie put her spoon down. "I don't think I can finish this."

"That's all right. Pup will be happy to oblige, but don't tell Ma I fed him out of our bowls." Nell smiled and set the stew and last of Annie's bread on the floor under the table and out of the way. While the dog finished off the food, Nell had Annie lean over a bucket and poured warm, soapy water over the girl's hair. Using Albina's fine-tooth comb, she untangled most of the snarls, killing half a dozen fleas in the process. After drying the girl's hair, she braided it, tying the ends with pieces of blue ribbon. Then she helped Annie stand. "I'm going to take you outside and pour warm water on you for a quick wash. After that, you can lie down in my bed, and I'll fetch the doctor."

Annie bit her lip. "What if Pa comes here?"

"He won't, but, if he does, Pup will protect you. He knows you're my friend, and no one hurts my friends."

Annie winced occasionally when the soapy water hit a raw spot, and Nell made fast work of the bath before getting her dressed again and opening the bedroom door to gesture her in. Albina had an extra night-gown, and Nell helped the girl change. Annie's body revealed bruises and burns, both old and new, and Nell's anger grew. When the girl was in bed with Pup at her side to provide comfort and warmth, Nell put soap and water in a bucket and added Annie's clothes so they could soak. Grabbing her hat, she said, "Try to sleep a little. I shouldn't be gone long."

At the end of the block, halfway down the hill, she met a neighbor boy and pulled a coin out of her pocket. "There's one more like this if you will find Dr. Mrs. Clarke and bring her back to my house."

"You bet, Nell." He took off running. Nell returned home to wait.

Half an hour later, the doctor arrived and Nell led her to the bedroom. "This is Annie, Mrs. McCarver's house girl. Her father beat her. I don't know how badly."

Nell carried a chair from the kitchen into the bedroom for the doctor, who worked swiftly but gently, squeezing Annie's arms and legs. She ran her hands up and down Annie's ribcage, then turned the girl's head left and right. After that, she sat back, considering the situation. "She may have some cracked ribs, but, except for the broken arm, I think she's otherwise all right. Straightening and binding the arm is going to hurt, though." Dr. Clarke opened her medical bag, removed a roll of bunting, and set it on the bed. "Can you find me a piece of straight, flat wood I can use as a splint?"

Nell went outside to the woodpile and shifted logs until she discovered a broken stave. She smoothed off the splinters, then returned to the house and handed the length of wood to the doctor. Dr. Clarke nodded her approval. "Do you have any whisky on hand? I was called out today and used all my laudanum."

"Ma keeps a bottle, for pain and such. It's hidden so Pa won't find it."

"That'll help. See if you can get some down her."

While Nell pried up a floorboard and rooted out the bottle, Dr. Clarke ran her fingers more intently over Annie's broken arm under the girl's wary gaze. "You'll have to hold her," she said to Nell. "I'll work as quickly as I can, but the muscles need to be stretched and the bones put in place." She turned to her patient. "I'm sorry, Annie, but this is going to hurt, and you will have to be as brave as you can. The whisky will help with the pain."

When Nell held a cup to Annie's mouth, she sputtered and coughed but swallowed most of the liquor.

The doctor nodded. "That's enough. Now hold her arm, here." She showed Nell where to put her hands. "When I start, Annie will naturally fight you; she can't help it, so don't let go."

Nell did as told but looked away when Dr. Clarke started working the muscles. Annie screamed once and then passed out, and Nell felt her throat fill with bile.

"Don't be sick, now," the doctor said.

Nell took several deep breaths. "I won't."

The bedroom grew warm. A moth fluttered around, getting in the way, and Pup jumped down to the floor and lay on his side, occasionally panting. For Nell, time seemed to stop as the doctor stretched Annie's arm straight and repositioned the broken bones. When she slid the stave under Annie's arm and started wrapping it in place with the bunting, she looked up briefly and nodded. "That's it. You performed well."

"Will she be all right?"

"I think so — unless she has internal injuries. Once the splint comes off, the muscles will be very weak, and Annie will have to exercise her arm. That will hurt. But unless she *is* hurt internally, and we'll know that fairly soon, she should be up and about in a few days."

The two of them looked at each from either side of the bed. Now that she'd done the best she could for Annie, Nell let her anger boil to the surface. "I'm going to make her father pay."

"How?"

"By going to the saloon where he drinks all Annie's wages and demanding that he do so."

"You can't do that."

"Oh, yes I can, and I'll let every man there know that he beat his daughter to the brink of death in order to guzzle beer with her earnings. This might be a rough town, but men don't generally cotton to that kind of thing, especially the younger ones, who often have little sisters at home." She stopped talking when voices reached her ears. "Here's Ma and the girls. I'd better tell them about Annie's being here."

Dr. Clarke repacked and closed her medical bag and followed Nell out of the bedroom. They met Amity, Josie, and Albina coming in the door. At the sight of the doctor, Amity immediately looked concerned. "It's okay, Ma." Nell took her mother's hat and hung it on a peg. "Josie, do you remember Annie Penny, Mrs. McCarver's kitchen girl?" When Josie nodded, Nell continued. "Her pa beat her and broke her arm; she ran away, and I found her sitting on our doorstep."

"Oh, the poor thing," Amity said.

Albina narrowed her eyes. "Where is she?" Albina wasn't reconciled to sharing a room with Josie and continually wheedled Nell to give her back her old room.

"In the little bedroom I've been using." Nell sighed, looking at her younger sister. "Her bruises and burns are horrible, and she passed out from the pain when Dr. Clarke reset her broken arm. She needs to be in a room where she won't be disturbed."

Just as she'd counted on, Albina's countenance immediately changed from suspicion to sympathy. "I can carry in her food and help her eat."

"Would you, Beanie? That would be wonderful. I don't think she has a friend in the world."

"Well, I'll be her friend — her best friend. You can move back in with Josie, and Annie and I can share my room. She can live here, can't she, Ma?"

Amity drew in a breath. "Ah . . ."

"We'll have to decide that later." Nell laid a hand on her mother's arm. "Don't worry, it will all work out." She took her hat from a hook and put it on. "I have an errand to run. I'll be home in an hour or so."

Amity looked anxious. "This late? Can't it wait?"

"No, not this time." Nell hurried out the door before anyone could ask what the errand was, with Dr. Clarke following.

"Where are you going?" the doctor asked.

"I only know of one saloon in Old Tacoma, and I'm guessing Mr. Penny will be there."

"But, my dear, you can't go into a saloon."

"I need to strike while the iron is hot. I'll shame him in front of his friends, and they'll make him pay."

"In more ways than one, perhaps."

Nell caught the meaning, and she and the doctor smiled at each other. "Well," Dr. Clarke said, "if you insist on going there,

I'll go with you."

"Are you sure?"

"I spent my medical school years as the only female in a class of men. I know how to take care of myself. I may not have any drugs with me, but I have several sharp needles."

Nell's grin widened. "Then it's on to the Madhouse."

"The Madhouse?"

"That's the saloon in Old Tacoma. It's on a hill overlooking the water, hidden in some trees."

Accompanied by Pup, the women started along the hill trail to Old Tacoma. Just before the main track dropped down to the water, it made a *T,* and Nell turned left onto a narrow trail barely visible among the salal, ferns, and brooding fir trees. They heard music and raucous noise before they saw the tavern. Breaking into a clearing, Nell and Dr. Clarke stopped and stared at the windowless, ramshackle building huddling under cedar and maple trees. At the sight of the women, three men standing outside under what remained of a shake awning straightened up. One whistled through his teeth. Another shoved his hat to the back of his head, and the third merely stared.

Nell walked purposefully forward. "I'm

looking for Mr. Penny."

"Mr. Penny, is it?" The whistler laughed. "Don't know if the old lush is inside or not."

The others also laughed, and Nell brushed them aside. "Never mind. I'll find him myself."

She pushed between them and shoved at a dilapidated door. It swung back and ricocheted off a wall, startling those nearest to it. Inside the Madhouse, the smells of stale beer, old smoke, and sweat assaulted her. The sudden presence of two ladies caused consternation among the drinkers. A fiddle player stopped halfway through his song, and a blowsy blonde woman slid off a man's lap, falling on the floor. No one paid any attention, and she sat there with her mouth open. Nell, with Pup beside her and Dr. Clarke close behind, paused to let her eyes adjust to the dimness. The room grew silent, and she waited until the men started to fidget as if uncomfortable in the silence before she spoke. "I'm looking for Annie Penny's father."

"Wha'cha want 'im for?" The question came from an Indian woman who leaned against the makeshift bar, arms crossed. She looked more curious than hostile.

"He owes me money for the doctor."

The room erupted in laughter, and Nell

flushed. A man sitting on the back two legs of his chair righted it to all four and stood. "I'm Roy Penny, and I don't believe I've had the pleasure of creating a reason requiring your need for a doctor." The polite words didn't match his unpleasant face with its pockmarks and crooked, broken nose.

Men slapped each other and whooped. Nell waited, not moving, until they stopped, and another uncomfortable silence fell. Her eyes drilled into Roy Penny's narrow ones. "You beat your daughter almost to death so you could take her pitiful wages and come here to drink with your" — Nell paused and looked around the room — "cronies. I need money to pay the doctor who's trying to save her life."

The drinkers looked at Roy Penny, and at each other, and muttered uneasily. Penny put on a fake smile. "I may have smacked her once or twice, but she's my daughter, and the money she earns goes to maintaining our home. She was tryin' to hold out on me."

Aware that a soft voice was often more effective than a loud one, Nell pitched her voice low. "Mrs. McCarver gave Annie money for a decent dress. Annie can no longer go outside because she has nothing to wear." Nell knew mentioning Mrs. Mc-

Carver's name would carry weight. "Mrs. McCarver told Annie she couldn't come back until she was properly clothed. Mrs. McCarver didn't want the embarrassment, you see, though apparently you don't care."

"Now see here . . ." Moving quickly, Penny grabbed Nell's arm. Pup immediately leaped forward and caught the man around the ankle, biting hard enough to make him cry out. When Penny tried to shake the dog off, Nell hit him across the jaw as hard as she could. Penny staggered, and Nell called Pup off. Her hand started throbbing, but she refused to show any discomfort.

"Don't you dare try to treat my dog the way you do your daughter. I want money for the doctor I had to call, and I want money to feed and clothe Annie."

Penny recovered his balance and sneered. "And who's going to make me?"

"The city marshal."

"Howard Carr?" Penny laughed.

Nell continued as if she hadn't heard him. "And Marshal Fulmer. Neither man cottons to child beaters. But here's the rub, Mr. Penny. I know most of the businessmen in both Old and New Tacoma, and I will ask them not to employ you. I will also ask the various ministers to preach, and sing hymns in front of your home, night and day.

Of course, you could try to leave town — try, I say — because you *can't* leave until we see if Annie will live or not." Behind her, Dr. Clarke made a huffing sound, which Nell ignored. "Murderers hang."

"Give her the damn money, Penny," someone yelled. Others chimed in with the same advice. Scowling, Penny reached into his pocket and pulled out some coins. He held them out to her, contempt in his face.

Nell made a point of poking at the cash with a finger and looking it over before taking what she felt would be enough. "You best watch out there, little girl," Penny hissed. "I got my eye on you." He staggered backward as someone grabbed him by the collar.

"And I'll have my eye on you." Nell was amazed to see Thurlow Monk holding Roy Penny's shirt and twisting the man's right arm behind him.

"You best get along out of here, Little Miss Counter Gal," Monk said. "It's late."

Nell backed up, straight into Dr. Clarke. Pup, however, seemed reluctant to leave the ankle he'd bitten. He growled once in Penny's direction before following the women out of the Madhouse. They hurried down the track, not stopping to rest until they reached the *T.*

"Can you really do the things you threatened to do?" Dr. Clarke asked.

"I could try." Nell laughed. "How much do I owe you?" She jingled the coins in her pocket before pulling them out. "Take what you're owed; there's plenty."

The doctor's eyes twinkled, and she laughed and shook her head. "And I thought I stood up well to the men at medical school." She fanned her face with her hat. "That was an impressive performance, Nell, very impressive."

CHAPTER 18

By the Fourth of July, things on the reservation had settled down. Dr. McCoy had opened a practice in town, and the Puyallups seemed to enjoy the holiday as much as everyone else. June's erratic weather had settled into warm days and nights. For a time, strands of white clouds floated lazily across the sky, creating the appearance of blue and white stripes. But then they disappeared, and the temperature climbed, making people restless and occasionally irritable and making sleeping difficult. On one particularly hot night, Nell tossed and turned in her stuffy bedroom until she finally gave up. "Come on, Pup," she whispered to the dog, who lay panting on the floor. Together they went outside to sit on the step, taking care not to wake Annie, who slept on a pallet near the stove. Pup quit panting, and Nell's feet cooled on the soil as she flapped her nightgown up and down, letting fresh air underneath. As they had for the past several days, her thoughts turned to John Calhoun.

She had been at work, reading the "Local Briefs" column in the *Tacoma Daily Ledger,* where the news seemed either repetitious — drunken brawls in the streets and fires in the shops — or bad: a giant tree falling on a corral of cattle waiting to be shipped and killing them all, and what seemed like daily accounts of the construction on the Tacoma Hotel. "I suppose it's just a matter of time before the Halstead Hotel is sold and I have to find another job," she'd said to Pup. She had folded the paper and laid it on the corner of the desk for someone else to read when the door opened and Albina's class-mate, Billie Yoder, came in long enough to hand her a sheet of paper folded and sealed with red wax. Nell hadn't gotten over her thrill at receiving mail, and she used a knife to carefully slit it open.

Dear Nell, her friend Sarah had written, *Dr. Culver says the weather coming our way from San Francisco will continue to be good, so I am having a little gathering at one o'clock this Friday. Mother's garden is looking its best, and with luck we can have lemonade and cookies under her apple tree. She and I are making rugelach and mandelbrot, which are very popular in Jewish families. Do come. I am asking Hildy, Ellen, Kezzie, and Fern, so it will be just like old times. Sarah.*

She refolded the paper and sighed.

"Is anything wrong, Miss Nell?" Fred's footsteps behind her were so soft, she hadn't heard him approach.

"I've been invited to a party on Friday," Nell said. "I have to see if Mrs. Halstead will let me have the afternoon off. I hate to ask, though, since she just gave me an evening to take my sister to the Humpty Dumpty picnic."

Fred handed her a cup of coffee and leaned on the desk, looking thoughtful. "Well now, Miss Nell, we just need to think on what to do, but you've made yourself mighty important to the family."

Nell laughed. "I certainly have tried."

"Might be, if you can find someone to sit in for you, Mrs. Halstead would agree."

Nell's eyes lit up. "That's a good idea, and I have just the person — my sister Josie. She owes me more favors than I can count."

Walking home later, Nell planned her strategy.

"Josie," she said the following morning while washing breakfast dishes, "you never told me if Mrs. McCarver noticed how nice you looked when you played the piano during her at-home."

"Oh, yes." Josie wiped a plate and put it on a shelf. "She said I looked as nice as a professional."

"That's lovely, isn't it." Nell hummed a little as she rinsed a cup. "You know, I was remembering how you begged me to leave Steilacoom the same day we arrived, and we did. Do you remember?"

"Of course I do. For sure and certain, I don't want to ever go there again."

"Certainly not. You never have to, but . . ." She handed Josie the cup. "I do favors for you, so you have to do some for me, sometimes. That's only fair."

Amity looked up from where she was sewing a button on Obed's shirt. "Do you need Josie to do something for you, Nell?"

"Yes, Ma." Nell dried her hands, sat down, and fished Sarah's invitation from her pocket. Handing it to her mother, she said, "Fred thinks if I have someone to take my place at the front desk, the Halsteads will be more likely to let me have the afternoon off."

"Can't one of them do it?"

"Well, the sons are trying to settle their own businesses so they can take over the hotel until the Tacoma Hotel opens and they decide whether or not to close, and the oldest daughter just had a baby and it's colicky."

While Nell twisted her hands in her apron, Amity looked at Josie. "Josie, since this involves you, you had better sit down and listen." Josie took a seat at the table near where Albina and Annie sat, listening with interest while they cleaned feathers. "Do you know what favor Nell needs?" Amity asked.

"No, Ma."

"Well, Nell would like you to sit at the hotel's front desk this Friday so she can go to a party."

Josie's eyes widened. "Oh, my."

"Do you think you could do that?"

"What would I have to do?"

"I'll have everything ready for you, so it will be easy." Nell took her sister's hands. "You sit at the desk, with a big book in front of you. If someone wants a room, you turn the book to face them and hand them a pen. They sign in by a number where there is no other signature, and you give them the key that has a tag matching that number. The keys are on hooks behind the desk and are all labeled."

"That doesn't sound too hard," Josie said slowly.

"It isn't, and Fred promised he will be close by if you have any problems."

"Problems?"

Nell hurried to cover her mistake. "Just in case. I've never had one, but it's best to know you can call Fred."

"What if someone asks me a question?"

"You answer it to the best of your ability. For example, if someone asks you where something is, and you don't know, you smile and say, "I'm afraid I don't know, but if you step down the street to Mr. Hohenschnild's dry goods store, I am sure he can help you." When Josie still looked hesitant, Nell added, "And, of course, you will be paid for your time."

"All right." Josie beamed. "I can save the money for a piano."

"Thank you, Josie." Nell kissed her sister's cheek. "I'll let Mrs. Halstead know."

Persuading Josie had been easier than Nell anticipated, but she wasn't looking forward to approaching Mrs. Halstead. *I don't know why,* Nell thought as she climbed the stairs to the family's apartment. *She's much younger than Mrs. Blackwell or Mrs. McCarver.* Nevertheless, she had to calm the butterflies in her stomach. Standing outside the door to the family's suite, she caught bits of conversations going on and took a deep breath. *If I don't ask, I* can't *go to Sarah's.*

"Well, now, dear, I just don't know," Mrs. Halstead said after she'd steered Nell to a seat and offered her a cup of coffee. "I can't be on hand should problems arise, what with the baby and all." Lowering her voice, she added, "And Jeanette is still trying to recover from Jacob's passing, and she takes most of my time."

Nell raised her chin, not caring for the implied insult to Josie's competence. "I am sure my sister is perfectly capable of sitting at the front desk for a few hours," she said.

Mrs. Halstead must have realized how her words sounded, because she hurried to make amends. "Yes, of course. Being your sister, she would be quite able, it's just that . . ."

Just that what, Nell wondered but remained silent and kept a steady gaze on her employer's face. Finally, uncomfortable with the quiet, Mrs. Halstead agreed. "As you pointed out, Fred will be here, and it is only for a few hours."

"Thank you." As Nell stood and smoothed her skirt, Jeanette called from the bedroom, asking for a cup of tea. Mrs. Halstead sighed, and Nell added, "I'll see myself out."

The following Friday, Nell laid three dresses on her bed and stood back, just as

Albina wandered in. "What are you doing?" Albina asked.

"Today is Sarah's garden party, and I'm trying to decide which dress to wear."

"Can I come?" Albina sat on Nell's pillow and crossed her legs.

"Were you invited?"

"Maybe Sarah forgot." Albina sounded hopeful.

"What about Annie?"

"No one knows Annie lives here."

"Well, I don't think you *were* invited, and you have your shoes on my spread." Nell tossed two hats on top of the dresses and eyed the garments critically.

Her sister shifted position so her feet hung over the edge of the bed. "It's so much trouble to be forever lacing and unlacing them."

"I know, but I don't want my blankets getting dirty."

"What will you be doing at the party?"

"Sarah's mother has a lovely yard, and we will walk around and admire her flowers and have snacks and talk."

"I can do that."

Nell smiled and shifted the hats. "Of course you can, but this party is just for our school friends. How about if we do something special on your birthday?"

"You can't have a garden party in winter."

"No, but you can have a hayride out into the country, and a bonfire picnic. Now, which dress and hat do you think?"

Albina glanced at them. "The blue gingham with the little blue flowers and the straw hat with the bow to match."

"I like those, too." Nell rehung the other two dresses and sat on the bed. "How are your feathers coming?"

"I have lots more chicken feathers, mostly white."

"Did you comb them clean?"

"Not yet. I don't like to do that. They smell."

"Aren't you enjoying making your own money?"

"Yes, but . . ." Albina pulled a piece of loose thread from the coverlet, twisted it between her fingers, and tried to look pathetic.

"Well, let me know when you have them cleaned and I'll help you dye them. I thought we could mix some of the yellow with blue to make a nice green." Nell left Albina sulking and went to find Josie.

"How nice you look," she said to her sister, who was busy winding her long hair into a chignon.

"Do you keep your hat on in the hotel?"

"No. There's a hook on the wall behind the desk."

Josie took a deep breath and picked up her hat. "Have a nice time at the party."

"I will. Now, don't be nervous, just enjoy yourself. Remember, Fred can help you with anything you might need." Nell kissed her sister and waved her off at the door.

Back in her bedroom, Albina was sleeping sideways on the bed, her feet hanging off the side. She woke when Nell came in. "I like the rickrack trim you put on Josie's dress," she said.

"A lady dropped it on the floor of her room," Nell said. "I found it after she was gone."

"You find lots of things, don't you?"

"Not really, mostly just newspapers." Nell removed her dress and corset cover. In the kitchen she loosened the corset strings, pulled off her chemise, and filled a basin with water. After a quick wash, she put on a clean chemise and retied the corset.

"Do boys have to wear as many under-clothes as we do?" Albina asked while Nell put on a fresh corset cover.

"Not much more than a union suit." Nell sat on the bed to change out of her work shoes.

"Why do we have to wear so many

things?"

"I don't know. I guess after Eve ate the apple, she just began covering up with all the leaves she could find."

Nell intended for her sister to laugh, but, instead, Albina looked pensive. "Annie doesn't have friends because her pa made her work all the time, but why doesn't Josie have school friends like you do?"

"Hmmm." Nell pulled her dress over her head and started buttoning it. "I guess it's because she didn't go to school very long."

"Why?"

"Because she had trouble reading."

"Like I do with multiplications sometimes?"

Pinning on her hat, Nell considered the question. "Most people easily learn the things that interest them. I think, when you have a ledger for your feather business, mathematics will start to make sense. For Josie, playing the piano is the thing she loves most, so it's easy for her. Probably not so much for you or me."

Albina swatted at a bee that had found its way in. "I wonder what Indiana can do."

Nell held back her uncharitable comment, saying instead, "She is a really good mother and wife. Now, how do I look?" She held her arms out and twirled around.

"You look beautiful."

Nell kissed her sister. "Thank you, love. And if you have some feathers clean tonight, I have been saving onion skins to make yellow dye."

Sarah and her family lived on E Street, in a house that had at one time been part of the Girls' Institute. A lady named Mrs. Bailey started the school, importing German, French, and Spanish language teachers from England. Before she attended public school, Fern had studied voice at the institute. By that time, Mrs. Bailey was gone, and a Mrs. Williams was in charge. "Schools don't open and close so quickly in Virginia," Fern had said to Ellen, Nell, and Hildy the day she started public school. Hildy's reply was, "The new Annie Wright School will no doubt offer many of the same classes. What a shame you're a little too old to attend."

Remembering sweet-tempered Hildy's remark, Nell grinned. She was still smiling when a male voice called her name, and she turned around to see George behind her.

"Good afternoon, Nell." He tipped his hat. "Where are you going?"

"To Sarah's. She's having a garden party."

"I'm headed that way myself. Perhaps we can walk together." Without waiting for an answer, he took Nell's elbow and matched his steps to hers.

Oh dear, Nell thought, as she felt his sticky hand. *There goes my sleeve. He'll get it all wrinkly.* She had never figured out why she didn't care for George; she really had no reason not to. True, when he was uncomfortable, his face turned red and blended with his freckles and red hair until his head looked like a giant tomato. But it wasn't just that. "The truth is," she once told Hildy, "he's just so unctuous." At which Hildy had laughed and said, "Goodness, what a word."

Now, Nell picked up her pace, saying, "How are things with your studies."

George beamed. "The Reverend Mr. Oakley has agreed to tutor me."

"That's wonderful."

"Yes, it is. If I can learn enough to pass tests for the freshman and sophomore courses, it will mean I can enter college as a junior."

"Do you have a school picked out yet?"

"No. Mama has family in Oregon, and she is looking for a Bible school there so I can board with relatives."

"Well, that sounds very practical."

"I guess. Say, Nell," George tightened his grip on Nell's arm and pulled them both to a stop. "The church is having a strawberry social after services Sunday. Would you like to come?" He looked so hopeful; Nell's spirits plummeted. *Thank goodness for the hotel,* she thought.

"I'm sorry, George, but I have to work. Mrs. Halstead was very reluctant to let me have this afternoon off, so I dare not ask for more time." She paused. "Why not ask Ellen? She's very interested in church matters. I'm sure she'd love to go." Nell started walking again, forcing George to release her arm.

Sarah's house was recognizable by its fenced yard and a large dogwood tree shedding the last of its blooms, and Nell increased her speed. "Here's my stop, George. Thanks for the escort. I know Ellen will keep us all up to date on your studies." She pushed the gate open before he could reach around her and hurried down the path toward the house.

The front door stood open, and the other guests milled around, talking and laughing. Seeing her, Sarah hurried to pull her inside. "I'm so glad you could come, Nell. I hope you don't have to hurry off."

Nell hugged her friend. "I am, too, and Josie is sitting in for me until one of the Halstead men takes over, so I have the whole afternoon free."

Sarah tugged on her arm. "Come on, everyone, here's Kezzie coming up the walk. Let's all go outside."

Nell stepped aside to join Hildy, and together they followed the others. Looking at the rough log fence bordered by beds of flowers that enclosed the yard, Hildy said, "The paper is always talking about Mrs. Wilkeson's flowers, but I think yours are just as pretty."

"Mother says we have lots of lovely things growing wild in the woods. Look." Sarah lifted a branch of small white blooms. "This is serviceberry. The flowers are almost gone, but soon the plant will be covered with berries that make the most delicious pies. And this pretty purple flower is harvest lily. Mama planted it here, next to this plant Mr. Pincus sent her. He knows she likes flowers, so he sent it down from Steilacoom. It's called Scotch twisting broom."

"Mama got one of those a few years ago," Hildy said. "I love the yellow color."

Fern sneezed. "Oh dear, excuse me," she said. Her words were followed by another sneeze. "They have a very — uh — pungent smell, don't they? I don't believe our flowers in Virginia are so very — uh . . ."

"Pungent?" Hildy said.

"Exactly."

Nell poked Hildy and rolled her eyes.

"Perhaps we should move away from it," Sarah said. She led the way across the grass to a table and chairs set up under an apple tree. Behind the tree, the last of the rhododendron petals had fallen and lay among daisies nodding their heads in the mild breeze. Nell took a seat in the shade and unpinned her hat. Before Fern could say anything, Hildy did the same, saying how good the fresh air felt. Seeing her sister's friends sitting around the table, Sarah's sister, Esther, came across the yard carrying a tray. She put it on the table and hurried back to the house, returning in seconds with a two-tiered dessert stand loaded with pastries.

"What a beautiful dish," said Ellen.

"Thank you. It's French. Mama found it in Portland when she was there last winter."

"What was she doing in Portland?" Hildy asked.

"Visiting her sister." Sarah lifted a pitcher of lemonade off the tray and began filling glasses. "Hildy, Mama will want to know what you think of her cookies."

Hildy grinned. "Which one is which?"

"The twisty ones are *rugelach,* and the

others are called *mandelbrot.* You bake them twice."

"Hmm." Hildy picked up a rugelach and bit into it, closed her eyes, and chewed. "I love cinnamon," she said after she'd swallowed.

"Me, too," said Nell, "but the *mandelbrot* is lovely."

"Nell." Fern picked up her glass of lemonade. "Did I see George walking you here?"

At the question, Ellen's head snapped up.

Nell kept her tone offhand. "Yes, I met him a couple blocks down on E Street, and he said he was coming this way." Without thinking, she tried to smooth the wrinkles his hand had left in the sleeve of her dress.

Kezzie laughed. "Well, he must be sweet on you. As soon as you were out of sight, he turned and started back down the hill."

"He'd better set his sights elsewhere, because I'm going to be a dressmaker."

At Nell's indignation, the others also laughed, and Ellen forced a smile. "Did I actually hear that you were on the wharf road without a hat a while back?" she said.

Dash it all, Nell thought. *I've done nothing to encourage George, and now Ellen will be surly all afternoon.* "Well," she said, trying to make light of things, "I lost my bonnet on the prairie that day and had to come home without it, so you may well have."

"You lost it on the prairie? How did you get from the prairie to the wharf?"

"It's a long story."

"We have plenty of time, don't we, Sarah?"

Hildy's foot nudged hers as Nell felt her face turning red. "I went to the graveyard," she said. "When the twins were sick, Ma sent Josie, Albina, and me to stay with our older sister, Indiana. We were still there when they died and were buried. I rented a horse to ride out to their graves. Then the horse tossed me, and I lost my bonnet."

Oblivious to Ellen's pique, Sarah said, "But how did you get to the wharf?"

"I was on the ground in Mr. Scott's cow pasture, unconscious, when two Puyallup Indians found me and took me to the gathering at James Lick's potlatch. When I woke up, a lady named Cheeta and her daughter Piney helped me."

"I know Piney," Hildy said. "Cheeta's brother is a friend of Samuel's, and he brought her to the bakery once."

"Mrs. Stair would be shocked, Hildy," Fern said. "Who brought her to the bakery, Samuel or her brother?"

Hildy laughed. "She must have been a good teacher for you to remember that. The brother, of course. I can't remember his name."

"Girls, please," Kezzie said. "This conversation is going all around Robin Hood's barn. Nell, what happened after you woke up?"

"Cheeta bathed my head with cold water and fed me Indian bread, and then she found a canoe and let me off at the wharf in front of the Blackwell Hotel. I walked home from there. It was dreadfully hot, and my head really hurt. The only good thing is, it was just an old bonnet I lost and not a nice hat." Nell laughed and took another cookie. "What has everyone else been doing lately?"

The conversation turned to Fern's trip to Seattle and Kezzie's mother's need for spectacles, and the doings of their various friends and neighbors. A hummingbird buzzed in and out of the foxgloves, and Sarah's cat appeared from under a fern to watch it. Sarah's little sister, Abigail, brought a doll out and sat under a maple tree, where the cat soon joined her. Hildy talked about her dough kneading machine, and Nell told the girls about receiving her first tip. Then Ellen mentioned her church work and it gave Nell a chance to redeem herself.

"While we walked here, George mentioned the strawberry social. I think they're shorthanded. Are you helping out?"

"I hadn't thought about it, but I certainly can," Ellen said.

"I have a feeling George would be very grateful. He certainly seems awfully connected to church activities." Nell took another cookie and pretended disinterest, and Hildy smiled.

"How is your needlework coming?" she asked.

"Slow but steady."

"As in, 'wins the race'?"

Everyone laughed, and the conversation shifted to Sarah's hanging her artwork in her father's shop and other topics of general interest. Esther brought out more lemonade, and, when the sun was low enough to create new shadows, the girls rose from their chairs.

"This has been lovely, Sarah," Nell said as she rescued her hat from the grass and re-pinned it. The others added their thanks, and everyone helped carry their glasses and napkins inside. Hildy left first, saying she had to set her dough for the next day. Ellen, Kezzie, and Fern followed, with Nell behind them. When they turned toward their own homes, she waved and headed down Ninth Street and then up Cliff Avenue to where a small secluded bluff overlooked the bay. She and Hildy had found it years before, and, though the new Steele Hotel wasn't far away, the secluded clearing was still hidden. With a happy sigh, she removed her hat and unpinned her hair. A wind coming off the water blew it upward, cooling her neck. She leaned over, undid her shoes, and pulled them off, then sat on the mat of moss with her skirt hiked to her knees. "Oh, lovely, lovely," she whispered, leaning forward slightly to see which ships were coming in. "There's the side-wheeler *Alaskan,* and the steamboat *Emma Hayward,* and there's the *Fairy.* Goodness, she's a long way from home. I wonder why she's so far from San Francisco?"

Nell was so busy watching people come ashore and cargoes being unloaded, she failed to hear someone pushing the foliage aside until an amused-sounding voice said, "May I join you?"

"Land sakes!" Nell pulled her bare legs under her skirts and made a grab for her hair. "What are you doing here? This is a secret spot."

Without waiting for an answer, John Calhoun sat next to her. "Not so very secret since yon hotel went up. Here, let me help you." He caught at the wisps of hair blowing near his face and handed the strands to Nell.

"Thank you," she mumbled through a mouth full of pins, and the strands quickly became a braid that she wound around her head and fastened under her hat. "If you'll turn your head, I can put my shoes back on."

Once she was settled, John said, "What do you mean by a 'secret spot'?"

"Hildy and I found it years ago, and no one else ever seems to come here."

John pulled his knees up and wrapped his arms around them. "Aye. That's why I like it, too." They were quiet for a moment, and then he looked at Nell. "You must know every ship on the bay."

"Not all, just the ones who regularly make port, those in the Mosquito Fleet and such." She changed the subject. "Did you bring the Scotch broom plants to Sarah's mother?"

"Aye. I like to see it; it reminds me of the hills back home."

"Where's that?"

"Scotland."

Nell propped her own arms on her drawn-up legs and turned to look at him. "Oh, yes, you mentioned Aberdeenshire, I think. I guess that explains the accent."

"You mean this accent?" John said, sounding like a proper Englishman. "Or this one?" The second question sounded distinctly Swedish.

"That's wonderful! How do you do that?" He reverted to his normal Scots burr. "Just a God-given skill, I guess."

"Hmm." Nell resumed looking at the bay. "How can a person tell who's the real you?"

John lost his teasing tone as he looked intently at her. "Those that I want to know will know." Their silence grew awkward, and he added, "Will you do me a favor?"

"What favor is that?"

"Will you tell me when you see a strange ship come in?"

"Why?"

"It will help me with some work I'm doing." He pulled something from his pocket and handed it to Nell.

"What's this?" She turned it over in her hands. The object was a thick, triangular-shaped chunk of glass.

"It's a Porroprism." He took it from her hands and held it up to her face. "Look."

"Goodness gracious." Nell leaned forward. Through the glass, the ships bobbing about seemed so close, she gave a start when men dropped a large crate. "I can see what's on the deck and all the people's faces and everything." She laughed as she took hold of the prism. "I can even see the gulls close up, if I want to." After a minute, she handed it back. "Is that what you do with them? Watch for strange ships and such?"

"Aye."

Before he could say anything more, a mill whistle sounded. They jumped up at the same time and bumped into each other. John grabbed Nell's arms, preventing her from falling into a prickly Oregon grape bush.

"Thank you." She regained her balance and, in what she thought later was a ridiculous gesture, put a hand to her heart.

He continued to hold her arms, and she caught her breath at his being so close. His gaze roamed her face, lingering on her eyes and stopping at her lips. He raised one hand to a wayward strand of hair and twisted it in his fingers. "Beautiful." It was barely a whisper. He ran his thumb down the side of her face and then pulled her tightly against him. Their lips met. Softly, tentatively at first and then firmly. They drew briefly apart, and his arms went under her shawl and around her waist. His body was firm and hard against her chest and legs and, when their lips met again, Nell's arms held him close. Then a train rushed by on a track below, and its noise brought her back to her senses.

"I'd best get home," she said, pulling away.

John let his arms fall to his sides. "You go on. I think I'll stay here a while." He took a small sketch pad from a pocket.

"Of course." She didn't move.

"People seeing us leave together would get the wrong idea."

"Yes — well — goodbye, then."

Nell hurried away down the path, checking her hair and making sure her hat was in place. And trying to catch her breath and still her heart.

Thinking about John as she sat on the step in the gentle night air, Nell remembered how her body reacted while she was in his arms, and how solid and safe they felt, especially when they kissed, and how his lips were both firm and soft, and how hers seemed to open of their own accord. In that one kiss, she knew what lay behind his dark intensity. And then, when her thoughts turned to Dr. Clarke's promise to tell her about babies, she had to force them away.

A mother raccoon and three kits appeared, and an owl hooted its interest. Nell wondered if she should shoo the raccoons away and let the owl go hungry, or let one kit be sacrificed. *Not fair to have to decide.* From there, she remembered the new hotels going up and the Halstead family's plans to sell theirs, having to find a job of which her mother would approve, and how much more money she needed to earn before she could buy a sewing machine. But memories of John Calhoun kept intruding, and finally she called Pup and returned to bed.

CHAPTER 19

After a spurt of warm, sunny days through most of July, the August weather once again turned capricious. Nell's days at the hotel dwindled while the Halsteads tried to decide whether or not to auction off the building and its contents. Her main source of income had become the needlework Mrs. Spooner allowed her to sell at Spooner's Millinery Shop, for which Mrs. Spooner took a percentage, of course. Fortunately, Obed's leg had healed, and he was working, so, except for Mrs. Spooner's commission, any income made there was Nell's own. Still, as she said to her mother, "I am so far away from having enough money for my sewing machine, I sometimes feel like giving up."

"I wish we could help," Amity said. "But why not just enjoy the rest of the summer and look for something in the fall?"

"I have to work as much as I can, but I

think I'll be home a lot more," Nell said.

She was working in the vegetable garden when a voice she recognized as belonging to Fern called out a cheery good morning. Since spring, Nell had only seen Fern the one time at Sarah's tea. She stood and turned to greet her friend with a smile. "Fern — and Ellen. How nice to see you. Fern, are you enjoying the warm weather? Is it more like Virginia?"

"Yes, but it does get hotter in Virginia, so this is nice."

Nell pulled off her gloves and dusted her skirt. She was dumbfounded that Fern had actually found something in Tacoma that she preferred to her former home. "What brings you here? Would you like to come in and sit down?"

Ellen took over the conversation. "I think not, but thanks, anyway. We're here to invite you to a picnic."

Ellen had hosted her first picnic when she was twelve. It had been a berry-picking picnic at the burn southwest of town near Gallagher Gulch. After that, she had a different kind of picnic every August.

"Promise me no bears?" Nell said.

"I've never forgiven that bear for eating all our berries." Ellen scowled; Fern smiled, and Nell laughed. "The tide will be low in the afternoon," Ellen continued, "so it's going to be on the beach at the almost military reservation."

"Point Defiance? That's a long way to carry food."

Before Ellen could reply, Fern spoke up. "Why do old-timers call it the Reservation That Never Was?"

"Because when Charles Wilkes explored here, he thought it would be a good place for the military to keep an eye on the comings and goings of ships in the Sound," Nell said.

"Well, that explains it." Fern smiled. "You certainly seem to know a lot of history."

"I do when it's about here, but not so much about other places."

"Anyway," Ellen interrupted them. "We won't have to carry the food. Father rented boats from Mr. Wren, and we're going to row."

"What fun." Nell's brown eyes lit up. "Who's coming?"

"Well, we will have three boats, so I'm asking you and Hildy for one boat. George and me for the second, and Fern and Frank Clarke for the third."

"Not Sarah?"

Ellen stiffened. "I'm taking corn on the cob and potatoes to bake in a fire. The boys are going to fish and dig clams, and Sarah doesn't eat shellfish."

"She eats salmon, though. I've heard her say how much she likes it."

"But if we don't get any fish, she wouldn't have anything to eat."

Nell refrained from saying *you don't fool me; it's because she's Jewish. How mean.* Sarah's family was related to Abe Gross, and her father was a tailor. Ellen was happy to shop at Gross's and attend Sarah's tea party, but not to socialize much with the family.

"What a shame. Remember the painting she did of us at the first picnic? She could make sketches."

Ellen's unhappy expression plainly said she hadn't considered that.

Looking mildly anxious, Fern broke in. "In Virginia, we eat littleneck clams and blue crab. They're terribly good. I miss Virginia food just awfully."

Nell took a deep breath and let it slowly out. "Well, anyway, when is it?"

"Saturday. Mr. Wren is bringing the row-boats to the Hanson and Ackerson Mill at ten o'clock."

Ellen still looked irritated, so Nell decided to turn on the charm. "It's so good of you to do this every year. I certainly know what a lot of work you go to. Lucky for me, it's a day away from the hotel. I'll be there for sure and certain. Would you like me to make a pie?"

Ellen unbent a little. "That would be lovely."

Fern said, "Back home we had an apple tree called Virginia Beauty. Maybe someday, Washington will have a tree named after it."

"Maybe." Nell's friends were beginning to wear her out, and she had to force a smile. When they left, their heads bent together as they talked, she let out a long sigh of relief. *Phooey on Virginia Beauty. And since none of our apples would pass Fern's muster, I'll just make blackberry.* She went inside to change for work, and her disposition immediately improved. *I'm so glad I don't have to stay home every day. But, if the hotel does get bought out, and I don't get rehired, August will likely be a very long month. I know it's mean, but I hope no one wants either it or the furnishings.*

She was fretting about this in the early afternoon when Hildy walked over to the hotel carrying a bag of cookies. Hildy sat at a table near the front desk, and Nell went to the kitchen to give a cookie to Fred and fetch cups of coffee. "Why isn't Samuel going to Ellen's picnic?" she asked as she

335

rejoined her friend.

Hildy laughed and shook her head. "Ellen got lucky. Samuel's on the coast, working."

Nell knew Hildy's beau worked for the Department of Agriculture, reporting on timber and logging, but she didn't understand what Hildy meant by Ellen being lucky. When she asked, Hildy said, "You know how Ellen feels about his Indian blood." She blew on her coffee, looking more amused than annoyed.

"She's asked Frank Clarke. Everyone knows he has designs on Katherine Tuttle." Nell smiled and nodded to a couple going out the hotel door.

Hildy shrugged. "Probably just to make George jealous."

"I don't think he'll care. Try as I might to push them together, George has never shown any interest in Ellen."

"Like I've said before, ever since he moved here, he's had eyes on either you or me. You know that."

"Well, he'd better shift his eyes elsewhere, is all I can say."

"You need a beau. That would discourage him."

"There just isn't anyone I fancy," Nell said, but she knew it wasn't true. "Say, will you do me a favor?"

"Of course."

"Would you ask Samuel if he's found out anything more about John Calhoun?"

"Who's he, exactly? Do you know?"

"That's just it, I *don't* know, but it seems as if I run into him all over the place. And he's always asking questions or talking to someone. Annie says he draws pictures of practically everything he sees — ships, people, all sorts of things."

"Who's Annie?"

Nell sipped her coffee, then grinned. "That brings me to another favor." She told Hildy about meeting Annie at Mrs. McCarver's and then about how the girl had run away from her abusive father. "She was so hurt, I sent for Mrs. Dr. Clarke."

Before Hildy could respond, someone rapped on their table. Nell looked up to see Thurlow Monk. With a deep sigh, she said, "I haven't had a chance to thank you for stepping in and helping me with Mr. Penny. Both Mrs. Dr. Clarke and I appreciated your assistance."

Monk's rictus grin didn't include his eyes. "You can tell me all about it when we take that walk."

Nell held his gaze. "There will be no walk, Mr. Monk. I have neither the time nor the inclination." She turned pointedly back to Hildy.

Monk huffed, then took himself off. "Gracious, who was that?" Hildy asked as he gave the reception desk a couple of raps and then headed for the bar. She dunked a cookie in her coffee.

Nell lowered her voice. "He's a smuggler who just happened to be at the Madhouse when I went to get money from Annie's father."

"The Madhouse!" Hildy choked until coffee came out her nose. She fished in a pocket for a cloth and wiped her watering eyes. "That's — that's the den of iniquity above Old Town, isn't it? Why would you go there, and weren't you afraid, and who's Mr. Penny?"

"Mr. Penny is Annie's father, and I was too mad to be afraid. Besides, I had Pup and Mrs. Dr. Clarke with me. Mrs. Dr. Clarke had to set the arm Annie's father broke when he beat her. She'll have to exercise it when the splint comes off. Which brings me to the favor."

Nell paused, giving Hildy time to look suspicious and say, "Which is?"

"Would you let her turn the handle on your dough kneading machine?" Before her friend could answer, Nell hurried on. "I know you don't want someone else in your bakery, but Mrs. Dr. Clarke said Annie will need to exercise the arm until it gets strong again, and it won't be for long. I'll give you some money you can give to her, so she thinks she's earning it."

"Well!" Hildy laughed. "Isn't that just the ticket. Mama and I have started canning and drying apples and things for winter, and having some help — just temporary, mind you — wouldn't go amiss. But . . ." She put her empty cup down. "I will pay Annie, not you. And don't argue," she added when Nell started to protest.

"You're a brick."

The girls laughed, and Hildy stood, picking up the reticule Nell had made her as a birthday gift. "I'll see you at the picnic. You can do the rowing."

Hildy left, and Nell went back to the reception desk. A few minutes later, a man carrying a bag entered the hotel. Nell smiled at him. "Are you looking for a room, sir?"

"Yes, thank you. A single, please."

"Of course, Mr. . . ."

"Tyler."

She turned the registration book to face him and handed him a pen. "Business trip, is it, Mr. Tyler?"

He nodded. "I'm here to oversee the

339

Tacoma Hotel."

"Oh." She struggled to maintain her smile. "I've read all the articles in the paper about it and visited the construction site. The racket is enough to wake snakes, but the hotel will certainly put New Tacoma on the map."

"It will, indeed." Mr. Tyler picked up his bag. "We will be hiring quite a lot of women. Maybe when the time comes, you'd like to work there as a chambermaid."

Not by a jugful would I like to, but I guess it will be a case of needs must. "That will certainly be something to think about, but it would be a step down for me after helping to run the Halstead Hotel. Of course, if the pay is higher . . ." Nell let the words trail off, and she and Mr. Tyler shared a little laugh. "Never mind." She stepped out from behind the desk. "Follow me, please, and I'll show you to your room."

On the day of Ellen's picnic, warm weather had returned, but a welcome breeze brought the temperature down. In her bedroom, Nell put on a dark-brown skirt and then fumbled with the buttons on her brown and white pinstriped blouse. "When I'm a famous dressmaker, I'm going to design dresses that don't require a corset," she muttered.

"The way you've laced yourself today, you might as well not be wearing one." Seated on the side of the bed, Amity shook her head. "I'm not sure you're decent."

"I'm decent enough. Look how loose the bodice and sleeves are. Isn't it lucky when I remade your old twill, I had enough good fabric for this skirt? Gosh, I'm glad women don't wear hoopskirts and crinolines anymore. Now, where's my hat?"

"Nell." Amity stood and gave her a little spank. "I've asked and asked you not to use slang. And 'gosh' is blasphemous, as you well know."

"I'm sorry, Ma. I keep forgetting." Footsteps sounded outside, and Nell hurried out of the bedroom. "Is that you, Hildy? Come in. I just need my hat."

Nell's hat was a straw one with brown velvet ties, a matching band around the crown, and an ostrich feather flowing from the crown down the back. She twirled it on one finger as Hildy admired it. "I was tidying up one of the bedrooms at the hotel and saw a picture like it on a cover of *Harper's Bazaar.* I got Ike to buy me a straw hat from one of the sailors and added the decorations."

"It's gorgeous. Won't Ellen be pea-green?"

"Look." Nell turned it upside down. "I used green fabric to line the brim and crown so the straw won't scratch."

"Well, I think it's just dandy."

Nell giggled. "Ma doesn't approve of slang," she whispered in Hildy's ear.

Nell had two berry pies tied into a flour bag, and Hildy carried a basket of rolls, their yeasty smell lingering as the girls left the house. Laughing and talking, they walked up the hill. Where the trail dropped down to Old Tacoma, George and Frank joined them. "We can always count on you to bring something good to eat, can't we?" George fell into step with Nell, inching Hildy off the path.

"Nell made pies," Hildy said, dropping back to walk next to Frank, who looked as if he wished he was elsewhere. "I just brought rolls. Of course," she looked at George and smiled, "Samuel says one of the best things about coming home after a trip is eating my bread and rolls."

"Who's Samuel?" Frank asked. He'd been away so much, and people came and went so quickly in New Tacoma, he no longer knew everyone.

"Hildy's intended," said Nell, and George scowled. If he shared nothing else with Ellen, he did share her general dislike of

342

Indians. When he looked as if he was going to take her elbow, Nell shifted her pies to that side, effectively putting a distance between them.

"It's lovely to have you with us." She turned slightly to smile at Frank and let him help her over a tree root. "Are you going to sing?"

"I hadn't thought about it." He took a handkerchief from his pocket and wiped his forehead. "I've been sick since I returned from college, and Mother wanted me to get some air. She and Ellen's mother work together on behalf of the new Fannie Paddock Hospital, so that's how I got invited."

Well, that explains why he's here, but he must be very uncomfortable. He's much older than us — at least twenty. Nell looked in the direction of the old hospital and shook her head. "Imagine a dancehall being turned into a hospital. Do you think the women's ghosts dance for the patients at night?"

"Ah — well — that is . . ."

"Oh dear, that was inappropriate of me, wasn't it? I apologize." Nell tried to think of something Frank might be interested in. "I'm sure you've seen a lot of changes in town since your return."

Her companion perked up. "Yes, indeed. The new hospital, of course, and the opera house, and the Tacoma Hotel."

"And the new Episcopal church. My brother, Ike, has been working on it. He said when the sandstone for the hotel comes down from Wilkeson, the quarrymen are bringing sandstone for the church, too." Nell had to raise her voice in order to be heard over the racket coming from Old Tacoma's salmon cannery, the barrel factory, and the numerous mills.

The trail began its descent. Ahead of them, tied to a piling at the Hanson and Ackerson Mill, they could see three rowboats, looking insubstantial as they bobbed near schooners that waited to have their cargoes of lumber unloaded. The sight of the little skiffs reminded Nell of John Calhoun and the trip home from Steilacoom. *As soon as Hildy and I are alone, I'll ask her if she had a chance to find out any more about him.*

Nearing the wharf, she saw millworkers hefting logs in the direction of the saws and heard them shouting to each other. Some of the younger men were casting glances at Ellen and Fern, who stood near the ladder leading from the edge of the wharf down to the water. The waiting pair looked glad when Nell and the others hurried to join them.

George climbed down the ladder first and stepped into the nearest boat. Frank handed him the food and looked to see who would go next. For a minute, the girls hesitated, then Nell took hold of the ladder's sides and clambered into a second boat with Hildy following. Watching George hold Hildy's hand for an unnecessarily long time, Nell snickered, and Hildy poked her before sitting down. *Make up your mind, George,* Nell wanted to say.

Having learned to row from Ike, Nell sat in the middle thwart with Hildy facing her. Frank untied their rope, and she used an oar to push away from the dock. Ellen scurried down the ladder and joined George, leaving Fern and Frank to share a boat. Watching sunlight sparkle off the water's slight chop, Nell wondered if Frank was strong enough to row.

Despite the light southern breeze and the boat's weight, Nell sent it skimming across the water's surface. From the mill, they started west toward Point Defiance. She and Hildy were in the lead when they passed a half-submerged log on which a great blue heron rested. At their approach, it lifted its large, supple wings and flew across the bay toward Vashon Island. Nell stopped rowing long enough to hike her skirt hem above bilge water swashing around.

"Look at that log boom," Hildy said, as a steamboat pulling a roped-together raft of wood passed them. "I heard mill owners are sending fir, cedar, and hemlock seeds clear to Europe, because over there, folks cut all their own trees down." Samuel had passed on to Hildy his concerns about how fast the woods were being timbered off. Nell wasn't sure how much she should worry about trees. As if guessing Nell's thoughts, Hildy said, "Samuel says thanks to timber companies, the midwest hardwood forests are all but gone. He doesn't want to see that happen here."

Nell resumed her strong and steady strokes as she said, "Did you have a chance to ask him about John Calhoun?"

"Yes, I did, and Reuben knows him, too. But they don't know much, only that he seems friendly and asks a lot of questions. Samuel thinks he works for the government."

"The territorial government?"

"He didn't say, and, before I could ask, he changed the subject."

A steamer headed north came from behind them, and Nell stopped rowing again to watch. "That's the *George E. Starr.* She's said to be the slowest boat on the sound.

Have you heard the poem about her?" When Hildy shook her head Nell chanted, "Paddle, paddle, George E. Starr/How we wonder where you are./Leaves Seattle at half past ten/Gets to Bellingham, God knows when!"

Hildy laughed, and Nell leaned into the oars, pushing the heavy boat and leaving the other two behind. Not to be outdone, both Frank and George picked up the pace, and Nell let them pass. Fern gave a small shriek when one of Frank's oars kicked up water on her. He laughed and waved his hat. Ellen and George hurried to catch up. Forty-five minutes later, Ellen gestured for the boats to put in at a spot just beyond the clay banks. George turned his boat toward the beach and the others followed suit. Nell leaned hard into her oars and sent her boat a foot up the shell-strewn shore.

"If George and Frank weren't here, we could take off our shoes." She looked over the bow at the water.

"And Ellen would strongly disapprove. Now, here come Frank and George, and, if you ask George sweetly, I'm sure he'll assist you." Hildy grinned, and Nell stuck out her tongue.

Frank grabbed the cleat rope and pulled the heavy wooden skiff up six inches more.

Then he extended a hand to Hildy. She handed him the rolls and pies, winked at Nell, and jumped out, landing just beyond the water. He followed her up the beach, leaving Nell and George. "The tide's going out," Nell said, "so the boats should be all right." She took the hand he extended. *I hope he helped Ellen, too, or she won't like this.*

Fortunately, Ellen had her back turned. She was spreading out an old blanket in the shade of some trees that leaned out from the bank and anchoring the corners with rocks. All around the area, driftwood and logs that had escaped from the booms nestled in the seaweed and shells to mark the high tide line. Frank took a deep breath and coughed. "The sand banks have quite a powerful odor, don't they?"

"I forget how nice the salt water smells." Nell took a deep breath, too. "When I was little, I was down on the wharf anytime I could escape from home. It smelled like this at first, until so many businesses went up and so many ships started coming in and out of the harbor. The air smells different in Old Tacoma. I'd near forgotten how much I missed this smell." She stooped to pick up a periwinkle shell and an unusually large barnacle.

With the blanket safely anchored down, Ellen stood, holding some pieces of driftwood. "We need wood for a fire."

"Where's George?" Frank looked around.

"He brought a hand line and walked down to the clay banks to try and catch a salmon." Ellen dropped the wood onto a little pile. "Would you like to rest on the blanket?" she asked Frank, who stiffened and turned red. "I brought a small shovel. I'll see if I can get some clams."

He walked off, and Ellen looked chagrined. "I shouldn't have said that. No man likes to be reminded of his illness."

Nell and Hildy exchanged looks, both of them surprised at Ellen's unusual display of sensitivity. "Make a fuss when he comes back, even if he's just wet," Hildy said. "There's always the one that got away, even if it's just a clam."

Fern laughed. "That's what my mama taught me."

"I will. Now, we need lots more wood and big rocks to make a fire pit," Ellen said. "Let's spread out and see what we can find."

Mindful of her hands, Nell let Ellen and Fern take care of the rocks while she carefully gathered pieces of dried branches for kindling. Hildy did the same, stopping once to pick up a round glass ball.

"Look at this." She held it out.

"Aren't you lucky." Nell took the ball and examined it. "The Norwegian fishermen use these on their nets to keep them from tangling up." She handed it back, and Hildy put the ball in her pocket.

When they had enough wood, Fern lined a hole in the sand with rocks, filled it with the wood they'd gathered, and started a fire. Then the four girls sat on the blanket.

"That's a pretty hat, Nell," Fern said.

"Thank you. It's a *Harper's Bazaar* pattern."

"Could you make me one?"

"Of course. I'd be happy to." Nell smiled.

"Isn't it lovely to be here on the water where there are no flies?" Hildy leaned back on her arms and lifted her face to the sun. "They've been the plague of the bakery all summer."

"Be careful or your face will get brown," Ellen said.

"I don't care. When there's a breeze, the sun feels good, and Samuel doesn't mind how dark I get."

"Well, of course, he wouldn't," Ellen said.

Hildy sat up, her eyes snapping. Nell nudged her foot. Ellen, oblivious to the insult, watched George pulling his fishing line in, hand over hand. At the same time,

Frank came up to see if they had something he could carry clams in. Sand and bits of seaweed covered his pants and arms, and he panted from exertion. Nell thought he'd be very glad when the day was over. Ellen handed him a three-legged pot and then started scattering the firewood to uncover the heated rocks. She re-covered the stones with damp seaweed, added the potatoes and ears of corn, and buried them under more seaweed. Then she started a fire over it all. That done, she went to help Frank with the clams he'd dug. Together, they rinsed them off, and Ellen put them in the pot, added a little water, and covered it with a lid. Frank carried the pot to the fire, and she set it where the clams would steam cook.

In the meantime, George cleaned a small salmon he'd caught, accompanied by dozens of gulls and terns that swirled around waiting for the entrails, fighting among themselves. He threaded chunks of the fish on pieces of wet wood and stood them upright in the sand where the fire's heat and smoke would cook the meat. While the food cooked, they talked about the telegraph line being extended to Tatoosh Island, and the move to ban horse racing on Pacific Avenue.

"I like the races," Nell said, "even if the horses do kick up a lot of dust. They're exciting." She laughed. "The races, I mean."

"I don't think it's seemly. I'm sure no one races horses down the middle of New York," Ellen said.

Fern agreed. "They certainly don't in Virginia, even though we have beautiful horses there, much nicer than the ones I see here."

Before anyone could think of an appropriate response, a side-wheeler came down the bay from the direction of Steilacoom, and the group waved. In turn, the ship's captain played "Yankee Doodle" on the vessel's calliope. "That's the *Eliza Anderson,*" Frank said. "The captain does that when the ship's in Canadian waters just to irritate folks." He sang the first verse of "Blow, Boys, Blow," and everyone laughed when he came to the part in the song about the ship flying the Stars and Stripes. When he was done, Nell asked if they'd heard about the ghost who had steered the *Eliza Anderson* to safety during a storm.

"Instead of loading the sacks of coal onboard, the ship's crew hid them on shore to save themselves the work," she said, "and the *Eliza* ran out of coal in the middle of a storm. The passengers and crew started burning the cabin furniture, wall partitions, and the wooden coal bunkers themselves to keep her going. And they wrote goodbye notes, put them in bottles, and tossed the bottles in the water. The captain ordered everyone into lifeboats, forgetting the waves had washed them overboard. Just when they assumed all was lost, a tall, ghostly figure with a beard and white hair, and wearing foul weather gear, walked into the pilot house, took the wheel, and steered the ship to safety. When she was in calm waters near land, he disappeared. No one knew who he was or where he came from."

Everyone was still and quiet, and for a few seconds the air around them seemed cooler. Ellen broke the silence when she started poking in the fire pit to check the food. "I think we're ready." She took the lid off the clams and used a stick to scatter the burning firewood that covered the corn and potatoes. Fern had brought plates and utensils, which she handed around, and George used a fork to push pieces of salmon off their wooden stakes onto the plates. Soon everyone was eating and praising Ellen.

"Where did you learn to cook like this?" George asked.

"Mama taught me. She learned from women on the wagon train when they were coming west, except for the clams and salmon, of course. She learned that here."

"Well, you were obviously an exceptional student." George tossed a clamshell over his shoulder, and Ellen beamed.

Everyone praised Hildy's rolls and Nell's pies, too. When they finished eating, Hildy carried the dishes down to the water, scrubbed them with sand, and returned with them and the cooking pot full of water. She doused the fire, watching for runaway embers. The tide had long since changed, and, when her hat flipped backwards, with only a large hatpin keeping it from blowing away, the group noticed dark clouds were moving in, and the wind was picking up.

"I think we should start back." Fern began putting her dishes in a basket. Nell and Hildy shook out their flour sacks and then helped Ellen and Fern. Everyone talked about what a delightful day it had been as they walked to the boats.

"I didn't realize how choppy the water's gotten." Nell steadied her boat while Hildy climbed in.

"Why don't I share the middle seat and help row?"

"All right." They took their places, and Nell pushed off with an oar. This time, George and Frank shared rowing chores, and Ellen sat in the back of her boat, facing

Fern and holding down the baskets of picnic supplies. A series of wakes rocked the rowboats as ships headed for shelter in the harbor. Out in the bay, Fern and Ellen quickly fell behind the others.

"I used to know every ship coming in." Nell watched a vessel from the Mosquito Fleet hug the shore, kicking up rollers. At a gasp from Hildy, she turned and saw Ellen standing to join Fern in the middle seat. Before anyone could shout a warning, the ship's wake caught the rowboat, smacking it hard. Ellen staggered, trying to catch her balance. Fern grabbed at her, too late. Ellen fell overboard.

Fern gave a strangled noise, pulled the oars up, and leaned over the side, trying to grab Ellen. "Help! Help!"

"George! Frank!" Nell and Hildy turned their boat and rowed as hard as they could to where Ellen flailed in the water.

The two boats reached the site at the same time, just as Ellen went under. Nell let go of her oar and frantically started undoing her clothes, ready to dive in, when Hildy shouted, "Samuel!" Nell looked up and saw another rowboat heading their way from around a Mosquito Fleet vessel. Hildy's beau was one of the men pulling at the oars. The other was John Calhoun.

Nell and Hildy waved their arms. Within less than a minute, all four boats bobbed and bumped against each other. John threw a rope toward George, and he and Samuel jumped in the water and dove down.

Nell turned to Hildy. "Hold my ankles." She turned her back to her friend and knelt down. As soon as she felt Hildy grab onto her, she went over the side of the boat.

As a child, Nell had spent a lot of time around the bay. She knew that the water where their boats bucked about was only seven or so feet deep, but the growing chop was stirring up the bay's floor, obscuring her vision. She strained to keep her eyes open, searching for Ellen in the opaque water. Seaweed and kelp caught in her hair; something slimy brushed her arm, and she jerked away. The jellyfish hereabouts didn't sting, but octopi sometimes used their suction cups to hold on.

"Over there, I think," Hildy said when Nell came up for air. Nell worked her way down the edge of their dinghy and plunged into the water again, as far as Hildy's grip allowed. When something seemed to grab at her face, she struggled not to panic. Another surface for air, and then, with flagging strength, she went back down. This time, something brushed her hand. It felt like a

356

boot, and she grabbed it.

Deeper down, she glimpsed John and Samuel swimming nearby. They seized something and gave it a mighty push toward the surface. Nell lost hold of the boot, but then felt Ellen's skirts brush her arm. She caught her friend around the waist and propelled her up as far as she could. Ellen surfaced, followed by the two men, who shoved her into the boat as Hildy struggled to keep control of it. Nell wiggled her way back in and saw Ellen lying on her back in the keel, where bilge slopped over her. Was she breathing? Nell wasn't sure, and her heart caught in her throat.

"Turn her on her stomach and see if you can push the water out," Samuel said as he and John struggled to get back in their own boat. "And, everybody, row for all you're worth."

George and Frank had roped Fern's boat to theirs. Sitting side by side, they pulled on the oars while Fern sat paralyzed with cold and fear, wringing her hands. Nell grabbed Ellen and managed to turn her over, while Hildy did her best to keep their rowboat steady. When Hildy's strength flagged, John grabbed her rope. "Nell, are you all right?"

"I don't think I've ever been this cold. I can't imagine how frozen Ellen must feel."

She straddled Ellen and began pushing on her back.

"Clean her mouth out," John shouted. Working quickly, he lashed his and Samuel's rowboat to theirs.

While the men rowed, Hildy and Nell raised Ellen's head so her face was out of the bilge water, pried her mouth open, and fished out bits of eelgrass and kelp. "Come on, Ellen," Nell shouted and pushed on her friend's back some more. "Breathe."

The water grew rougher. Whitecaps slapped the boats, making them hard to maneuver. After a sudden surge of waves smacked them, Ellen flopped up and then down, hitting the support in the hull hard. The impact was enough to start her coughing and spewing out water and clumps of red and brown algae, followed by bits of salmon and corn, stained purple from Nell's pie. "Thank God for the seventh wave," Hildy said, while Nell helped Ellen sit, first in the hull and then on the thwart, all the while rubbing her back.

"The dock isn't far now," Nell said.

"How far do you think?"

"I don't know, but we have to get her on shore and warmed up." Nell wrapped her arms around Ellen, but with both of them wet through, she doubted it would do much good. Ellen was shuddering, and her face had turned pasty white.

George and Frank rowed to their leeward side, and Frank said, "Can we help?"

"For Pete's sake, give me your jackets," Nell said. "Can't you see she's going into shock?"

White faced, both men unbuttoned their coats and tossed them over.

The brusque wind blew sodden clouds across the sky, and harsh, stinging rain fell. Ellen shivered violently, and Nell wondered why she'd had to ask the men for their jackets. But even with them she worried about Ellen. Fighting against the wind, they approached Old Tacoma and saw an Indian pulling his canoe up the beach. Samuel shouted something in the Puyallup language and waved his arms until he caught the man's attention. When the Indian turned around, Samuel shouted something else, and the man pushed his canoe back in the water. A few strokes brought him to the boats. While John and Samuel kept the canoe steady, Nell and Hildy helped Ellen get in.

"Where take?" the Indian said.

For a moment, no one spoke. Then Nell said, "Grandma Staley's house. Do you know who she is?"

"Hyasklootchman." He used his paddle to push away.

"What does that mean?" Fern shivered as she watched his sure strokes send the canoe skimming toward land.

"Important woman." Nell's teeth clattered against each other. "As soon as we get back, we should all go to Grandma Staley's, too. We're frozen."

Ten or so minutes later, all four boats reached the mill. The high tide covered most of the ladder, making the scramble up short. The storm had put a halt to mill work, and the wharf was deserted. Hildy put her arm around Nell and hustled her to land with everyone else following. "Can you believe Frank and George?" she said. " 'I'm too frail.' 'I can't swim.' I call them disgraceful."

"At least Frank has an excuse," Nell said through chattering teeth, "and neither Samuel nor John wore jackets, but George? I will never look at him in the same way again."

The storm had forced most Old Tacoma residents inside, and the streets were empty. Because the previous few weeks had been so dry, the dirt was slow to absorb the rain. Water found channels down which to flow, filling potholes along the way. "I don't know why we're bothering to sidestep them," Hildy said. "Even our shoes are soaked through."

Hildy hurried Nell along until they reached Grandma Staley's house. As they approached, the woman opened the door. "Come in, quickly. I've built up the fire and have a pot of soup heating on the stove."

Inside, everyone rushed to the fire while their hostess found blankets. The men turned their backs while the girls peeled off their outer layers of clothes. Hildy had rescued Nell's hat, skirt, and blouse and draped them over a chair. Then the men turned back and took off their shirts and boots, choosing to keep their breeches on.

"I'm cold to the insides of my bones," Nell said. She spied Ellen lying on a narrow bed, wrapped in blankets and surrounded by deer bladders full of hot water. "How's Ellen?"

"I've given her hot water and Holland's Balsam of Spruce." Grandma Staley began ladling soup into bowls and handing them around. "Who pulled her to the surface?"

"Samuel and John dove in and pushed her up." Nell ignored her spoon and drank from the bowl. To her amazement, Fern followed suit.

"You did your share," John said. "Right,

Samuel?"

"Absolutely."

"Well, she wouldn't have lasted much longer." Grandma Staley stepped over to check Ellen and moved some of the bladders to her feet and chest.

"Does that mean she'll make it?" Hildy cradled her bowl, warming her hands.

"If she doesn't get chesty, she will, in body at least. She was underwater a long time. That can do things to the mind."

While she spoke, the house shuddered under an onslaught of wind. It came down the chimney, making the fire leap and dance, throwing sparks with abandon. A cat slunk into the room and sat by the stove. Grandma Staley took their bowls to the dry sink and returned with cups of something. "This should help warm you even more."

"What is it?" Hildy sniffed the beverage.

"Honey and whisky."

The girls cautiously sipped, and George and Frank coughed and sputtered. John drank his with no apparent problems, and Samuel set his aside untasted. They watched their hostess mix flour, dry mustard, and water into a paste, which she spread on a cloth and put on Ellen's chest. "I can make mustard plasters for all of you," she said, but the others declined.

The room fell quiet. Outside, the wind and rain slowly abated and then stopped altogether. Through the lingering clouds, the sun made a tepid appearance, and birds came out of their hiding places to peck at the ground. Nell checked her clothing and decided it was dry enough to put on. "I'd best get home," she said. "Ma will be terribly worried."

She hushed as Ellen stirred and half sat up. "Where . . . where am I?"

"Old Town, warm and safe," George said.

"She'll feel better if you sit by her." Hildy looked at her own clothing and then at the men. "Turn around, please." She giggled as she tried to pull her dress on and realized she still wore her hat. "My poor hat," she said. "I fear it will be the casualty of this picnic, just like the berries we picked at the first one."

Nell looked at her own saturated straw hat and sighed. "In spite of your best efforts, mine too."

Warm and fed, they all lingered by the fire for a little longer, going over the events of the day. In the background, Ellen and George talked quietly. Nell snuck a look at them and saw Ellen clutching George's hand. She was still holding it when the others started to leave. They were effusive in their thanks, and Grandma Staley said she would keep Ellen at least until the next day and asked them to tell the girl's parents.

At the door, Nell wrapped her arms around the older woman. "You said I'd be back, but I didn't expect it to happen this way."

"Neither did I, dear. Life is full of surprises."

They were going out when suddenly Ellen leaned against George. "Wait, everybody. Listen. George said he had no idea how much I meant to him until I fell overboard and nearly drowned. He has asked me to become his wife." Still holding his hand, she fell back on the pillow.

Nell's mouth dropped open, and she exchanged looks with Hildy. Then she caught a glimpse of George's face. He looked stricken.

CHAPTER 20

The day after the picnic, Nell sat at the Halstead Hotel's front desk, alternately drinking hot coffee when she was cold and cold water when she was hot. Her eyes watered, and her throat was scratchy, but the worst was her drippy nose.

"I'm so tired of blowing my nose," she said to Pup. "I don't know how it can be plugged up and runny at the same time." But it had been a point of honor to come into work. The bar had already been leased to a man named Gerald Bott, and John Muntz, the blacksmith, had approached the Halsteads asking them to forgo the auction and lease the hotel to him. Her employment was by no means guaranteed, though.

"The only good thing about having to be a chambermaid," she told Pup, "is that I will be able to see the ladies' hats and dresses."

When she returned home the previous

day, she'd found a note from Mrs. Halstead asking her to work the following day rather than that afternoon and evening. The morning had been quiet, but at dinner time hotel guests drifted in for a noon meal. Nell kept busy serving bowls of stew, hot rolls, and coffee. For those who wanted it, there was apple pie. She and Fred cleared the tables, and no sooner had she returned to the front desk than the door opened and Fern came in.

"Goodness me," she said, as Nell succumbed to a coughing fit. "You caught cold yesterday, didn't you? I was just in to see Hildy, and she has one, too. I told her I thought she should close the bakery until she was better, but that helper she has as good as said I should mind my own business. I didn't know she had a helper. Who is she?"

"She just started. Her name is Annie Penny, and she used to work for Mrs. Mc-Carver. Hildy was very lucky to hire her away."

Fern ignored the answer and looked around. "So this is where you work."

Nell took exception to something in Fern's tone of voice. "The Halsteads are lovely people. Are you making calls today?"

Fern looked surprised. "I don't call on

folks while they're working."

"Oh, of course not. I wasn't thinking," Nell wiped her nose and decided to wait her friend out.

"Actually, Ellen sent me."

"Not another picnic."

"Of course not, don't be silly. No, it's decided that George will be going to Linfield College in a few weeks, and she wants to be married before then so she can go with him. She wants you to make her wedding dress."

Nell was dumbfounded. "Why, that's wonderful — about the dress, I mean."

"Mrs. Coffey went to see Ellen at Grandma Staley's house, and, once she learned about the engagement, she thought that, since the Coffeys have kin in McMinnville where the college is, Linfield would work out perfectly for the newlyweds. She reckons they can stay with the family, and Ellen can help George with his studies."

"It doesn't sound like George had much say in the matter."

"He just seems so overcome with everything; I think he was glad to have the decisions taken out of his hands."

"And Ellen's going, too. Goodness, how grown up we're getting to be."

"Bound to happen, isn't it?" Fern waited

while Nell blew her nose. "She asks, could you come by sometime this week with a few ideas. Of course, she has ideas, too, but then so does her mother, and, so far, they aren't agreeing."

"Do you know why?"

"Ellen wants more than her mother says is practical. Mrs. Coffey says money should be a tool and is not to be abused."

"Surely Ellen knows preachers don't make a lot."

"She figures she can tutor and help out. Anyway, it isn't good manners to talk about money."

Several men came in, and Fern stepped toward the door. "In Virginia, we used to go to Charlottesville for our bridal clothes. That was Thomas Jefferson's home, don't you know."

And there it is. Nell thought. *The reference to Virginia.* She smiled sweetly. "Did your wedding cakes also come from there?"

The remark went over Fern's head. "That would have been very difficult."

"Perhaps Hildy can make them for Ellen."

"Is she capable?"

"Of course. She has requests all the time for things we don't see in the bakery." Nell didn't know if that was true or not, but she refused to let Fern slight her best friend.

A Chinese man appeared carrying a pile of laundry, and Fern inched closer to the door. "Can I tell her you'll make her dress, since she can't go to Portland to shop?"

"I would love to."

"It certainly will be wonderful advertising for you, won't it? Ellen is such a generous friend." With a farewell nod, Fern left.

No sooner had she gone than Ike came in. "Hey, Nell." He ambled over and sat at the table closest to the reception desk. "Ma said you had a cold. Is the barkeep giving you whisky?"

"I almost wish, but I'm off after supper, and that's not long." She coughed, and then sighed. "I'll get us some coffee."

She went to the kitchen and returned with two steaming mugs. "What are you doing here, anyway?"

He took one of the mugs from her. "Frieda Faye's ma is visiting."

Nell laughed. "Well, that explains it. Has she gotten over having to cancel the necktie party?"

"The least mention is always good for a sulk." Nell snickered at that, and her brother continued. "Did you hear old Mrs. Caddy finally died?"

She hadn't. Nell sneezed into a soggy rag, then said, "Lloyd took care of her right up

369

until the end, didn't he? He was a good son."

"Well, he wants you to have his ma's clothes. Asked could you come by sometime today and get them. He's signed onto a ship taking lumber to San Francisco."

"That's awfully kind."

"Lloyd was always sweet on you."

"He was? I didn't know."

"Just too bashful to let on, I guess."

"Well, I get off work in a couple of hours, so I can go for the clothes then. Do you think I'll need something to wheel them home in?"

"Couldn't say." Ike finished his coffee over the racket of two men pushing and shoving their way into the room.

"Lordy," said Nell as they shouted for a bartender. "Isn't one of those men Mr. Gordon, who writes for the *Ledger*?"

Ike snorted. "He celebrated when his dog was stolen, and he celebrated when he got it back. That's all he does, is find reasons to celebrate."

"I know, and Mr. Radebaugh is so soft-hearted, he's all the time firing him and then hiring him back." The men's loud calls for the barkeep made her head ache, and she rubbed her forehead.

Ike frowned. "Ma know about these kinds

of goings on?"

"Fred will soon have them sorted out." Seeing her brother's disapproval, Nell added, "I don't suppose this is the first saloon they've visited today, and the Halsteads don't allow rowdy behavior."

As if he'd heard her words, Fred appeared and took each man by an arm. "Come on, boys, you know the rules. I reckon you best get over to Levin's."

He ushered them out the hotel door, and Ike took his leave. Nell thought she'd have a minute to breathe, but then the hotel's equipage — a large buggy drawn by a team of horses that regularly brought folks up from the wharf — stopped in front of the door. A family climbed out and came in, then asked for a room. After Nell registered them, she darted into the kitchen for more coffee, heavily laced with cream, and a thick slice of buttered bread. "I pretend the soggy bread soothes my throat," she said to Pup, "but I purely love dunking. Don't tell anyone." She gave him a piece of crust, closed her eyes, and rested her head on her hand.

The previous day's storm had blown out, and the rain had laid the dust. Now, humidity hung heavy. Charles Halstead came to relieve her, and the door opened again. /

371

don't care if it's Thurlow Monk, she thought. *Pup will put him gone. I'm just going to get the clothes from Lloyd Caddy and go home to bed.* As it turned out, though, it wasn't Monk who came in; it was John Calhoun.

"I dropped by your house to see how you were doing," he said as he removed his hat. "Your little sister said you were sick. I have a buggy waiting to take you home."

Nell put on her hat and picked up her shawl. "Oh, I'm so grateful. My head hurts something awful, but I do have a stop to make."

Outside, John helped her into the buggy. She snapped her fingers for Pup, who hopped in and sat in the middle of the seat. John got in, picked up the reins, and gave the dog a dirty look. "Where do you need to go?"

Soon they were heading up Seventh Street to D Street, where she had him turn left. The Caddy home was two stories and had a small covered porch all made of salvaged boards. "I won't be a minute," Nell said. "Pup, you stay here." Before John could help her, she jumped down and hurried up the dirt walk to where the door stood open. When she went inside, Lloyd had the items neatly folded and in a pile. A bed shoved against one wall showed that Mrs. Caddy had spent her final days downstairs rather than in one of the two small bedrooms overhead.

"Lloyd," Nell said, looking at the clothing, "I'm so very sorry, and this is really good of you, but can't I pay you for all this?"

Lloyd's face went white, and he turned away. After a moment, during which he cleared his throat and blew his nose, he said, "Don't seem right to be selling Ma's dresses and such. You take 'em and welcome. Mebbe you can use 'em in your sewing."

"That's very kind, and, as it happens, Ellen Coffey — do you know her? No? — Well, anyway, she's marrying George Meyer, and she asked me to make her wedding dress. Your mother's things will help start a bride on her way."

"Well, now, that sure is nice. Ma'd be proud."

"Ike said you're bound for San Francisco." Footsteps sounded on the porch, and two children came in, followed by a woman who began looking at the few pots and pans. Nell held out some coins. "How about you take these, and any old magazines you stumble on, especially if they have pictures of ladies' clothes in them, you send up to me. I can write back, and that way I won't lose an old friend."

Lloyd smiled. "That I'll do, Miss Nell."

The piles of garments were surprisingly heavy, and John helped her put everything in the back of the buggy. He had turned it around and was starting back down the D Street when they heard people shouting. A small carriage pulled by a runaway team of horses was headed in their direction and teetered dangerously from side to side down the road. On the seat, General Sprague pulled frantically at the reins while his wife clung to the seat sides. It soon became clear why the buggy was out of control: one of the horses had managed to get a front leg over the carriage's tongue. His eyes rolled as he squealed in terror at being unable to extricate himself.

Men and dogs came from every direction, the barking adding to the confusion. Dirt and rocks flew; one stone hit a well-dressed man in the chest, and he yelped in pain. Nell grabbed Pup's lead in time to prevent his jumping from their buggy. In frustration, he nipped at her hand. Then the general's front buggy wheels hit some ties and rails with such force, he was pitched headlong over the dashboard onto the road. He lay stunned, while Mrs. Sprague held on until the vehicle slammed into a stump, and she was thrown out and over a picket fence.

John pulled their own buggy to a halt. "Stay here," he told Nell, then climbed down and joined the crowds of people surrounding both prone figures. Someone shouted that Doc Munson should be called. A woman rushed out of a nearby house and knelt by Mrs. Sprague. "Best take her inside," she said. Several men helped lift the unconscious woman, and one of them carried her in.

Meanwhile, John and others assisted the general to his feet. "I have to go to Julia," Nell heard Sprague say. "Will someone take care of the horses?"

"Don't worry sir, I'll see to them," John said.

"Thanks, John." With help, General Sprague got to his feet. He brushed leaves and twigs from his beard and hair and put his dusty hat back on.

The stump and overturned buggy had made it impossible for the horses to keep running. John approached them slowly, talking softly. When he was able, he grabbed the nearest animal's cheek piece and stroked the horse until it calmed down. Then he went to the other horse and painstakingly freed its leg. The animals stood quietly, blowing from their exertions, while he unharnessed them both.

He led them to the buggy where Nell sat. Pup jumped and barked, frantically trying to get loose. "Quiet, Pup," Nell said, her scratchy voice barely audible. While John tied the two horses to the back of the buggy, she blew her nose, wondering how red it was, wondering if she would lose her voice altogether, and thinking the day would never end.

John climbed back onto the seat, and they rode in silence for a bit. Finally, he spoke. "I would like to call on you."

Oh, Lord love us. I'm just not ready for this. Nell hugged Pup while she tried to choose her words. "I'm honored, John," she said, "but I don't think that's a good idea."

"Why?"

"Because I don't want to get married and have children. I want to be a dressmaker. I've wanted that all my life. That's why I work so hard. To save money to buy one of Mr. Singer's sewing machines."

Her earnest statement was spoiled when John laughed. "I'm not proposing, Nell, I just want to be able to call in from time to time." While Nell was thinking she'd never been so embarrassed in her life, he added, "And now I've made you turn all red. It's just, you see, I'm a long way from home, and I have no family here. I think of you as a friend and would like to see you and maybe visit with your little sister. I have one at home who's just about her age."

Friend? After their closeness on the bluff and his lovely kisses, Nell thought she should be outraged. Instead, her eyes filled with tears. *How foolish I have been.* She blew her nose to hide her emotions and said, "Of course. Please stop by any time. If I'm not home, Albina loves company."

John shifted position on the seat and flicked the reins. They soon reached her house and were greeted at the door by Amity, Albina, and Annie. Nell introduced him to her mother. Despite Albina's pleading, John left after helping to carry the clothing inside.

CHAPTER 21

For the next few days, Nell spent every spare minute unpicking seams and cutting off worn or stained spots from Mrs. Caddy's clothes, then cleaning and ironing the remnants. The result was a pile of eclectic pieces of fabric. "I promised Ellen I would make her wedding gown," she said to her mother. "It will be a challenge to come up with something appropriate from this."

"Mrs. Caddy didn't have many things," Albina said. She'd watched her sister with interest, all the while combing out a batch of newly dyed feathers. She looked at the remnants spread out on Nell's bed. "The colors are awfully dark, aren't they?"

"That's because Mrs. Caddy was an older woman." Nell overlaid the fabrics, with the largest pieces at the top. "Pastels wouldn't have been appropriate."

"When I get old, I'm going to wear any color I want." Albina lifted a length of black linsey-woolsey to look at some dark-gold taffeta underneath. "This feels nice; linsey-woolsey itches."

"It is pretty, isn't it?" Nell pulled the gold-colored material out and took a tape measure to it. "I think this will work." She hugged her sister. "Thank you, Beanie. Ellen has hazel eyes, so this should be perfect."

With the fabric chosen, Nell sat at the kitchen table, drinking coffee and going through her collection of clippings from newspapers and magazines. "So many of the dresses would take much more yardage than I have to work with, but this might do." She handed a newspaper clipping to her mother, who was knitting a baby jacket. "What do you think?"

Amity hesitated as she looked it over. "Well," she said after a moment, "Ellen is small, and the style is good, but it is rather plain, even with the buttons."

"They're not really necessary. They're just for decoration. As you said, Ellen is short, and they'd weigh her down — make her look even shorter. I'll use other fabrics to fancy it up and make her look taller."

"Well then, I think it sounds lovely." Amity handed back the clipping and picked up her needles again.

Despite her confident words to Amity, it

was with trepidation that Nell showed Ellen the fabrics and design a few days later — trepidation not misplaced.

"It's beautiful." Mrs. Coffey rubbed her fingers over the taffeta.

"But I want a white dress," Ellen said. She, her mother, and Nell sat in the Coffey family's parlor. "Ever since Queen Victoria wore one, they've become all the rage."

Mrs. Coffey sighed. "We've gone over and over this. This will be your Sunday dress until George makes enough money for you to have a new one. White would be dirty in a matter of days." She rubbed her temples, while Ellen turned her back on her mother and Nell and picked up her cup of tea.

"Can't I have a traveling gown to wear?" she asked after a moment.

"No. You have very little in your trousseau, remember. That must take priority."

"But . . ." And Ellen was off on a litany of arguments.

Nell picked up her own tea and glanced around the parlor, doing her best to ignore the increasingly heated discussion. Despite Ellen's airs, the Coffey family lived modestly. Their parlor was attractive but much like Frieda Faye's. Nell actually liked Ellen's mother better than she did Ellen. She sipped tea and sat back to reconsider her ideas, until finally Ellen's mother said, "Ellen, enough. What Nell has shown us is stylish and beautiful. If you don't want it, you can be married in your navy blue."

Nell took swift advantage of the momentary lull. "Ellen, I've always thought you have the most beautiful hazel eyes, and I think this lovely piece of dark gold taffeta will be beautiful with them. I can trim the cuffs and make a V-shaped bodice with it, and I'll add bits of bronze satin. You can carry bronze mums and white orange blossoms and have a white veil. The dress can easily be re-accessorized for your wedding trip."

"That all sounds very strange," Ellen said, just as her mother said, "Oh, how lovely, and so unique." Ellen subsided, and Mrs. Coffey continued, "Why, we can have a regular bower of flowers and concentrate on your trousseau." She gave Nell a grateful look. "Well, I call today a great success. What good ideas you have, Nell."

Nell breathed a little easier. "While I'm here, I'll take Ellen's measurements, so I can get started right away."

They spent the next little while doing exactly that, though Ellen still looked mulish. With the necessary measurements in hand, Nell took her leave. She was halfway down the walk when Ellen came out the door, saying, "But what about a going-away hat?"

Nell made herself smile. "Just leave it to me."

Since Ellen had been forced to give in to her mother, over the next few days she pouted and flounced through her fittings. As Nell later told Hildy, "It's almost enough to make me want to be a teacher instead of a dressmaker."

Hildy laughed. "Too bad you can't rap her fingers with a ruler."

At last, the dress was done, and the day of the wedding arrived. From where she knelt on a bedroom floor adjusting a bit of hem that had come loose during the endless fittings, Nell looked up and smiled at Ellen. " 'Something old, something new, something borrowed, something blue.' "

" 'And a silver sixpence in her shoe,' " Mrs. Coffey added.

Nell knotted off her thread and leaned back on her heels just as Ellen's youngest sister, Daisy, entered the room. "Oh, Ellen. You look so pretty," she said, and Nell smiled gratefully.

The Coffeys didn't have a full-length mirror, but refracted light coming through a window allowed Ellen to see herself. She turned and tucked and patted and pirouetted, watching herself in the glass.

"Nell was right, the color certainly makes your eyes stand out," Mrs. Coffey said. "You'll be the envy of every woman who sees you."

Only Ellen had remained silent. Now, she looked at Nell and smiled. "It's so nice, Nell, so elegant." In fact, Nell told Hildy later, she'd never seen Ellen smile so broadly before.

"Thank you." Nell snipped the basting thread and stood. "Walk around the room, please, Ellen. Let's see how the gown moves."

As Ellen dutifully paraded up and down, more women wandered in for a look at the bride, until it seemed as if the room was full of them. So many women, many unknown to Nell, had been in and out since she'd arrived, she wondered if the dress would be a surprise to anyone.

"What processional are you having?" asked one lady.

"Vivaldi's *Four Seasons.*" Ellen stroked the collar of her gown and ran a finger under a cuff. "It's meant to say that our love will last through all the seasons — all the year."

"Queen Victoria marched down the aisle to a blare of trumpets," the woman said. "And her wedding cake was plum and weighed three hundred pounds." Still watching Ellen, she said to Nell, "You do lovely work."

"Thank you."

"How do you know all that about the queen?" Ellen asked.

"I have an old newspaper clipping a cousin sent me about the royal wedding."

"I think the queen must have had a lot more people to give cake to than Ellen and George do," said Mrs. Coffey. "Now, if you're done, Nell, let's everybody leave the room so Ellen can finish dressing."

Outside the bedroom and away from the cloying odors of powder, perfume, and humanity, Nell took a deep breath. The house was abuzz with activity: ladies' voices coming from the parlor, Mr. Coffey talking to the minister, and a man named Paul Boulton warming up on his violin. The Boulton and Moore Combination had been performing at the Alpha Opera House to very small audiences and was due to go up to Carbonado to play. *They probably need all the money they can earn,* Nell thought.

She went to look for Hildy and found her friend outside, enjoying a gentle wind that was bringing in Commencement Bay's briny taste and smell but also bruised-looking purple-gray clouds. "Where's the cake?" Nell asked.

"Mrs. Coffey created a place for a small table in a little alcove where Ellen and George can sit and serve it."

"How did you get it here?"

Hildy giggled. "In the back of Mr. Scott's hay wagon, with Dovie and me on each side holding it and Reuben driving the team."

"Well, I just learned that Queen Victoria's cake weighed three hundred pounds."

Hildy snorted. "I'm not surprised. Plum cakes are heavy. We had quite a time getting this one out of the wagon and into the house." The wind pushed coils of madrona bark across the yard. "The wedding should be over by the time the rain begins."

"Did you see all the canoes in the bay? The Indians are going to the valley to pick hops."

"I did see them, and I saw Sarah making sketches. I bet she can sell them back East."

"I think it's lovely that she's making a sketch book of the wedding for Ellen, in spite of the way Ellen treats her."

"So do I." Hildy held out a hand. "Is that a mist I feel?"

"Their romance started with a rainstorm,

385

and now so will their wedding tour." Nell saw George standing near a copse of trees. Several other men nearby talked and laughed, but George seemed to have distanced himself from them.

"The vine maples are really red," Hildy said. "They turn so quickly, it seems as if they want to push summer aside and jump into winter."

"They're pretty, though," Nell said. "Their color makes a nice change from all the green foliage."

"George looks pale, doesn't he?"

Nell glanced at him again. "I don't think he's happy. But Ellen adores him, and she'll be a wonderful minister's wife."

"I hope he comes to realize that." When George's faraway gaze shifted to them, she said, "Let's go inside, shall we?" They nodded to George and went in, then made their way to the parlor, where the doors stood open and people were finding seats.

Thanks to the Ladies' Guild, the room was full of flowers. *The mums and dahlias will be so pretty with Ellen's dress.* Someone sitting at the back of the room sneezed, and Nell wondered if it was Fern. A minister stood on one side of a small altar, the violinist on the other. At a signal from Mr. Coffey, the music grew louder. A few seconds later, George walked down the aisle, followed by a cousin Nell had yet to meet, and then by Lacy, Ellen's oldest sister. When they were all in place, the *Four Seasons'* joyous notes filled the room. On her father's arm, Ellen started down the short aisle between the rows of chairs. She reached George and turned to face him with a brilliant smile, and Nell was pleased to see him return it.

"Dearly beloved," the preacher began. As the ceremony proceeded, Nell saw Hildy look down and smile. *Holy Moses,* Nell thought. *I hope she's not next. Even if she doesn't tell my secrets and things to Samuel, nothing will be the same if she's married.* Much troubled, Nell missed most of the ceremony, only dismissing her thoughts when people began to stand.

In lieu of a wedding breakfast, the Coffey ladies had set a large table with coffee and punch and small sandwiches and cookies. In the alcove, Ellen and George boxed pieces of cake and handed them to guests. Knowing she had to go from the wedding to work, Nell ate three sandwiches and drank two cups of coffee. Then she congratulated George, kissed Ellen, and headed for the hotel.

CHAPTER 22

"I've got good news for you, Nell," Fred said when she pushed through the hotel door, bringing wind and rain with her.

"What?" Nell draped her jacket over the back of the chair and shook her wet skirts. She had purposely worn a dress appropriate for the wedding and for work.

"That there Thurlow Monk checked out. He won't be pestering you anymore."

"Oh, that *is* good news, especially since I just came from a wedding and had to leave Pup home."

Fred looked out the window. "In June the farmers were praying for rain, and now they're praying the storms will stop." He shook his head. "I heard even the peanut vendor is thinking about moving to some other place." Indeed, the peanut vendor, who often stood by the front door, was gone. Every time someone went out or came in, rain accompanied them, until the floor was wet and muddy. As the afternoon wore on, Nell helped clear the dining-room tables and lay them for the next meal, but she had to set mugs on top of the napkins to hold them in place. Nearing the bar, she caught snatches of conversation.

"Ugly night," a man muttered.

"There'll be mischief, though," his companion said. Curiosity piqued, Nell slowed her work and listened.

The first man said, "You hear something?"

"Monk's sailing when the bay calms down. You know what that means."

"For sure and certain there'll be men missing tomorrow."

"Charlie Sweeny off the *Carrie Hayden* went missing in March and hasn't been heard of since."

"Best to stay away from the Pacific. Bartender there is known to be hand-in-glove with Monk. Think the Halsteads will let us stay here for the night . . . here in the bar, I mean?"

Nell thought about the Chinese men dumped on the beach near Steilacoom, a man missing off a schooner regularly seen in the bay, and Thurlow Monk. When the two speakers moved to a table in a back corner, she beckoned to the bartender. "Henry, did you hear any of that?"

"Been hearing rumors about Monk for quite a while," Henry said. "Heard 'em while I was at sea, too."

"Do you think those two men will be able to stay here for the night?"

"Mebbe; if they ain't drunk."

"That tavern they mentioned, the Pacific . . ."

Henry lowered his voice further. "Monk's got a system. He buys a likely-looking fellow a drink and slips 'im a mickey until he passes out, hauls 'im out to a wagon, and gets one of his men to take 'im to a place on the bluff somewhere off A Street where he's got a tunnel. Down the tunnel, onto his boat, and off to sea."

"And with the storm, there won't be many people on the streets to see it happen."

Henry dried the glasses he'd washed and set them on the counter. "Where's your dog?"

"Home. I came straight from a wedding."

"Well, you watch yourself. I seed that Monk took a shine to you, and you can't be too careful."

Nell replied with more confidence than she felt. "I always have a hatpin handy."

"Well, mebbe I can get one of the men to walk with you."

"I'd certainly appreciate that."

Henry went to serve a newcomer, and Nell returned to her desk, much troubled. She spent the rest of the night mending sheets and, when that was done, sketching ideas for a combination bedroom/sewing room on scraps of paper. It was near eleven when Charles Halstead came down from upstairs.

"You should stay here tonight," he said.

"We're full up." Nell put her jacket on. It had dried out since she got here but promised little protection from the rain that still gusted outside.

"You could sleep on Ma's sofa."

Remembering the itchy horsehair, Nell declined with thanks. "But if you have some sort of coat I could borrow, I'd appreciate it."

"I've got just the thing, if you don't mind a big old piece of canvas duck a man left behind."

Nell laughed. "Any port, or should I say old piece of canvas duck, in a storm."

"Well, it smells a mite, but it'll keep you dry."

Charles went to look for the canvas duck. When he brought it back, Nell draped it over her head, hoping the fish smell would come out of her hair. She tied the folds around her waist with a piece of rope. "I'll dry it out and bring it back."

Outside under the awning, she saw that water drowned the newly laid gravel and that someone had laid boards from one side of the road to the other. Unfortunately, they were already sinking. Lights and noise came from Levin's saloon nearby, and she wondered if Mr. Levin knew about Thurlow Monk's tricks. Pacific Avenue was rarely so deserted as right now, and Nell stood listening to the thrashing trees, loose shutters slamming against walls, and the pattering of rain on her canvas duck. She was just getting ready to try her luck on the boards when a wagon coming up the wharf road pulled to a stop in front of Levin's.

Nell kept still as the driver got down and went inside. After a few minutes, a man came out, carrying something long and heavy over his shoulder. As he hefted it into the dray, Nell realized it was a body. *Dear Lord, either it's a corpse or someone's being shanghaied!*

One of the horses whinnied, and the driver climbed back onto the seat and drove off. Not giving herself time to think, Nell started after the wagon as it disappeared into the darkness.

A squeaky wheel, and the lamp hanging off one side of the wagon, let her track its progress. Hugging the wall of the building, she followed the wooden sidewalk to the Standard Steilacoom Beer building next door. The Hebrew house and store were two blocks farther, and after that was the Ouimette Block. Neither of these buildings had awnings, but Naubert's Gent's Furnishings at Ninth and Pacific did. When the dim lamp light and the sound of the squeaky wheel had almost disappeared, she dashed through the rain and took shelter there, in the nick of time. The rain-drenched buggy drew closer, and horses' hooves squelched in the mud. The driver cussed and shouted something over his shoulder to the person in the wagon bed as he turned east toward A Street and the bluff above the bay.

Very clever, Nell thought. *Captain Clancy and General Sprague have houses on A Street, so no one seeing the buggy will suspect anything, just wonder who was out in such foul weather.* Then she remembered their houses were further north of here. Recalling Henry's story about Thurlow Monk brought to mind a one-paragraph article in the *Ledger* last April — some men were seen repairing a cave-in on the bluff where Seventh Street ended. Apparently, no one had thought to question the peculiar action, as she didn't recall any follow-up.

She risked getting closer and, in the light of the side lamp, saw one of the horses switching his tail up and down. *I know what that means. He's upset and will probably buck.* Sure enough, the next second he began kicking, upsetting the other horse. The driver yanked on the reins, then jumped down to try to calm him. While he fought with the unhappy animal, Nell darted through the shadows, heading for the back of the wagon.

As if sensing her presence, the man in the bed looked up. Shock jolted through Nell as her gaze met John Calhoun's.

He was tied — his hands bound behind him, another rope around his ankles. The wagon rattled as the spooked horse kicked and whinnied. She gathered her wits and spoke as softly as she could. "Where are they taking you?"

"To the cave on the bluff, then down a tunnel to Monk's old boat out in the bay, probably to be dumped overboard."

Another shock, that Monk meant to kill him. "I'll go for the marshal —"

"There's not enough time."

"What can I do?"

The horse was calmer now, quieting down. "Get to the tunnel," John murmured, his voice barely a breath. "The cave's by a giant boulder, with bushes in front. Get through, hit the driver if you get the chance —"

The wagon tipped as the driver resumed his seat. The next second, it was moving again. Nell followed as closely as she dared. The sewer line trenches had advanced to Seventh Street, and the wagon had to go down one side of the rutted road, giving Nell an opportunity to run to where piles of dirt made the street even darker. Her shoes squelched in the mud, and the canvas duck flapped, letting in rain. Fortunately, the noise of the storm and the still fractious horse slowed the driver, and she was able to run ahead. Where was the boulder? She peered through the rain, straining to see, stretching her hands out in front of her. A rough, roundish shape loomed — the boulder, surely. Bushes in front, John had said. The creaking wheel and the clopping hooves drew closer; any minute, the wagon would be near enough for the driver to spot her. Nell's hands met scratchy wet leaves, festooned with what felt like soggy spiderwebs. With seconds to spare, she pushed through the foliage and stumbled into a damp-smelling, dark space.

The swinging side lamp on the approaching wagon cast just enough light for her to see an ominous black hole in the cave floor.

Nell heard the wagon creak to a halt and the driver jump down, felt the bushes shake as he tied the horses. She sat by the hole and swung her legs over the edge. With nothing but air under her feet, she let go, dropping onto the muddy bottom of a narrow shaft. Her abrupt arrival frightened a cave cricket, and she gave a small squeak, shuddering to think of what else lived in the tunnel.

Water dripped from the low ceiling onto her head and ran under her feet. The frigid air stank of mold. Unable to stand, she bent at the waist and walked as fast as she could away from the opening, fighting claustrophobia. Behind and above her, the wagon driver shouted at John to "get a move on it."

The tunnel was black as pitch. Nell trailed a hand along the rough wall to keep her bearings. For a few yards, the tunnel stayed fairly level, and then it sloped downward. Nell tripped over unseen roots. She put her free hand out to catch her balance and touched something slimy. Jerking her hand back, she tripped again, hit her knee on a jagged piece of granite, and cried out.

Behind her, the wagon driver shouted, "Who's there?"

Nell froze. John said, "What's the matter,

are you afraid of a wharf rat?" Nell heard a scuffling noise and wondered if the driver had hit him. When she heard their footsteps start up again, she moved, too.

If there had ever been any warmth in the shaft, something had long since swallowed it up. Nevertheless, she sweated with fear even as she shivered with cold. It was impossible to know how far she'd come, or how far the tunnel went. *What if it goes deep into the ground? I just assumed it comes out somewhere near the bay, but what if it doesn't?* The further she went, the more water she encountered — dribbling down from the ceiling, seeping through the walls and up from the floor. Hadn't she read an article less than two months earlier about a waterlogged embankment on the Puyallup Reservation giving way? *And there's been so much more rain since,* she thought. *The bluff here has to be saturated.*

The thought of a cave-in brought on a wave of hysteria that she struggled to control. Her dress was soaked and had picked up mud, weighing it down. The men's footsteps behind her sounded closer, and she frantically tried to think what to do if they caught up with her. Then, mercifully, a pinprick of light shone in the distance. It grew larger as she crept toward it, and the moldy smell disappeared, replaced by the odor of low tide. She'd found it unpleasant before, but now it seemed sweet.

The tunnel ended abruptly. With no choice in the matter, Nell jumped down. Not far, luckily, since she landed on a mass of flotsam and jetsam left by the last high tide. She ducked behind a massive tree root swept down from the bank, not a moment too soon. John rolled out of the tunnel and onto the beach, thanks to a boot to his backside. The driver followed, clutching the lamp from the wagon.

The rain and wind made the lamplight sputter and buffeted the surrounding vegetation. Tree limbs waved, and moorage ropes holding ships in the harbor strained audibly. While Nell shivered and tried to think what to do, a figure appeared from out of the dark. *Thurlow Monk?*

The figure reached the driver, who stood by John's prone body. When he spoke, she recognized Monk's voice. "Were you followed?"

"Down the tunnel? Not bloody likely."

"Well, get Calhoun on his feet again and let's go."

He started back down the beach. Nell felt around the pile of flotsam, picked up a hunk of wood, and heaved it as far as she could.

It ricocheted off something with a loud thump and skittered down the beach. "Who's that?" Monk shouted as he whirled around.

Nell held still, barely breathing. "I'll check it out," the driver said.

"You stay here. I'll do it."

As Monk melted into the darkness, Nell's fingers closed around what felt like a broken board. Gripping it tightly, she left her hiding place, crept up behind the driver, and whacked him behind the knees. He made a startled noise and went down. She hit him over the head, then knelt by John. His hands were still bound, though they'd freed his legs so he could walk down the tunnel. "We've gotta get out of here," she said, helping him to stand.

"Aye. I hear Monk coming back."

"Where can we go?"

"Back up the tunnel."

She took a precious few seconds to untie the rope at his wrists so he could climb back into the tunnel mouth, then suppressed a gasp as he grabbed the collar of her dress. To the sound of it tearing, she found a foothold and followed him inside. Hunkering down, they heard Monk return. A muttered curse, followed by, "Boone! Get up!" told them he'd discovered his cohort lying on the beach.

A few noises followed before Boone muttered, "Someone hit me."

"You dumb fool. Who hit you?"

"How would I know? He came from behind."

"Where's Calhoun?"

"Dunno."

"Come on. He can't be far."

Outside the tunnel's entrance, sand crunched. Nell shivered, and John leaned close. "Throw a rock into the bushes," he whispered into her ear.

Groping in the mud, she finally brought up a stone small enough to throw, but big enough to make noise. She took a deep breath, leaned toward the opening, and tossed the stone into the vegetation. It made a satisfying noise. "This way," Monk shouted, as he and Boone started up the embankment.

John grabbed Nell. "Come on," he hissed.

She balked, suddenly terrified. "I don't think I can go back."

"What's it to be, the tunnel or Monk?" Without waiting for an answer, John jerked her arm. Nell whimpered but started back up the moldy-smelling, cramped shaft behind him. Bent double, she occasionally hit her head on the ceiling. From John's muffled grunts, it was even worse for him. The water underfoot had increased to a steady stream and had broken through the wall in places, pushing out dirt and debris. After they'd gone a decent distance, John said, "What's the first thing you'll do when we get out?"

"What?" How could he make conversation at a time like this?

As if he'd heard her thought, he said, "Talking will take your mind off things."

Oh. "Get out of these clothes and take a hot bath. What about you?"

"The same, I guess. Ouch! Watch the stone on your left, it's sharp."

She ducked away and avoided it. "Does the tunnel seem steeper than it did going down?"

"Aye."

A chunk of dirt fell from the ceiling between them, and Nell wiped muddy water off her face. "Why did Monk shanghai you? Not even that — he meant to dump you overboard, you said."

"I work for the government. I reported his activities."

"Is that what you do? Report on kidnappers like Monk?"

"Aye." John sighed. "What else will ye do when you get home?"

"Eat something. Maybe I'll eat while I'm in the bath."

"Do you have a tub?"

"Not really, just an old barrel, but it's big enough to squeeze into. I'll put lots of hot water in it and pour more over me."

"My maither liked to do that, too." His Scots burr was more pronounced now, likely from fatigue.

"Is she still alive?"

"Aye, and I've a wee sister as well."

"I remember your mentioning her. What's her name?"

"Kirstie."

They crept along in silence, until John said, "And what food will ye eat while bathin'?"

"Hot buttered toast, which I'll dunk in coffee. Ma doesn't like me to do that but —" She stopped when John made a noise. "What? What is it?"

"We've reached the end."

He crawled through the bushes, then turned and did his best to help Nell. Once outside, she lifted her face to the sky and let the rain wash down it. Her muscles ached, her fingernails were broken, cuts and scratches on her hands stung, but she was free, and with him, and she felt happier than she had any right to, considering the situation. They sat on the edge of the muddy road, and John began rubbing feeling back into his rope-chafed wrists and ankles. She helped him to his feet, supporting him until full feeling returned. Then they started walking.

"General Sprague lives just yonder," John said. "He can send for the marshal."

"I'm going home," Nell said.

"What about the hotel where you work?"

"You go there, or to the general's house if you want, but I'm going home."

John chose to stay with her, and they retraced their earlier trip on Seventh Street, then turned onto Pacific Avenue. The road was deserted, but, ahead, noise and light came from the Grotto Saloon. When they reached it, John pulled Nell against the wall. "Wait here," he said and shoved through the doors. Seconds later, his voice carried clearly to her: "I've just come from the bay. Thurlow Monk's drugging men and taking them to his ship."

The crowd inside had likely been drinking most of the afternoon and evening and were easily stirred up. When John mentioned a woman being involved in the shanghaiing, angry voices rose, and men pushed out the door, headed for the bay. Despite shivering with cold, she was laughing when John rejoined her. "We must get thee to the bath," he said.

"And you." Nell snuggled close when he put an arm around her.

"Aye. But where I come from, it can get very cold, so I'm used to it." His arm tightened around her shoulders. "I'd like to take you there — to see my home. The hills behind it are covered with gorse, and in spring there are little burns rolling down the tors. And, if you're lucky, you might see a *capercaillie.*"

"What's that?" Nell was breathless, from his words as much as the hurried walk.

"A bird. It looks black but it has feathers of all colors: dark blue, green, white, and brown."

Before Nell could respond, he pulled her to him. His lips were wet and a little gritty, and their kiss was long. Afterward, Nell held him close and rested her head on his chest. Then, holding on to each other, they continued up the road toward her home.

AUTHOR'S NOTE

Mr. Singer's Seamstress, like its predecessor, *A Feather for a Fan,* is based on stories covered in the local newspapers of the time. I spent hours reading two years' worth of the *Tacoma Daily Ledger* in order to make *Mr. Singer's Seamstress* as authentic as possible, right down to the strawberry social mentioned in Chapter 18, which actually happened. A section in the *Ledger* called "Local Briefs," a society page of its day, provided hundreds of items that brought the people to life.

Nell and her family and friends are fictional, but the Blackwells, the Halsteads, General John Sprague, Grandma Staley, Prussian Pete, and Frank and Nellie Alling, among others, were actual Tacoma residents. The site of the Alling fruit farm is now a park. The Puyallup Indians' protest in Chapter 1, over their children being taken to boarding schools in Oregon where many of them died, did take place, but on the reservation, not in town. My command of the Chinook language is shaky, but I did my best. And Dr. McCoy did eventually quit working with the Indians.

The trip to Steilacoom and all the people mentioned there, except John Calhoun, were real, as were the roads and buildings. The nuns, the Rigney twins, Mr. Pincus, and descriptions of Steilacoom are, to the best of my ability, true to the times, as is the sad history of Albert Balch. The smuggler Jimmie Jones was briefly mentioned in the *Ledger.* As for James Lick's potlatch, I was very lucky to stumble on a lengthy description of it. The story of the Chinese girl was in the paper as well.

The Blackwells, their hotel, and the furniture bought from Jay Gould are historically accurate; Mrs. Dr. Clarke briefly had an office in Tacoma; and Mr. Bonney's Sulphur Room and carbolic crystals were noted in *Hunt's History of Tacoma.* The Blackwell Hotel, Halstead Hotel, Alpha Opera House, coal bunkers, and Tacoma Hotel were real places. Pacific Avenue did have large holes in it, and the businesses were often not level with the sidewalks. Madame Rive-King, the Humpty Dumpty picnic, the gypsies, and the Conestoga wagon with "In Bunch Grass

We Trust" on its canvas cover all came to town as well. And the Madhouse was a notorious dive hidden away in Old Tacoma, and the cave-in on the bluff got a brief mention in the *Ledger.*

"Historylink.org" is the best place to read up on the two Tacomas. Captain Quincy and his Chinese wife were residents of Old Tacoma. When Mrs. Quincy disappeared from town, it was believed she was kidnapped and taken back to China by men her father hired. Local legend has it that her spirit haunts the hill where her home stood.

When I had a radio program talking about Tacoma history, Jacob Halstead was one of my favorite Tacoma settlers. Before the hotel, he had a mobile chuck wagon, which he regularly moved to where the lumber companies were working in order to feed the men. It was a pleasure to put him in this book. Another unexpected pleasure was stumbling on the Fawcetts' first days in town. The Fawcetts came to Tacoma to open a seed and farm implements store. Modern-day Tacoma has a street named for Angelo Fawcett, who served as mayor three times between 1896 and 1928.

I did have to fudge on a few things. Marietta Carr married in 1869 and drowned in 1875, when the ship she was on sank. General Sprague's buggy accident happened as described, but on a different street. The shoe repair man did have a three-foot-wide shop, but it was on the wharf, not in town, and the Rector shooting was actually a murder-suicide. However, to the best of my ability, this book depicts what life would have been like for a young woman living in New Tacoma in the early 1880s.

ABOUT THE AUTHOR

Karla Stover graduated from the University of Washington with honors in history. Her classmates say she was writing stories as far back as they can remember. Locally, her credits include *The* [Tacoma] *News Tribune,* the *Tacoma Weekly,* the *Tacoma Reporter, Senior Scene,* and the *Puget Sound Business Journal.* Nationally, she has published in *Ruralite* and *Birds and Blooms.* Internationally, she was a regular contributor to the *European Crown* and the *Imperial Russian Journal.* Her short story "One Day at Appomattox" won the 2008 Christell Prize. For more than fifteen years, she talked about Tacoma history on KLAY AM 1180. She is a member of the Daughters of the Pioneers, the Daughters of the American Revolution, and the Tacoma Historical Society.

The employees of Thorndike Press hope you have enjoyed this Large Print book. All our Thorndike, Wheeler, and Kennebec Large Print titles are designed for easy reading, and all our books are made to last. Other Thorndike Press Large Print books are available at your library, through selected bookstores, or directly from us.

For information about titles, please call:
  (800) 223-1244

or visit our website at:
  gale.com/thorndike

To share your comments, please write:
  Publisher
  Thorndike Press
  10 Water St., Suite 310
  Waterville, ME 04901